FATAL SILENCE

CAROLYN RIDDER ASPENSON

Severn River
PUBLISHING

Severn River Publishing
www.SevernRiverBooks.com

This is a work of fiction. Names, characters, businesses, places, events and incidents are either the products of the author's imagination or used in a fictitious manner. Any resemblance to actual persons, living or dead, or actual events is purely coincidental.

ISBN: 978-1-64875-321-3 (Paperback)
ISBN: 978-1-64875-322-0 (Hardback)

ALSO BY CAROLYN RIDDER ASPENSON

The Rachel Ryder Thriller Series

Damaging Secrets

Hunted Girl

Overkill

Countdown

Body Count

Fatal Silence

Deadly Means

To find out more about Carolyn Ridder Aspenson and her books, visit

severnriverbooks.com/authors/carolyn-ridder-aspenson

For Jack
For always believing in me

PROLOGUE
JULY 4TH

Sweat trickled from his temples. His shirt clung to his body. He took no pleasure in fixing other people's mistakes, but there was no other option.

If not found immediately, the atrocious heat and stifling humidity would leave his victim bloated, an invitation for bugs to feast on her remains. That was unacceptable. He needed her perfect, or, given the unfortunate, uncontrollable circumstances, as perfect as possible. They needed to discover her as she was when her heart stopped, glorious in the justice she so deserved.

He must be vigilant not to disturb the scene. Transporting her from such a distance had not gone as easily as he'd planned. The unintended struggle wasn't visible on her remains, but it was on him. He did not like deviations from the plan, but the job was finished. He would address the deviation later.

A bee buzzed past. He breathed in and held it. He was allergic and had left his EpiPen in his vehicle for fear he would lose it and leave himself vulnerable. Keeping it on his person was too great a risk. He stilled, holding the girl sitting up steadily on the ground. Her weight grew heavier in his hands as the bee circled around him.

He understood the bee well. It could take their lives. Choosing something that was necessary, yet could lead to tragedy, was a risk, but he knew his choice was worthy.

He required her to suffer. She was not worthy of life. The pain and suffering she had inflicted upon others were her crimes, and she must pay for them. It was his responsibility to cast judgment upon her because his victims were not victims at all. They had chosen their path, made a decision that required justice. He provided a service to eradicate their injustice without time wasted through trivial court battles.

He added the final touch near her hand, the sweat on his face even heavier as it pooled in the creases of his skin. Though not as he had planned, he was pleased with the final work, and they would understand he had returned.

Was she pleased with her decision? Was it easy for her? And most importantly, had she regretted it as her heart raced and she lay there dying? He hoped so.

She was not his first, nor his last, and he would accomplish his goals regardless of the obstacles presented. It was his responsibility to seek out evil and eliminate it. He *must* send a message. She would lie in the glory of her deserved punishment where her final justice was served.

Just like the others. He was the mastermind.

1

I waved my hands near my face and grimaced at the oven. It wasn't, was it? I bit my bottom lip. No, it couldn't be that. Not with everyone I cared for close by. But it was, and I'd never hear the end of it. The scent seeped into my nostrils. I worried it would permeate into the kitchen walls. Chicken feces stink, the kind ripened in the sun for days, wasn't the impact I'd wanted to make my first time at Michels's house.

The scalding sun beat down on us. Michels's had central air, but my sweat slicked anyway. If the heat was the whipped cream on a sundae, the humidity was the cherry on top. The two combined teetered at an unbearable level as sweat built up behind my knees. The environment was already ripe for stench, and the funk penetrating from the oven only made it worse. I cringed. The burned ammonia scent brought back memories of the time Tommy and I had volunteered at a chicken farm. I'd suffered from chicken feces PTSD ever since. And there I was again, in the thick of it.

Smoke swirled from the oven. I must have been in shock because I stood there, my feet glued to the ground, watching it billow out and fill the small kitchen with a cloudy odor. The inside of the oven glowed in soft ambers and yellows. Flames. The inside of the oven was on fire.

"Crap! Crap! Crap! Michels's oven. My beans!" I stared at the oven like a mother who'd discovered her child had scribbled across the wall with a permanent marker. Where was the damn potholder?

I couldn't deny it any longer. It was my fault, and I'd never hear the end of it. Damn. If only I'd received an easy potluck assignment. I could buy bags of chips with the best of them. Baked beans didn't rank high on my list of successes. I waved at the smoke detector, but my five-foot-five stature didn't let me reach high enough. I flipped the oven knob to the off position.

I stretched two big steps toward the sink. I'd use the faucet to spray the stove, but that was stupid. The hose wouldn't reach. "Oh, hell. I hate beans. Do these people not even know me?" I coughed into my inner elbow. "Dear God, that's awful."

As I searched the room for a potholder, Bishop and Cathy walked in and froze. Bishop's brow furrowed as he stared at the smoke seething from the oven. "What the—?"

Chatting wasn't an option. A volcano of baked beans and bacon was about to erupt from Michels's oven. A loud, piercing sound only dogs should have been able to hear penetrated my ears and sent sparks of pain through my head. "The smoke detector," I yelled. "I need a fire extinguisher."

Bishop coughed and pointed to the oven as he searched for it. "Are you cooking chicken feces?"

I glanced at Cathy, who'd pressed her lips together to trap a laugh ready to burst. She checked under the sink and grabbed a fire extinguisher from the back of the cabinet. "I found it!" She stepped closer to Bishop and handed it to him.

Bishop posed in a split leg lunge with his head back, the extinguisher held in outstretched arms. "Open it," he said.

"And back away. God only knows what's coming out of that thing."

Where was everyone else? Were their ears immune to the brittle screeching of the smoke alarm? And that smell? How could they ignore it? People across the state would get a whiff of it soon enough. Why were the rest of them avoiding the catastrophe imploding in Michels's kitchen?

Probably fear.

Small flames flickered through the oven window. "I need a potholder." I twirled in a circle. "Doesn't Michels own any potholders?" I glanced at Bishop and pointed to the smoke alarm. "Can't you do something and turn that thing off?"

"Shouldn't we eliminate the fire first?" he asked.

Cathy grabbed a broom from the pantry and waved it at the smoke alarm.

I curled my shoulders inward and flipped around, knowing what was coming but also not wanting to destroy Detective Michels's kitchen further. I grabbed the oven handle and jerked it away. "It's hot! I need a damned potholder!"

Cathy searched through the drawers, found two, and tossed them to me. She used the broom to whack the heck out of the fire alarm as I pulled the oven open, and Bishop sprayed my burning baked beans until the flames died out.

Cathy opened the window over the sink and fanned the smoke toward it.

I heard Bubba, the department's tech genius, say, "What is she cooking in there?"

Bishop stepped back, set down the extinguisher and coughed. He wiped his nose and swiped his hand across his sweaty head. "What the heck was in there?"

"It's my baked beans." I blew out a breath.

The corners of Bishop's eyes crinkled as he smiled. "You mean it *was* your baked beans?"

Cathy raised both her eyebrows and shoulders and pressed her lips together again. "Excellent use of past tense, Rob." She laughed.

The smoke lessened, and I removed the beans from the oven. I frowned at the charred mess and tilted the heavy dish so Cathy and Bishop could see it. "They're ruined."

Bishop leaned toward the beans but stayed a few feet away, as if he was worried they'd jump out of the dish and attack him. He gave them a cursory examination and lifted his eyes to me. "Are you sure those were beans?"

"Be nice. I don't get how to use this oven." I set the dish on the stovetop and put my hands on my hips. "Why do you people always make me cook? Can't I bring a storebought pie or something?"

Bishop scurried over and motioned for me to move to the side. He studied the beans again, dipping his head to the right and shaking it. "We're going to need Dr. Barron to confirm what they really were."

Cathy snorted. I shot her a death stare. She cringed and held her palms up. "I didn't mean to laugh out loud."

Bishop waved his hand in front of his face. "The scent is worse now than earlier."

"Rob," Cathy said. "Not everyone is born a chef."

I pointed to her. "Yeah, what she said."

"Beans from a can. How could someone ruin those?" he asked.

"Rachel has a very specific skill set," Cathy said. "Let's celebrate those instead of this." She smiled, and another laugh slipped out. "Sorry, I...they're so bad. I've never seen anything like it."

Bishop chuckled.

I shrugged. "I've never claimed to be a cook." I'd never been interested in cooking. My mother once called me Hurricane Rachel, and rightfully so. I destroyed her kitchen with every dish I attempted to make. Takeout and simple sandwiches? Those were my specialties.

"And you shouldn't," Bishop said. "Tossing a few cans of beans into a casserole dish and sticking it in the oven isn't exactly cooking, partner."

"I used a recipe that included bacon, which, by the way, I cooked to perfection. So shut it, *partner*. And I added spices which made the dish smell delicious. Not like this. I considered it a win."

"Which you turned into a loss." He shook his head. "You have the oven set at five-hundred-fifty degrees. You should have warmed them at three-fifty max."

I bit my bottom lip. "It shouldn't have mattered. Again, it's not my fault. I wanted to buy a pie. You guys all made me cook."

He slid the burned Pyrex dish and the cooling pad farther away on the kitchen counter. "We put ourselves through the suffering, too."

Cathy laughed again. We both stared at her. "Sorry, but it's beans. I don't see how anyone can fail at beans."

Bishop laughed. "Rachel's an excellent detective, but she's a horrible cook."

Kyle walked into the kitchen. "Why does it stink like burned chicken—"

I held up my hand. "Hold up and think before you speak."

He noticed the baked beans on the counter. His eyes widened, and a smile crept across his face. "Those—"

I jabbed my finger at him. "Don't you even."

He raised his eyebrows, held his hands in surrender, and slowly backed out of the room.

I yelled, "Chicken!"

"Feces," Bishop added.

I couldn't help myself. I laughed. I turned toward the oven, which was still sending out small smoke signals. I stared at it and sighed. "Is this thing okay?" *Please don't be ruined. Please don't be ruined.*

Bishop peeked inside and cringed. "It'll be fine after a good cleaning. The fire was only in the dish."

"I'll pay the crime scene cleaners to give it a whirl," I said.

"Probably wise."

Kyle returned with two large cans of Bush's Baked Beans. "I brought reserves in case something happened."

Bishop and Cathy laughed.

My eyes widened. "Way to have faith in your woman."

Kyle smiled. "I have faith in everything you do except cooking."

"Totally warranted," I said. I pointed to the cans as he placed them on Michels' counter. "Those are your responsibility."

Savannah walked into the kitchen. "I smelled something coming from the window. What's—" Her smile morphed into a scowl. "Sweet baby Jesus, why does it stink like my grand pappy's chicken coop in here?"

The three traitors pointed to me.

She spied the glass dish full of burned baked beans, glanced at me, and then at Kyle. She waggled her finger at him. "You did not make her cook!"

He shook his head. "It's a potluck party. I claim no responsibility for this event."

I rolled my eyes. The man could chase down drug cartel members, tackle two of them at once, and rip the drugs from their pockets, but my best friend put the fear of God in him. "He's right. It's Michels's fault. He handed out the potluck assignments."

She shook her head. "Erm, I'd expected him to be smarter than that."

I needed to get away from the scene of the crime. "I'm getting a cold beer and sitting on the back deck where I should have been all along. The oven needs to cool down, and there's nothing we can do about the stench right now anyway. Also, I need to apologize to Michels." I marched out of the room with my chin held high.

"Wait a minute," Savannah said. She yanked me by the collar of my shirt and flipped me around toward the stench. "Get rid of those." She pointed to my dish. "Before the smell kills someone." She flicked her chin at Bishop and Kyle. "And you two, find air freshener or something."

I shrugged her grip off my shirt. "Drama queen."

She smirked. "It's my best trait."

Bishop handed me the two potholders. "Take them out by the mailbox and set them on the curb. I'll toss the whole thing in the garbage when I leave tonight."

I pursed my lips. "This is an expensive Pyrex dish."

He glanced at the others and leaned his head to the side. "You think someone's going to steal it?"

I jutted out my chin. "They can clean the dish."

"Listen, sweetie," Savannah said. "Unless they're trying to ward off evil spirits, nobody's touching that dish."

"Ouch." I grimaced. "But I can clean it."

Bishop shook his head. "There ain't no cleaning that thing."

I stomped out with my dish and stormed toward the living room, nearly bumping into Bubba. He jerked his head back and plugged his nose. "Who died?"

I scowled. "Et tu, Brute?"

His dark brown eyes widened. "Huh?"

I headed out the door and walked down the sidewalk to Michels's driveway, muttering to myself.

Nikki, our crime scene tech, stepped out of her car next to the mailbox as I set the beans down. She glanced at the dish and then back up at me. "Why do they always make you cook?"

"Thank you! At least you see the stupidity in that."

We both stared at the dish. I crossed my arms over my chest and sighed.

Nikki sighed, too. "May they rest in peace. Whatever they were."

I laughed. "They were baked beans. Bishop told me to put them here so they don't stink up the house more than they already have."

"Ouch, that had to hurt."

"A little." We turned back. I warned her about the stink and hoped my Pyrex would survive. I'd make Bishop pay for a replacement if it didn't. I headed around back for a beer and an apology to Michels.

Jimmy Abernathy, the chief of the Hamby Police Department and my best friend Savannah's husband, thrust a squirming, chunky, bawling-up-a-storm baby at me. "I swear the funk in the air isn't from her. But please, take her. She won't stay in my arms." Sweat pooled on his temples as his eyes pleaded for help. "It's hotter than hell out here, and this humidity is sucking the air out of my lungs. Scarlet's miserable. Please, take her to her mom. She'll kill me if I do it." He held her with outstretched arms, her front side toward me. Her little face was red and wet. "Please."

The chief of police, who had taken down violent and dangerous criminals with his own two hands, was a desperate, weak mess when it came to Scarlet. I laughed, even though he was clearly panicked. "Wow. Way to be a tough guy there, boss. Give me a minute. First I have to apologize to Michels. I messed up the oven. Have you seen him?"

"I should have realized the odor belonged to you. I heard you all inside, but I had my own problems out here." He flicked his head to the side of the house. "He's back there messing with the wires for his speakers." He bounced from one foot to the other. Poor little Scarlet's scowling face blushed a deeper red, and a scream so high pitched it rivaled the smoke alarm bellowed out of her tiny mouth. Jimmy's eyes pleaded with me. "Help me."

I bit the side of my cheek. "Two minutes," I said, and rushed to the side of the house.

Michels cursed as he worked to unknot several multi-colored wires from a speaker resting on the windowsill. I walked close to him, and the scent of cedarwood and sweat overpowered the beans and filled my nose. I caught my breath as my heart burst open and memories flowed like blood through my veins. *Tommy.*

He turned around, and his face changed from a scowl to a smile. "Hey."

I swallowed hard. It was cologne, but it had the power to toy with my emotions.

He set the tangled mess on the sill. "Is my kitchen okay?"

I shook off the memories and forced a smile. "Why are you blaming me?"

"Everyone knows you're anti-kitchen. I should have suggested a dessert or something."

"The oven is fine, but I..."

He worked with the speaker wires again as he spoke. "You burned your beans and almost set my kitchen on fire. Kyle told me, and the damage has permanently set into my nose hairs."

"Don't worry. In a few years, you'll be pulling those out anyway," I mumbled. "Traitor," I added under my breath.

Michels laughed.

"I'll pay to have the oven cleaned."

"No problem." He sighed. Scarlet screamed nearby. He rested his head on the windowsill. He lifted it back up and smiled. "The chief has Scarlet, doesn't he?"

I giggled. "How can you tell?"

On cue, Scarlet screamed louder. Michels winked. "I'm a detective."

"I'm on it. Sorry again," I said and jogged around to the back of the house.

Scarlet's screams bounced off every object in sight. It was impossible for Savannah not to hear her child. The entire neighborhood echoed with the screams. It must have stretched her heart strings taut, but the woman had the strength of a Titan and didn't come outside. She wanted Jimmy to handle his daughter's outbursts, not pass a sopping mess of tears and snotty baby back to her every time. Jimmy, on the other hand, struggled with the concept.

I fought the urge to help and took a cold beer out of the cooler. I popped it open and set it on the table. Since Bishop and I were on call, O'Douls would have to do.

Jimmy rocked his hips back and forth, but poor Scarlet couldn't settle. I caved. "Give me that sweet thing."

He stretched out his arms. "This is harder than tackling an armed robber."

"Just wait until she's a teenager." Scarlet wiggled into my arms. Hints of jasmine and baby powder emanated from her soft, sweaty skin and infiltrated my nose. Her baby scent was a world better than chicken feces. I smiled at her. "Hey, you little bundle of perfection!" I tapped her nose with the tip of my finger. "How's my sweet goddaughter?" Her screams softened to small mutters and broken breathing. She hiccupped. "It's okay, sweet thing. You're fine." I hopped from one foot to the other like Jimmy had. Scarlet's body was warm from the sun and the exertion of her crying. Exhaustion usually caused her Texas-sized fits, and her little body was worn out. She sat like a dead weight in my arms. Poor thing. "Geez, she feels like a brick."

"Tell me about it. I'm thinking of putting her in peewee football in the fall."

I laughed. A lot of years needed to pass before that happened. Scarlet hiccupped again and laughed. I giggled, too, and talked baby talk to her. "Did you just hiccup?" I pretended to hiccup. "Oh, excuse me!"

She'd been smiling, but she hiccupped again and her smile flipped upside down. When her brows furrowed to a point at the bridge of her nose, and her mouth opened to the size of an underpass on Chicago's I-90, I prepared myself. I'd experienced it before. I held her out in front of me and waited for the verbal explosion, which hit right on cue. "*Maaaaaamaaaa!*"

Jimmy laughed. "I saw it coming."

"I'm telling Sav you handed off your child while she was screaming her head off."

He carefully extradited the screaming ball of baby from my hands. "I'm not afraid of my wife." Before he pushed open the back door, he said, "Okay, a little." He called for Savannah, but I could barely make out his voice over Scarlet's screams.

I loved kids. Other people's kids. Crying? Need a diaper change? Throw up all over themselves? Easy fix. Hand them back to their parents. I was perfectly fine being the fun aunt. My plans for spoiling that child rotten were already in full force.

Bishop and Cathy walked onto the back deck. "Wow, that kid's got a set of lungs," Bishop said.

"Have you met her mother?" I asked.

He laughed.

Cathy laughed too. "My granddaughter has them, too. Boys are loud when they're around five or six, but girls are loud all the time."

"How many grandchildren do you have?" I asked.

"Only one. Her name is Ida, after my mother."

I'd spent so little time with Bishop's lady friend. I wanted us to be friends because whether he would or could admit it, he was in love.

The back gate on the left side of the house opened and Ashley Middleton walked through it, a big toothy grin on her face. "Hey, y'all." She strolled over to the three of us.

I hadn't seen Ashley in ages. We hugged. "How are you? I had no idea you were coming!"

"It's great to see you!" She whispered in my ear. "Is that Bishop's girlfriend?"

"Yup," I whispered back. We let go, and she introduced herself to Cathy.

Ashley was once the crime scene tech for the department. She'd done a great job, but she needed something more fulfilling, so Kyle and the Drug Enforcement Agency stole her from us. I was happy for her, but sad for us. She was my first female friend in town and an excellent crime scene tech.

"I'm so excited to see everyone," she said. "Where's Justin? Is he inside?" Her face flushed, but it wasn't from the heat.

Justin? Nobody called Michels by his first name. I cocked my head to the side. "Justin?"

Her cheeks turned bright red. "I mean Michels. Is Michels inside?" She bent her head and looked to the right. I turned away and smiled. Calling Michels by his first name was no mistake.

I grabbed her arm. "Let's go see. I believe he's trying to get his speakers to work out here." I dragged her inside and past the kitchen.

"Oh, wow. What smells?"

"Bishop burned the baked beans. I swear, the man is a disaster in the kitchen." I kept her moving past a small bedroom where Jimmy held Scarlet facing away from his chest. She still screamed, but it was a little softer than before. He raised a brow as I smiled at him. I mouthed, "Something's up."

He hitched Scarlet back onto his hip and followed, her screams softening to a tolerable mutter. Savannah was in the family room with Michels and a few other officers as well as Mike Barron, the coroner.

"I wasn't...I wanted to say hi," Ashley said. Her face was still red, but she was full of smiles and giggles. I positioned her behind Michels. He was busy cursing a mess of wires behind his entertainment system.

"Hey," I said. "Someone's here to see you."

He turned around with a scowl on his face that was quickly replaced by sparkling eyes and a bright smile. "Hey, hon—" he stopped. "Ashley." The entire room stared at him, and his face turned beet red.

Ashley's shoulders curled in. I stepped back and gave them a tilted head, hand-scratching-chin look. I played scenes from my past on a loop through my mind. Michels and Ashley laughing. Ashley handing Michels case files first in the investigation room. Michels smiling at Ashley in the middle of a murder investigation. Michels and Ashley. Michels and Ashley. There were a lot of *Michels and Ashley* scenes I hadn't paid attention to, and I was a better detective than that.

"It's, uh," Michels stuttered. "It's nice to see you."

"Erm," I said, turning toward everyone else and smiling at Mike Barron. "Male victim's eyes are glossy, pupils dilated. He appears to have flushed skin and a rapid heartbeat. Female victim is jittery with a slight giggle ready to escape her lips." I glanced at the couple, and back at Barron, who was smirking beside Michels. "It appears to be an obvious case of secret romance busted. Do you concur, doctor?"

Barron placed his finger on his chin and nodded. "I definitely concur, detective."

Michels held up his hands. "I confess to nothing."

Ashley turned to all of us, her face red as a tomato and a big smile still plastered on it. She elbowed Michels. "I think they know."

"We do now," I said. "Calling Michels *Justin* is a dead giveaway." I glanced at Kyle who had walked in with a similar smile across his face. I caught his eye, and he dropped the smile and studied the carpet.

"Hey, you," I said as I pointed to him. He made eye contact again. "You knew, didn't you?"

He raised his eyebrows but kept his lips zipped.

Michels wrapped his arms around Ashley's waist. "A year plus. We planned to tell you all today."

A year?

Everyone crowded into the shrinking space.

Jimmy's jaw dropped. "A year?"

"I'm with him," I said.

Michels shrugged. "We wanted to make sure it was serious before we said anything."

The entire room applauded, me being the loudest. Ashley was a great woman—smart, funny, honest. Michels was a great man and a damn good, by-the-book detective. They were a perfect match, and I was glad to see them looking happy together.

Once the dust of the surprise settled, they turned the tables to poking fun at my beans. I let them have their fun, walked outside to the deck, and popped open my non-alcoholic beer. I wasn't a big drinker, but there was nothing like a cold beer on a hot day, regardless of the alcohol content. I sat in a comfy chair and sipped the beer like it was a gift from heaven. Kyle stepped up behind me and placed his hand on my shoulder. I frowned up at him. "Traitor."

"It wasn't my secret to tell."

"Aren't couples supposed to share everything?"

"We're in law enforcement. We can't."

I tipped my head down and examined my bottle with feigned interest. "Their dating isn't law enforcement, but nice try."

"It is when they work for the law, too."

I rolled my eyes. "Whatever."

Ashley walked over. "Hey Rachel, can we talk?" She smiled at Kyle. "Privately?"

My eyes shifted from Kyle to Ashley. I waved my hand near my face. "Oh, don't worry about him. He's a great secret keeper."

She laughed. "I can attest to that, but this is for you." She glanced at Kyle. "No offense intended."

"None taken." He stepped back. "I need to check on my beans. God knows we don't need another chicken feces situation."

"Did you put them in the oven?" I asked.

He chuckled. "I don't think anyone wants fire extinguisher flavored baked beans. I wiped up the mess and set the oven to clean itself. They're in the microwave." He headed back inside.

Ashley motioned for me to follow her. We walked toward

the back of the yard. Clearly, whatever she had to say was secret enough to warrant serious privacy. We stood in front of a grouping of pine trees. She bounced on one foot and picked at a branch on one of the trees, pulling the little needles off one by one. "I...I, uh." She studied the ground.

I touched her arm. "Ashley, it's no big deal. I understand why you didn't want us to know."

She wore a red, white, and blue short jumper with sleeveless arms and front pockets. She let go of the branch and needles flung from it as it reset itself. She stuffed her hands into her pockets. "No, it's not that. I wanted to talk to you about something else." She paused. "I need to find the right way to say it."

I tilted my head. "What's going on?"

She exhaled and stared down at her hands as she twisted her fingers together. "It's about the Chip Stuart case."

My heart rate immediately rose. Chip Stuart was a serial killer in both Birmingham, Alabama, and Hamby, Georgia. He'd robbed six men of their futures, killed the hopes and dreams of their parents, then left vinyl sticker numbers in baggies with the victims to leave his mark. The problem was that the numbers were out of order, and if there were another three numbers in the middle, we'd been unsuccessful at locating them anywhere in the country. When we'd caught Stuart, instead of telling the truth about the missing numbers and facing justice, he'd committed suicide. As he lay dying, he repeated something over and over, and though the cases were officially closed, with good reason, his riddle had haunted me ever since. *"One, two, three, you can't pin on me. Seven, eight, nine, I'll add to my crimes. Four, five, six, add to the mix."*

Stuart was a sociopath. Final answer. But for the rest of the teams in both Alabama and Hamby, they determined the intent of his riddle was simply to leave us with an unknown.

To torture us. To keep us awake at night contemplating its meaning.

And I was the only one who had.

Something evil lurked in the shadows. Stuart's crimes weren't finished.

"What about it?" I asked.

My cell phone rang with the department ringtone. I had to answer. I raised a finger as I dug into the back pocket of my cut-offs. "Give me a second. I'm on call."

"No worries," she said.

I stepped aside to answer. "Detective Ryder, I have a call for you and Detective Bishop," our dispatch operator said. "May I patch it through?"

"Sure," I said. "I'm with Bishop, so I'll grab him."

"Okay, thank you. I'll patch it through. Happy Fourth of July."

"You, too." I smiled at Ashley and mouthed, "I'm sorry."

She waved me off like it was no big deal, but her bouncing knee and twisted hands told me otherwise. "No problem. We can talk later."

"Plan on it," I said.

She and I jogged over to Bishop who had stepped outside with Cathy. "Call for us."

He glanced at Cathy. "I'm sorry."

"It's your job," she said.

We walked toward the fence for some privacy, and I put the call on speaker. "Detective Ryder here. I have Detective Bishop with me."

A man with a low and deep voice said hello. "Detectives Ryder and Bishop, this is Deputy Greg Grimes with the Forsyth County Sheriff's Office."

I glanced at Bishop. "How can we help you?"

"I've got a female victim and a murder scene with your

names on it, ma'am, and I'd like you to come on out and have a look."

"Detective, this is Detective Rob Bishop. I'm not sure I understand what you're saying."

"Our crime scene. Your names are stickered onto a piece of paper in a baggie pinned to the victim."

I flashed back to Chip Stuart's dying words. *"One, two, three, you can't pin on me. Seven, eight, nine, I'll add to my crimes. Four, five, six, add to the mix."*

We informed the detective we would be enroute, and as Bishop finished the call, I searched for Ashley. It couldn't have been a coincidence that at the same time she mentioned Stuart, someone discovered a murder victim with a baggie. Like our victims.

I jogged over to Michels when I couldn't find Ashley. "Where's Ash?"

"She ran to the store for me. What's up?"

"I had a question. No worries, I'll call her cell."

He pulled a phone from his shorts pocket. "She left it on the table, but she'll be back in thirty minutes, tops."

"Bishop and I are heading to a crime scene in Suwanee. Tell her I need to talk to her. It's important." I headed toward the front door.

"Wait," Michels said. "Is everything okay?"

"I'm not sure," I said and rushed outside.

2

Even with the air conditioning on high and my seat temperature at cold max, Bishop's vehicle was still a sauna. "This humidity and the heat," I said. I didn't bother finishing the sentence.

"I expected it would be bad. When it's above ninety in late May, the rest of the summer will be hotter than hell."

My shirt stuck to me. "I feel like I need another shower."

We didn't speak of the death scene during the twenty-minute drive from Michels' place in Alpharetta to the crime scene in Suwanee. We understood what was coming, why our names were there. But the victim was a girl? Why? That stumped us. Talking about it would make it real, and we weren't ready for that.

Stuart's murders were some of the worst I'd seen, and coming from Chicago where people were murdered daily, that said a lot. With his first murder, we were called to the scene of a burning horse barn. The barn was a concern, but more so for us was the dead body close to the scene. That case grew from one murder to three in a short amount of time, along with the three in Alabama three years prior, and ended with

Stuart's weak and pathetic escape by shoving a knife through his gut.

Six months prior we'd investigated a string of horrific serial justice killings. The killer, a man named Chip Stuart, left vinyl number stickers stuck to pieces of paper in baggies near each victim. We'd kept the vinyl sticker detail out of public knowledge, so the stickers in Suwanee were somehow connected to the Stuart murders.

Bishop's tense jaw told me our feelings were the same. We needed to process the news of another murder, though we didn't do a good job of that. When my partner was stressed, he kept his jaw locked, his shoulders stuck high near his ears, and he breathed in and out through his teeth.

I tapped my sneakered foot on the floor of his vehicle and chewed on my bottom lip as I stared out the window and focused on my breathing. Counting to keep calm and focus would do no good. I wasn't calm, but I would be when we arrived at the scene. I understood the game. Detectives fought to stay impartial and show no emotion at crime scenes, but sometimes, it wasn't possible.

Bishop's knuckles gripped the steering wheel with so much force they turned creamy white. I moved to touch his arm and tell him everything would be all right but stopped. It wouldn't be all right. A young woman died, and that was likely on us. We both understood that. I wasn't much calmer than he was, but my eyes weren't slitted like a snake, and though the pounding in my chest was fierce, my heart rate was only slightly elevated. Bishop, on the other hand, glowed a deep red from the neck up.

I glanced back at his knuckles. They were still white, and my breath hitched from the degree of red his face and neck had become. "Are you okay?"

"No."

"Because of Stuart?"

"Stuart's dead."

"I'm aware of that."

He honked at a car going under the speed limit, swung to the left, and roared past it. "Get the hell off the road if you can't drive the speed limit," he said.

I exhaled. "We both have to chill out before we get to the crime scene."

"We will," he said as he zipped past another vehicle.

"You want me to drive?"

His eyes shifted toward me but reverted back to the road. "No."

"Okay." Normally that would cause an argument, but not that time. Bishop teamed up with karma to work against me and their partnership smacked me in the face. Two months prior, I was the one at the wheel enroute to an armed home invasion in The Manor Golf and Country Club neighborhood. I'd slowed my official vehicle at a red light with the lights and siren on to alert drivers to yield. The cars stopped. I accelerated and moved into the intersection.

But not everyone had stopped.

A teenager t-boned us on my side. My vehicle had spun around, smacked into a car waiting at the light, and veered off the side of the road, flipping to a stop on its roof. Bishop had cursed up a storm, damning me to hell and back the entire time. I hadn't blamed him.

The sixteen-year-old boy received the ticket, and witnesses verified he was speeding. I'd sympathized with the kid, but not enough to push for fewer charges. He'd been on his cell phone and had his stereo blaring. He admitted that he hadn't seen us or heard the sirens, and he'd needed to learn the importance of that lesson.

Even before the accident, Bishop was uncomfortable with

me at the wheel, claiming I drove like a Chicagoan on steroids, and each time he climbed into the passenger's seat he inched closer to God.

"Turn right on McGinnis Ferry," I said.

"I've played golf at Laurel Springs. The golf course is right off the club house on the main road."

I chuckled at the image of Bishop playing golf and appreciated the reprieve from the angst of what lay ahead, but the break was short. My body switched into fight mode, where it landed every time we had a call, and where it stayed until the case closed. Fight mode prepped me for the evil coming, and, with it, my senses heightened in preparation to catch a killer. At that moment, my senses were extra amplified as my brain fired off scenarios wrapped around the stickers on the scene and the question of the girl. Why were our names left at the scene of a dead woman?

We arrived at the gated community. "No fire, though I didn't expect there would be," I said.

"Didn't see any smoke on the way," Bishop said.

An older woman with perfectly applied makeup opened the glass window at the entrance gate. Bright red lipstick, blue and cream eye shadow, and a sweep of blush across her cheeks were applied better than my makeup ever was. Her bun of gray hair on top of her head didn't have a flyaway anywhere. Kudos to her for knowing her look and running with it. She waved her long, bright red nails at us and snarled. "No lookie-lous. Make a U-turn through the gate."

Bishop flashed his badge. "We're the law, ma'am."

She squinted as she scrutinized his badge. She opened the gate and said, "So terrible. That poor girl."

Bishop's eyes shifted my direction. His subtle eyebrow raise confirmed our agreement. A female victim didn't fit, and our killer was dead, but there we were, our names at the scene an invitation to the surprise party we didn't want to attend. The dread lingering inside the pit of my stomach forced its way to the surface. Bile burned the back of my throat.

As Bishop said, the clubhouse was about fifty feet off the main entrance, and the street was packed with Forsyth County Sheriff's vehicles, fire trucks and ambulances. He drove past the crowded area, turned left onto a side street, and parked there. Before turning off the vehicle, he turned to me and asked, "Any chance one of those reporters leaked the details about the stickers?"

"I believe only Jessica Walters had the information, and she promised to keep it out of the news." I hoped I was right.

"She's a reporter. You can't trust her."

"She hasn't reported anything about the stickers in the news."

"Right. What about Stephanie Miller?"

"Her son was abducted, so wouldn't she have said something about them if she did?"

"Possibly. Reporters are good at keeping an ace in their pocket."

"I agree, but if they did have the information, I never saw it reported. I've kept tabs on them both."

An investigative reporter named Jessica Walters had received intel about the Stuart murders. She refused to reveal how she got it, but she also promised to not release private information to the public. The other reporter, Stephanie Miller, was the mother of Stuart's only surviving victim.

He nodded. "I've kept up with them, too." He exhaled. "You ready for this?"

"As ready as I can be. You?"

"Right there with you."

I clenched my fists several times, begging the tension to release with each break. Scenarios ticked through my brain at warp speed. What would we see? Would the scene be the same as the others? "Alright. Let's roll." I stepped out of the vehicle, grabbed my badge from my bag, and clipped it onto the right pocket of my shorts. I glanced over at Bishop. His heavy eyes and down-turned lips hadn't changed since we left the party. "Weapon." I said, more to myself than to him.

"Don't leave home without it."

I slid my weapon into the back of my denim shorts.

A deputy stood on the opposite side of the crime scene tape with his legs out and arms crossed, a pair of sunglasses hiding his eyes. He wasn't tall, but he was beefy, his muscles bulging and nearly splitting his uniform at the seams. He sweated profusely. I empathized, though his uniform had to be stifling in the heat and humidity.

He removed his sunglasses, eyed my cut-offs and casual top, and gave me a creepy once over that left me wanting to scratch the slime off. I turned to let him see my weapon and my badge attached to my side. His creepy gaze stopped at the sight of my weapon.

I bumped into his outstretched arm while walking under the yellow crime scene tape. "This is a crime scene. Unless you've got a badge to go along with those weapons, I'm going to have to ask you to hand them over."

"Seriously? I'm sorry, I could have sworn you saw it while ogling me." I grabbed my badge clipped to my pocket and flipped it open. Bishop did the same. "We're here at the request of Deputy Grimes." I shoved the badge close to his face. "Can you see it now?"

He closed his eyes and, through gritted teeth, said, "My apologies, detective. Playground's on the right. Detective Grimes is the one dressed in jeans and a black t-shirt."

I smiled and said, "Great job, kid," and then I ducked under the tape.

He called me something I'd been called thousands of times as I walked away.

"Don't let him get to you," Bishop said.

"He's an a-hole and not my problem."

Bishop chuckled. "Making friends and influencing people on this fine holiday."

"Making friends is my superpower."

"Right."

The crowd of law enforcement on scene raised the already steaming temperature to completely intolerable. I was sweating everywhere, and I was confident I smelled worse than my burned beans.

A helicopter roared over us, stopping the urgent chatter of law enforcement surrounding the scene. It dropped lower, sending a rush of hot July air blowing down at us. From a short distance, a man with a booming voice spoke sternly through a bullhorn. "This is an active crime scene. Get back now!"

I glanced up at the helicopter. "The media," I yelled to Bishop. "Figures."

The same voice bellowed from the bullhorn again. "I'll hit you with at least a dozen charges if you're not out of here in thirty seconds!"

The helicopter lifted back into the sky and sped away. I pictured the pilot doing his best Han Solo impression and laughing as it disappeared. "Idiots."

Bishop nodded. "All about the headline."

The man with the bullhorn walked over to us, and I instantly recognized him. "Sheriff Rodney," I said with my hand extended.

He shook my hand and made eye contact. His dark eyes lacked the joy typical of the July Fourth holiday. "Detective Ryder." He half smiled at Bishop and extended his hand.

"Detective Bishop. Sorry to see you under these circumstances. Let me bring you to Deputy Grimes." He handed us each a set of booties and gloves, examined our bare legs and said, "Stay right here. Let me get you each a Tyvek suit."

"Thank you," I said. I groaned as he walked away. "Great. Tyvek. My favorite." I wasn't a fan. While standard with crimes scenes for most departments, the suits' densely compressed fibers suffocated me like a soggy, locked box, and my borderline claustrophobic tendencies kicked into high gear each time I had to wear one. Given the heat and humidity, I'd be a puddle of melted flesh by the time I climbed out of the thing. The Hamby Police Department policy only recommended the suits, so most of us didn't wear them.

We followed him toward the truck where they kept their gear. I'd worked with Sheriff Rodney in previous joint investigations, and he was an excellent sheriff, so I complied without argument.

"I hate these things," I said to Bishop.

He flicked his head toward the guy the deputy had pointed to earlier. "He's not wearing Tyvek. Wonder why we have to?"

Sweat dripped from places no woman ever wanted to sweat. My armpits stuck to the side of my chest and even my palms were wet. It wasn't comfortable, and it would only get worse. "Rodney's showing us who's boss?"

"Could be."

After settling into our gear, we headed to the crime scene.

A sheet of painter's plastic stretched like a walkway of death to the victim's remains and Deputy Grimes. The memories of past crime scenes with vinyl stickers taunted me, bringing back a tightness in my chest I preferred to forget. Yellow evidence cards dotted the area surrounding the body. I studied the items they'd tagged. A broken, heart-shaped pendant necklace among other things, and a baggie with vinyl sticker letters stuck to a piece of paper. I didn't need to see it to know what it said.

"Detectives," Grimes said. "I'd say it's a pleasure but given the circumstances...."

We both nodded. Even with the body odor penetrating the area, the stench of blood hit my nasal passages hard, raced down to my stomach, and urged it to send the Mexican dip and chips I'd eaten at Michels's place back up for a visit. I swallowed hard and stepped closer to the victim. She was attractive, but death, in its ironic twist on life, would take that away. There was no beauty in death, no peace for the deceased, and never ever any for the ones left behind. My heart hurt for her family. She was young, probably early twenties. She'd had so much life left to live. A career, love, even marriage and children...so many things she wouldn't experience. Things her parents had imagined since she was born would never be, and they'd be left to deal with the pain.

I crouched down and examined the slice in her neck and the large, clear plastic baggie with a piece of paper inside. It was folded in half, but I recognized the outlines of the letters. *Ryder.* I stood. "Where's the other one?"

"On the ground there." Grimes pointed to the side of the victim a few feet away. "The one on the ground has Bishop's name on it, and the one on the victim has yours."

"I could read mine." I breathed in and out in short, quick breaths.

One, two, three, you can't pin on me. Seven, eight, nine, I'll add to my crimes. Four, five, six, add to the mix.

His riddle was clearer than ever. Stuart took ownership of the deaths in Hamby, but the three other deaths in Birmingham, Alabama, three years prior, weren't his.

And we'd just found number four.

3

We stayed back from the victim's remains and let the tech crew and medical examiner do their jobs. A Forsyth County deputy handed us each a cold bottled water. I guzzled it down quickly and smiled as Deputy Grimes and Bishop eyed me. "I was thirsty."

"Clearly," Bishop said.

Grimes picked up and opened the baggie with Bishop's name inside. "Any idea why your names would be in baggies at our crime scene?" His face was blank and his tone flat. He wasn't accusing us, though I wouldn't fault him if he had been.

Bishop and I made eye contact. Giving information to another law enforcement officer on a closed investigation wasn't uncommon, but Stuart's case was sensitive to us, and we were territorial, especially given the stickers. His slight nod gave me the go ahead.

I caught Grimes's eye and flicked my head toward a more private area. We walked over to a small, wooded area between the golf course and residents' homes.

Bishop motioned for me to start. "The Chip Stuart case, you know it, right?"

"Everyone in the country knows it." He turned back toward the deceased. "Don't tell me you believe this is connected. Didn't your suspect commit suicide?"

"Yes, but there were details about the scenes we kept private."

"And those details match my crime scene."

We both nodded.

He sighed. "The stickers."

"Each of the six male victims had vinyl stickers, numbers on pieces of paper in baggies, either attached to their bodies or close by."

Grimes rubbed his small beard with his fingers and thumb and dragged his hand down it. "Holy hell."

Bishop nodded. "Initially we assumed the numbers were a count of the victims, but they were out of order, and we couldn't find any murders with numbers or letters anywhere else."

"Until now," Grimes said.

Bishop nodded. "To the best of our knowledge only one person outside of law enforcement had any knowledge of the stickers."

Grimes raised an eyebrow. "And that person is?"

"Jessica Walters."

He blinked. "The reporter? How'd she get the information?"

"We aren't sure," Bishop said. "But she never reported on it."

"Even after the fact," Grimes said. "I wonder why she's holding out?"

"She wants an exclusive," I said. "But we agreed to wait a year in case the missing numbers showed up."

"Looks like she might be getting that exclusive sooner than expected," Grimes said.

I was afraid that was the case, too.

"There was also Stephanie Miller," Bishop said. "If you don't remember, her son was abducted by Stuart."

"She knows about the numbers?" Grimes asked.

"We can't confirm that at this time," Bishop said.

"I'll check with both of them and confirm who knows what," I said.

He nodded. "I may call her in for an interview," Grimes said. "In the meantime, can you provide access to your case files?"

Bishop nodded. "Shouldn't be a problem, but we'd like the same from you."

"Not a problem. I'll send them over daily if we have updates."

"Appreciate it," Bishop said.

"Did you ID the victim?" I asked.

"Yes, ma'am. Natalie Carlson. Twenty-four. Suwanee address."

"Had she been reported missing?"

"No," he said.

"Have you had any missing women reported recently?"

"This is a big county. We have missing women reported several times a week, but, thankfully, most of them return home without incident," Grimes said. "The family will give us a last seen date which should help with a timeframe."

"I'd appreciate that information," I said. I dug into my bag and handed him a card. "My cell's on there. Shoot me a text."

"No problem."

"Any other female deaths recently?"

"No, ma'am. No female deaths, no still missing women. We've only had two males die on us this week. It's been a good week considering the holiday. Things always get busy during a holiday."

"Right," Bishop said.

Things weren't adding up. The crime scene was completely different from ours or even Detective Johnson's in Birmingham, but that didn't stop the red flags from sending shivers down my spine. I glanced back and spoke more to myself than Bishop or Grimes. "Whoever did this didn't have access to our files."

Grimes tilted his head. "What makes you say that?"

"The crime scene," I said.

"It's sloppy. Unorganized. Rushed even," Bishop added. He pointed to where the woman's remains lay. "First of all, your victim is female. She's got blood on her. Her clothes aren't freshly cleaned and pressed, and her hair is messed up. Stuart bathed his victims, washed and pressed their clothing, and set up the crime scene meticulously. From how he positioned the bodies, to what surrounded them, even their location in relation to the fire, it was all planned. He left no traceable DNA, nothing that could connect him to the murders."

Grimes pressed his lips together as he nodded. "It sounds like someone got ahold of the sticker intel and ran with it, using your names to...what? Taunt you?"

"Sounds about right," Bishop said. "The question is, why?"

"That's the million-dollar ticket," Grimes said.

I shook my head. "No, something's not right." I couldn't put my finger on it, but it was there, waiting for me to make the connection, and I would, eventually.

"Murder is never right," Grimes said. "I'd appreciate it if you'd take a more detailed look at the scene, see if you can find any small similarities," Grimes said. "Anything that might help connect our killer to your murders."

Bishop and I made eye contact.

We walked back over to the victim as another helicopter circled above. Sheriff Rodney got back on his bullhorn and yelled up at the pilot and the cameraman and reporter inside. Their station call sign painted in large white letters, stood out like a sore thumb on the side of the thing. Once Rodney threatened them, they took off like the other helicopter had. A minute later he rushed past us cursing under his breath. I caught *news, reporters,* and *shove it* from him, and I didn't need the rest to get the point.

I stood sweating my butt off in the crime scene suit wishing I was back at Michels place giving him grief, instead of at a crime scene dressed as some deflated version of the Michelin Man. "What was called in?" I asked Grimes. "The girl or something else?"

He angled his head to the right. "Something else?"

"Our scenes started out with a fire."

"Only the girl. Mother walking a kid in a stroller found her. No one at the pool or on the course saw the vic."

I glanced back at the pool. Seeing her where the killer left her wouldn't have been hard. She'd been dumped in a shaded area a short distance from the pool at the edge of the golf course. Given it was a holiday and hotter than hell, the pool was crowded, but people weren't paying attention to what happened outside of the fence. Aside from the smell, which was getting worse in the heat, it was unlikely anyone would notice her unless they were up close and personal. "Have you talked to the golf staff?"

"They closed a few hours ago. According to gate security, all players were off the course, but we're going to contact the list from earlier."

Bishop rubbed his nose. "The smell isn't as strong as I'd expect."

"Someone was having a barbeque party," Grimes said.

"Makes sense," Bishop said. "I do get a hint of curry."

I eyed him. "Seriously?"

He shrugged. "I have a strange ability to smell spices. I can't help it."

Grimes chuckled. "You've worked a lot of crime scenes together?"

We nodded.

"I can tell, you handle them at an arm's length."

"Don't you?" I asked.

"Yes, ma'am, but I don't have a partner."

"You can have mine," Bishop said smiling.

I ignored Bishop's snide remark. "Does the victim live in this community?"

"Yes, ma'am, near the back entrance."

I circled back to the scene details. "And aside from everything we mentioned earlier about the other murders, the area around the victim was intentionally raked and smoothed over to remove any footprints or impressions." I studied the scene. "Like yours, so that's one similarity."

"It's a golf course. Maintenance is their most important feature," Grimes said.

"Except there would be something showing he was here. Something around the victim, but there are no evidence markers." I tapped my foot onto the ground and stepped away. "Look at my print and the ones surrounding here."

"Those are our guys." He rubbed sweat from his forehead. "Jesus, he removed his prints."

"That's what we assume," Bishop said.

"Was this Stuart guy ever in law enforcement?" Grimes asked.

I rolled my eyes. "Not smart enough, but he watched a lot of true crime TV."

"I swear that stuff alone creates more criminals than anything," he said.

"Outside of the internet," Bishop added.

"Amen," Grimes said. "It's not a coincidence that there are vinyl letters in baggies and your names. That's a message."

"There's something you should know," I said. Bishop pressed his lips together and nodded. I read that as confirmation to continue. "When Stuart was dying, he said, 'One, two, three, you can't pin on me. Seven, eight, nine, I'll add to my crimes. Four, five, six, add to the mix.'"

Grimes placed his hands on his hips. "Did he clarify what that meant?"

"Unfortunately, no."

"The initial murders were in Birmingham, correct?"

"Yes," I said.

"Did you prove he was in Alabama?"

Bishop cleared his throat. "We had evidence, but he had alibis, though they were slim. It wasn't our case, and we couldn't move it forward."

"Understood. They closed their investigation with his suicide, am I right?"

"Yes," I said. "But like Bishop said, it wasn't our jurisdiction, and we didn't have a say in the matter."

He kept his eyes focused on mine. "You didn't consider that a good decision?"

"After what Stuart said, I had my concerns."

"I've read about you, Detective. Strikes me as odd that you didn't push back."

"Again, it wasn't our jurisdiction. Detective Johnson was given the information, and he and his team decided based on the evidence. It was not my place to argue their decision."

"But it's bothered you ever since, hasn't it?" he asked.

"More so now than ever."

4

I peeled out of that marshmallow suit in dire need of a shower and a glass of ice water. Bishop opened my door for me.

"Wow. Such a gentleman. You sick?"

"What are you—" He shot me a slitted eye glare. "Chivalry isn't dead."

"But it was asleep for the past few years. You've never opened my door before. Is this practice for Cathy?"

"I guess I'm used to doing it for her, so it came naturally."

"I'm not going to argue." He smiled as I climbed into the vehicle. I was surprised he wasn't as rattled as me. As he sat, I asked, "So, you assume it's connected, too?"

"I'm still deciding. Tell me your take on it."

"It fits Stuart's rhyme, and this is number four. Five and six are coming, Bishop. We need to be prepared."

"Stuart's dead."

I leaned my head back in the seat. "Again, I'm aware of that. A copycat doesn't fit the scenario with the numbers, but I guess we can't rule that out. It's possible Stuart set up an additional three murders."

"By what, asking someone to kill for him in case of his demise?"

"He was all over those true crime sites online. It's not unreasonable to assume he made some connection and set it up offline."

"We've only had one murder, and it's not even in our jurisdiction. This could be someone we arrested before messing with us."

"With something similar to a serial killer's crime scenes? I'm not falling for that. Besides, who have we arrested that isn't serving time?"

"What if your reporter friend—"

I interrupted him. "She's not my friend."

"Whatever. What if the reporter leaked the information or someone found it in her notes? Some twisted nut job could have gotten hold of the information, and here we are. It's all for attention, but that doesn't mean it's connected to our numbers."

"*One, two, three, you can't pin on me. Seven, eight, nine, I'll add to my crimes. Four, five, six, add to the mix.* That right there tells me it's connected."

He exhaled and waved at the gate attendant. It was past nine, and the older woman was already gone, replaced by a younger black man who waved and flashed a big smile at us.

"I'm not saying this girl's death isn't related," Bishop said. "All I'm saying is that it doesn't mean this is the missing victim and that horror is starting again."

"But the—"

He interrupted me. "Not our investigation. If Grimes wants us involved, he'll involve us."

"I'm not sure. This murder proves my theory about Stuart's riddle."

"That he didn't kill the Alabama victims."

"And that there would be three more."

He rubbed a temple as we sat at a red light. "What about the crime scene? It's entirely different from ours and Johnson's. It's sloppy, and it's a female victim, and with all her body parts attached, I might add. The men were murdered in some whacked-out judgment killings to pay for their sexual assault or rape crimes. So, why a woman? The only link is our names, and it's a slim one at best. I'm going with copycat who had limited information about our scenes."

"Fine. I won't rule out a possible copycat either, but we can't downplay the stickers or the riddle. *Four, five, six, add to the mix.* We questioned that before, so what if we were right?"

He tapped his finger on the steering wheel. "I didn't question it. Stuart wanted us to think there were more murders coming. He wanted to mess with our heads."

"Maybe." I wasn't letting it go. "And regarding the missing body parts, the Alabama victims' penises were still attached, but that case closed despite the differences to ours. Slim or not, it could be connected, and we should treat it as such."

"I can agree with you on that, but, again, it's not our case."

"Fine. But let's work through this." My mind raced through possible theories. "Let's say you're right about Miller. Not only could she have known and leaked the information, but we've got a department full of staff as well as the entire Birmingham police department to consider as leaks. Any number of people could have purposely or mistakenly said something about the numbers and the rhyme. What if during the murders in Alabama someone from law enforcement let the details slip on one of those serial killer sites, and Stuart found out? He could have copied another killer. That would justify his little rhyme. Maybe, and I hate the thought of this, someone on the site is planning the murders and doling them out to nuts obsessed with the site."

Bishop sighed. "That would mean we'd have an infinite number of possible suspects. I don't have any idea how many of those sites are online."

"So, what do we do?"

"Nothing. The murdered girl isn't ours. We can provide information to Grimes, but it's not our case."

"And we risk two other people dying."

"Yes, but we aren't psychic, Rachel. We can't predict if and when someone's going to be murdered."

Bishop dropped me off at Michels to pick up my vehicle. The house was dark. Everyone had gone to the fireworks. I checked my watch. It was after nine, and they'd start any minute. I considered going, but instead of turning right toward the park, I turned left, toward our first victim six months prior. Jacob Ramsey's crime scene.

I drove my Jeep through the grass of the former horse farm toward the now demolished barn. Jacob Ramsey had been left near the barn and by a tree. I parked on the opposite side of the tree and walked over to the spot where Stuart left Ramsey's body. Nothing had changed since we first came to the scene. It was as though Ramsey never existed, that his remains were never part of the land.

I crouched down and ran my hand along the dirt and grass. Ramsey wasn't killed there. None of Stuart's victims in Hamby were killed where he left them, and we never located the murder sites. Experts tore Stuart's computer apart, stalked his chatrooms, and searched through everything in his home, yet we'd found nothing to tell us where he killed his victims.

There was evidence out there somewhere, the place where he killed his victims. Once we found that, we'd have the truth.

5

I fell onto my couch next to Kyle. Our legs touched, and that familiar buzz of ease mixed with energy raced through me. Kyle provided comfort without even trying, but sometimes even that comfort couldn't stop my brain from reeling. "I think it's Johnson."

Kyle scooted over a bit and turned toward me. His broad shoulder still brushed against mine, his face only millimeters away. He hadn't shaved in a few days, and the stubble on his face was prickly but sexy. I touched it with my hand. "I like the gruff."

"You can't drop that bomb and change the subject." He cocked his head to the right. "I'm going to need a little more detail, please."

I rattled off the highlight of those past hours, starting with the fact our names were left on scene. I ended with, "Maybe Detective Johnson is the killer after all. He could have framed Stuart. My dislike for him was obvious, so what if he decided to give us one more murder and drop our names to get us on edge?"

Kyle laughed. "The places your mind goes."

"If you've seen what I've seen, yours would go to dark places, too." I wanted to stuff those words back into my mouth the second I'd said them. Kyle worked for the Drug Enforcement Agency. He dealt with horrific things all the time. Murders, dead children, overdoses, things no one should see daily. I offered him a half smile. "I'd like to retract that, please."

"Accepted. Do you really see Johnson for this?"

"No. Yes. Maybe. But I'm confident it's connected. It could be a copycat. Someone could have leaked the vinyl numbers. It could be that Stuart planned these before he killed himself, and then he assigned them to someone else. It could be someone in those online true crime chatrooms he frequented. He could have planned it all and had three different people committing the murders." I inhaled and blew out a frustrated sigh. I needed to stay logical and rational, but my emotions wanted to take over. "And I'm kicking myself for not pushing the Birmingham PD to continue their investigation. I knew Stuart didn't kill the men there. I just knew it."

"You had no control over what Birmingham did, Rach, no matter what you said or didn't say, and they had evidence that proved he did it."

"A prosecutor would have torn his alibis apart." I leaned my head onto his shoulder. "I don't want to talk about it any more. Tell me about the fireworks. I'm bummed I missed them."

He kissed the top of my head. "How about we work on helping you forget tonight, and we make our own fireworks?"

I sent a text to Ashley.

Call me when you're free.

I tossed my phone on my bed and finished getting dressed. Kyle had left a few minutes before. I stared at my shirts hanging in my closet, realizing my choices were slim. Black casual, crewneck t-shirt. Black casual, v-neck t-shirt. The same in white and dark blue, a few Hamby PD short-sleeved, collared shirts in black, white, blue, and bluer. They were ugly and boxy on me, and when Savannah had caught me wearing one, she'd begged Jimmy to change the women's cuts, but he'd refused. I also had some dressier items Savannah forced on me, but I wasn't in a TV police drama where the female detective wore heels to catch killers. It was real life, and female detectives didn't chase down the bad guys in stilettos. Just the thought made my ankles hurt.

I picked a white Hamby PD shirt, threw it on and tucked it into my jeans. I connected my SIG Sauer, checked my nine-millimeter, loaded my magazine into it, dropped one into the chamber and secured it onto my belt.

I grabbed my work boots, the uncomfortable ones, and slipped them on, and after checking it the same way I had the other weapon, I added my second, personally-owned SIG Sauer P265 into my boot holster.

I dropped a few pellets into my Beta fish Louie's round castle and smiled as he joyfully rushed to his breakfast. Louie was as handsome—or pretty, I wasn't sure of the gender—as Herman, and I loved him, but we didn't have the same emotional connection. Herman had helped me through my husband Tommy's murder. His sympathetic looks told me he understood how I'd blamed myself for not acting fast enough, how I held no remorse for taking out his murderer, how with the help of loyal friends in the Chicago Police Department, I'd brought down the man who hired the killer, and how I barely held onto my sanity during my grief. Louie experienced happy Rachel. He'd yet to see the real me, the one with the darkness below the surface waiting for bad things to happen. Because bad things always happened.

I checked my watch. It wasn't too early to call Jessica Walters and Stephanie Miller before heading to the department. I searched the internet for Stephanie Miller's contact information and found her at a local Atlanta TV station. She'd changed jobs. How'd I miss that? Maybe I hadn't paid her the attention I'd thought. I dialed the number.

A woman with a pleasant and professional sounding voice answered on the third ring. "Thank you for calling WYTM, please hold."

I waited.

"Thank you for holding, how may I direct your call?"

"Stephanie Miller, please."

"May I tell her who's calling?"

"Detective Rachel Ryder, Hamby PD."

"One moment."

An instrumental version of a Lady Gaga song blasted into my ear. I hit the speaker icon and adjusted the volume as Stephanie Miller answered.

"Detective Ryder," she said in a happy tone. "What a pleasant surprise. What can I do for you?"

I doubted she'd feel pleasant for long. "I've got a few questions about the Stuart murders. Do you have a moment?"

Her voice dropped an octave and turned serious. "Chip Stuart? What's going on?"

I couldn't tell her any details about the woman found the night before, but her team was likely already on it. "What did you know about the murders when you first came to the department?"

There was a long silence until she said, "I'm not sure I understand. Are you saying I had information on the murders and didn't inform you?"

"Did you?"

"No. My son was abducted by that sociopath. I told you everything. Is there a reason you're asking?" Papers ruffled in the background. "Does this have anything to do with another murder?"

"We have no active murder investigations in Hamby, Ms. Miller. I'm finalizing some notes for the case file," I lied.

"Really? It's been months. I'd expect that was completed by now."

"There were a lot of notes to go through."

"I understand. As I said, I shared what I had, but I promise if I do hear that something has leaked, I'll be sure to get it to you immediately."

"Thank you," I said.

"Detective, I didn't get to this position because of my looks. Whatever it is you're really working on, I'd like to help. Off the record, of course."

She was a smart woman and read between the lines like an expert. I said thank you again and disconnected the call, and then I searched for Jessica Walters and gave her a call.

"As promised, I haven't reported on the numbers," she said. "But if you're ready for that exclusive..." She left the rest of the sentence for me to unravel.

"Not quite yet."

"Has there been another murder?"

"I'm working on some theories," I said. It wasn't a lie. "And I wanted to make sure you didn't tell anyone about the numbers."

"I haven't. I made a promise to you, and I expect you to keep yours made to me."

"I will," I said.

She asked a few more questions, and I suspected she understood exactly what I wasn't saying, but I did my best to put her off course.

"Detective Ryder, whatever is going on, I'm going to find out, and it's my duty to report the facts."

"I'd expect nothing less of you," I said, and I hung up.

I dialed Detective Johnson but got his voicemail. Whether I liked the guy or not, we owed him a call about the recent victim. I still toyed with the idea of him being connected to the murders, but not enough to jeopardize the investigation into the girl's murder. Grimes would likely be in touch also, but I had a few questions for Johnson myself. I left a message and asked him to return my call at his earliest opportunity.

I picked up coffees for Bishop, Michels, and me, added a dozen donuts in various flavors, and headed to the department. I chastised myself for eating two of the chocolate iced donuts before arriving. I slid the box onto the counter in the kitchen near the pit, the large open room where officers on patrol sat. Bishop, Michels, and I had cubicles on the outer perimeter of the pit, but the chief and a few other big wigs had actual offices with real walls, doors, and windows with a view. Granted, the view was a parking lot, but it was a view. I walked into Bishop's cubicle and handed him his coffee. Michels sat in one of the chairs by Bishop's desk, so I gave him his, too. Bishop was head down in his laptop. He grunted a thanks and cursed at his screen.

I sat in the chair beside Michels and flicked my head toward my partner and leaned toward Michels. "He having a bad morning?"

Michels smirked. "He's playing that word game and losing his ass."

I narrowed my brow at him. "Which word game? Words with Friends?"

Michels laughed. "What year do you live in? It's Wordle. It's creating high blood pressure problems across the world. I'm shocked you haven't played it."

"I don't play games on my phone or any electronic device. I do other things with my time, kind of like you."

His eyes shifted to me and back to Bishop cursing at his laptop screen.

"Come on," I said. "Spill the tea."

"You know what spill the tea means, but you don't know Wordle? Are you even human?"

"I'll never tell."

"Yeah, well, neither will I." His chin jutted forward. "My relationship with Ash is private."

I furrowed my brows. "You're no fun." A loud burst of baby-age screaming penetrated the cubicle. The partitions shook. "Scarlet's here?"

Michels nodded. "With the chief."

I patted his knee and smiled. "Thanks, Justin, baby."

I walked out of the cubicle to his saying, "Bite me, Ryder," but I ignored him and skipped in my excitement to see my goddaughter.

Scarlet sat on Savannah's lap wailing up a storm as her mom bounced her on a knee.

I stood in the doorframe with my arms crossed over my chest. "What have you done to my sweet Scarlet?"

"She's still teething," Jimmy said. "We felt one growing in last night."

Savannah's head whipped toward me. "This child is

possessed by the devil himself." She held her out toward me. "See for yourself."

I forced myself not to smile. "She is not possessed."

"Oh, yes, she is. That comes from Jimmy's family."

"Hey, now," he said.

"I speak my truth," Savannah said.

I eyed the sweet little girl. Her poor, chubby-cheeked face was red and swollen. She rubbed her eyes. Tears and baby snot covered her lip. I set my coffee on Jimmy's desk, grabbed the burp cloth hanging over Savannah's shoulder, tossed it over mine, and relieved Sav of her *not possessed* child. I wiped her little mouth and nose and kissed her on the forehead. "What's your momma doing to you, sweet girl?"

Scarlet sniffled, stared straight into my eyes, and wailed like she'd had her ear pierced. I handed her back to her mother. "Nope."

Jimmy laughed. Savannah pointed two fingers to her eyes, then to him and repeated it twice. He shut up. She rubbed some numbing solution on Scarlet's gums and stuck a chew toy in her mouth. Once the baby calmed down, Jimmy asked about the scene in Suwanee. I filled him in.

"Let me get Bishop in here." He walked out of his office. A minute later he returned with a donut in his mouth and Bishop behind him.

Bishop had hunted down the donuts and snagged a few for himself. Jimmy stole one from him. I no longer felt remorse for eating two on the way in.

The baby was calm and cute in no time. "Scarlet needs to greet her people," Savannah said. "She's their queen." She walked out of the room and into the pit. She was right. The men loved her baby, partly because she was the chief's child and they were sucking up, but Scarlet didn't seem to care either way.

Jimmy finished the donut and eyed Bishop sitting where Savannah had earlier. "Tell me your thoughts on the situation last night."

I took the seat next to Bishop and waited for him to act like it was no big deal.

Jimmy crossed his arms and tilted his head to the side as he prepared to listen.

"Stephanie Miller assured me she had nothing other than what she'd told us initially," I said. "And Jessica Walters kept her promise to keep quiet, too."

"Perhaps it's a leak at the Birmingham PD. Call Johnson. Clear the air," Jimmy said.

"I did," I said. "I got his voicemail."

"He'll call you back," Jimmy said. "You grew on him."

I grimaced. "Gross."

"You don't think it's a leak?" Jimmy asked.

"It's possible, but it's also possible it's not."

"How so? Stuart's dead."

Why did everyone keep telling me that? Did they think I didn't know? I repeated my theories, and when I finished, Jimmy leaned back in his chair and cursed. "This isn't our investigation," he said.

"Grimes has my number," I said. "We've already discussed most of this. He asked for us to help if needed. We said we would."

Jimmy nodded. "I'll get in touch with Sheriff Rodney, let him know we're here to assist."

"What if another girl is murdered?" I asked.

"Unless she's a Hamby resident, there isn't much we can do about that, Ryder. You know that."

"It sucks."

"It does." He leaned forward and placed his palms on his desk. "Now, since we're blessed to have no crimes worthy of your skills committed in the past few months, and given that you got called out last night, once you write up your call to Suwanee, y'all can take the rest of the day off. You're on call, but let's hope we don't have to see each other until tomorrow."

6

I stood and stretched, having typed out two thousand words of detail on the Suwanee woman's murder. Most of the details were my opinion on its relationship to the Stuart murders. I wanted things in writing for when they turned out to be correct. I dialed Johnson again and left him another message.

As I was preparing to leave, Savannah walked in without Scarlet.

"You're still here? Who has Scar?" I asked.

"Granny Abernathy picked her up a few minutes ago. It's easier for her to meet us here than come all the way to our place." She glanced at my closed laptop. "Jimmy said you're done for the day?"

I nodded. "Your husband was gracious enough to let Bishop and I have the rest of the day off."

"Oh," she said, smiling. She grabbed my arm. "Let's do lunch. We both need some serious girl time."

I would never admit she was right about me needing girl time, but she was. "Sushi?"

She inhaled through her nose and shook her head. "Ew,

no. Last time I ate the stuff I left it on the sidewalk outside the restaurant, if you know what I mean."

I cringed. "I do, but you were pregnant. That was a long time ago."

"Still not over it," she said. She grabbed my arm. "Let's go to Taco Mac. I'm dying for wings."

Taco Mac was a chain of restaurants in the metro Atlanta area with an outlier in Chattanooga, Tennessee. The place specialized in beer and wings, but their chips and salsa were good, too, though I never quite got their name. They had tacos, but it wasn't their main sell.

People gathered in their large bar area for the TVs and beer, while the restaurant was usually filled with families and youth sports teams. It was always crowded, and we were lucky when there wasn't a wait.

Savannah preferred the Taco Mac on Market Place in Cumming to the one close by in Alpharetta. She despised the traffic in downtown Alpharetta, and I agreed. The Cumming location was also close to a T.J. Maxx and HomeGoods combination store, and she loved those stores more than she loved her husband. The last time she roped me into going to that Taco Mac, she drove, and I spent three painful hours searching through racks and racks of clothing I would never wear for something she swore would be perfect for me. She found eight things for herself and three for me. I found nothing, and I politely declined her colorful choices for me. Orange may have been the new black, but she'd never get it on me.

From that point on, I committed to driving my own vehicle whenever Savannah and I had plans.

There was no easy route to the restaurant. I considered taking Highway Nine, but everyone used it to avoid the highway, and congestion was a major problem for the two-lane road. I hated taking Georgia 400 in the summer. It was always backed up with people coming and going to Lake Lanier, but it was the most direct route.

I needed the time with my best friend. We'd been close since shortly after I moved to town, but not from my doing. Savannah had a way of pushing herself into your life whether you wanted her there or not. Turned out, I wanted her there. I'd been without a best friend since a tragic accident in Chicago took my lifelong best friend Jenny Dolatowski. Savannah was my fresh start, and I loved her for it.

She was there already, sitting at a table, and sipping a pinkish orange drink. "I'm only having one, I promise." She twirled her finger around the edge of the glass. "Took you long enough. I was concerned." She winked and sipped her drink again.

A server walked up. I ordered a half sweet, half unsweet iced tea and chips and salsa. "Not concerned enough to call me."

"I had faith."

I laughed despite the slow fire burning in the pit of my stomach. "So, how's things?"

"Oh, bless your ever-loving heart. As if I came here to talk about myself." Her Southern drawl was thick, something she pulled out of her bag of tricks when she wanted to make a point. She took another sip from her drink and smiled. "Have you told him yet?"

The server brought my tea, and I busied myself sipping it to avoid her question. "I've been busy."

She exhaled and said, "Pfft. Watching you lie is as painful as watching a prized pig go off to slaughter."

I nearly spit out my tea. "Did you just make that up?"

She beamed with pride. "I did, but trust me, you do not want to see a pig go off to slaughter. It's heartbreaking."

"But bacon."

"Oh, bacon. I'm conflicted about that." She shook her head lightly. "So, why haven't you told him? He'll be happy. Kyle loves you."

"What makes you say that?"

"Because I've seen the way he looks at you. Women miles away can feel the heat coming off those taut muscles of his every time you're nearby." She fanned herself with her hand. "My oh, my. If he wasn't my best friend's man toy, I'd be drooling over that man on the daily."

I stared at her with a blank expression. "That is the worst of the worst of your Southern belle impressions, and he is not my man toy. Gross."

She gasped. "I am a Southern belle." She sipped her drink again and said, "But, really, that boy definitely has love written all over his face."

"So, how 'bout them Cubbies?"

"Don't change the subject. Besides, my Braves are doing better, anyway."

"Not by much. As for your first question," I said, working hard to avoid the love subject, "I'm honestly not sure how he'll react, and I have been busy."

"Liar."

I exhaled. "I'm not lying. I'm not sure how he'll react, and I don't want to talk about work."

"I am completely fine not talking about your work. I have Jimmy. I don't need to hear it from you, too." She took another sip of her drink. "Now, relationships and love? Those are things in which I excel. And you need to tell him."

The server brought the chips and salsa and asked about

our order. Savannah ordered twenty wings in one of their special sauces, saying we'd share.

"He knows it's something you intended to do. Why are you afraid?"

"It's a promise I made to my deceased husband, and I didn't keep it after his death before meeting Kyle. Okay, maybe I tried, but we saw how that turned out. Don't you see? If I tell him I'm taking riding lessons after all this time, he'll feel like I haven't let go of Tommy."

"You haven't let go of Tommy."

That took the wind out of me, but only because she was right. I'd never let go of Tommy. You don't fall out of love with someone because they die. That love continues, sitting there in the depths of your heart with nowhere to go. "I mean, he's not coming back. I get that. I don't sit and actively miss him like I used to, but I do miss him, and he'll always be in my heart."

"I understand. No one can really get it unless they've been through it."

"No, they can't. Tommy's in my heart, and something reminds me of him daily. It's like his memory floats into everything I do, and I can't push it away."

"That must be hard."

The sadness of the loss never disappeared. Sometimes it lay dormant, but when it showed itself, it hit like a brick to my chest. I turned away and rubbed my eyes to keep the tears at bay. "Grief is weird. One minute I'm driving home, singing along to Brooks and Dunn or something, my mood totally fine, and I walk in the house and feel the emptiness from him not being there. Grief is like a virus mutating to adjust to a new environment. My mind knows Tommy was never in my Georgia home, but sometimes it feels empty without him anyway. The realization that he's gone hits me like the first time I slept in our bed after his murder, and other times it's a brief, but intense, wave of sorrow washing over me. I'm not sure it'll ever go away, but I don't want Kyle to assume my love for Tommy discounts how I feel about him."

"How do you feel about him?"

"I'm still trying to put words to it."

She smiled. "Nice dodge there."

"I don't want him feeling someone else has all my heart because that's not really what's happening. I can't explain it, and I need to be able to find the right words when I tell him about the lessons. So he understands."

"Okay," she said. She put both palms flat on the table. "First of all, that someone else was your husband who you watched die. Kyle will understand. But you need to tell him. You started when you were ready, and it's been months now. He's going to think you're cheating on him."

I drew my brows together until it was almost painful. "He will not."

"You're gone three days a week for two hours at a time. That's enough for a quickie at the Hampton Inn."

I laughed out loud. "And a shower and a stop for lunch."

"Ain't that the truth."

We both laughed.

"He'll understand. Give him a chance."

"I will," I said. "I'm getting there."

"Now, about these words you're trying to find for the way you feel about him. I have a suggestion—"

I cut her off and pointed to the server coming with our wings. "Oh, look! Food!"

"Rach." Her tone turned serious. "If you don't feel this thing between you two can go anywhere, you need to tell him. He deserves to be with someone who wants a future with him."

"I didn't say I didn't see this going somewhere, or that we don't have a future together."

She raised an eyebrow. "Is that what you can't find the words for?"

The server dropped off our food and asked if we needed anything else. We both said no. As she walked away, I said, "It's that—"

Savannah bit into a wing and spoke with her mouth full. Manners flew out the window when Savannah ate chicken wings. "Tommy would want you to be happy. He'd want you to find love again."

"My brain knows that."

"What's your heart say?"

"That telling Kyle how I feel is letting go of the past, and I'm not sure I'm ready for that."

"Did you hear what you said? You said *telling Kyle how I feel*. Your heart is good to go, it's your stupid brain that's in your way."

"I love how you're so supportive and kind."

She shrugged and bit into the wing again. "I am a Southern belle. Any-hoo, Jimmy's birthday is coming up, and I thought we could all go roller skating."

I blinked. "I'm sorry. Did you say roller skating?"

"I did."

"Well, that's a big nope for me. I haven't done that since I was a kid, and I wasn't all that good. My entire junior high celebrated their birthdays at the rink, and I never missed one even though the lights and party rooms made me ill. Those disco lights and the psychedelic paint in the little rooms? Made me sick every single time."

She shook her head and laughed.

"Besides," I said. "We're a little old to be taking that kind of risk with our bodies. We might as well break each other's ankles and call it done."

She laughed. "For a tough detective, you have no guts."

My cell phone rang. I didn't recognize the number, but I answered anyway. "Ryder."

"This is Detective Edward Anderson from the Birmingham Police Department. I understand you left a message for Detective Johnson."

Savannah mouthed, "Is it work?"

I held up a finger to tell her to hold on. "Yes," I said to Detective Anderson. "Is he available?"

"I'm afraid I have some bad news. Detective Johnson took his own life this morning."

7

I whispered to Savannah that I'd be right back and headed to the restaurant's exit.

The right words escaped me. "Oh, I...I'm so sorry." I walked to my car and leaned against it. The sun beat down on me. I squinted and walked back toward the door where there was a small, covered space I could stand under. It wouldn't stop the heat, but it would get me out of the sun.

"Thank you. We weren't partners for long, but he was a good man, and I respected him a great deal."

"I understand. Would you let me know if there are services? I'd like to attend, and I'm sure my partner will, too."

"Of course. I'll be in touch. May I ask why you called? Perhaps I can help."

I wasn't sure how to answer that. I didn't know Anderson that well. He hadn't been actively involved in our investigation. "It's about the Stuart murders."

"Those were closed six months ago."

"Yes, I'm aware. Did Johnson tell you what Stuart said before he died?"

"Only that he wasn't making sense."

"It sounded as if he didn't kill the men in Birmingham. I wondered if Johnson had any concerns."

"I don't think he did. In fact, we spoke of it the other day. He said he was happy with the investigation and felt Stuart was trying to confuse things with the rhyme."

"There was a female murdered in Suwanee, Georgia, on July Fourth. The killer left vinyl letters spelling mine and my partner's names near the body."

"With all due respect, Detective, you and your partner were interviewed regarding the murders. It made national news."

"The information on the stickers was not released to the public, unless they were from your department?"

"To the best of my knowledge, they were not. I'm sure you understand that anyone could have decided to wrap you into their murder for attention. The letters could be mere coincidence."

I didn't care what he said. Natalie Carlson was connected, but how? "Understood," I said. "I was wondering if—"

He cut me off. "Johnson's suicide had nothing to do with those murders. You can trust me on that."

"Did he leave a note?"

"No, ma'am. It wasn't about the Stuart case. It was something else, and it's inappropriate for me to share that with you. It would be disrespectful to his memory." He took a breath and said, "Don't let the Stuart murders haunt you. We all need to move on. Johnson did, and he'd worked the case for over three years."

"Yes, that's true," I said.

"I'll keep you posted on the services," he said and disconnected the call.

I walked back into the restaurant. The food was already packed up in to go containers. "I'm sorry," I said.

"It's no biggie."

I checked my watch. "I have an appointment in a half hour. I should probably go."

"Don't get thrown off the horse." She winked.

In the car, I did a quick Google search for William Johnson in Birmingham, Alabama, and found two addresses. Bubba, Hamby PD's genius tech wasn't in, and I didn't want to bother him on his day off, so I ran a check for Johnson's license. I recalled him mentioning being divorced, and I wanted to make sure I found his wife.

Joey was an informant I'd used several times working for the Chicago PD. I'd used him a few times since moving to Georgia, but our contact had lessened over the years since I'd moved and worked with Bubba. He was as good as Joey, but he didn't break any laws for the intel. Or so I assumed.

Joey picked up on the third ring. "Holy balls, long time no speak. I thought you died or something."

"And I thought maybe you moved out of your mother's basement."

"I'm Italian. We don't move out until we're kicked out. What can I do you for, Detective?"

"I need to find the ex-spouse of Detective William Johnson in or around Birmingham, Alabama. Can you find me a number?"

"Got her first name?"

"No, sorry."

"No worries. I'll call you when I—"

"Can you check now, please? It's kind of urgent."

"Fine, but you owe me dinner."

"When you come to Georgia, it's on me."

"Uber eats, babe. Just pay and have it delivered." His fingers tapped on computer keys. "I'm feeling pizza."

"I'll Venmo you the cash."

"I'll send you an invoice. Okay, Elizabeth Johnson, and yeah, they're divorced like most cops. Want her cell?"

"Does she have a landline?"

"Nope."

"The cell, you doofus."

He laughed and gave me the number.

I dialed, riddled with self-loathing for making the call right after her ex-husband killed himself. What was I stepping into? Did they hate each other? Was the divorce amicable? Would she sob into the phone? I never handled crying well, and the phone didn't make it any easier.

"Hello?" She didn't sound like she'd been crying.

"Elizabeth Johnson?"

"Who's calling?"

"This is Detective Rachel Ryder with the Hamby, Georgia, police. I worked with your husband—"

"Ex-husband."

"Ex-husband on the Chip Stuart investigation. I was hoping I could ask you a few questions."

"Bill is dead."

"I know. I'm sorry for your loss."

"Thank you. Though we're divorced, it's still a tragedy. Bill was a good man. Unfortunately, he wasn't the right man for me. We hadn't spent a lot of time together lately, though he had come by a few times in the past few months. I can try to help you. What are your questions?"

"I was wondering if Detective Johnson ever said anything to you after the Stuart investigation was closed. Maybe referring to his belief about the killer?"

"Bill was very committed to that investigation. He lived

and breathed it since the day they discovered the first body. It's part of the reason our marriage ended. He couldn't walk away, even after it grew cold in those three years before the killings started in Georgia. Even after the case closed, he couldn't let go. In fact, the last time I saw him, he told me he thought he'd missed something, and he was planning on looking into it." She sighed. "Twenty years I spent with that man, and his life boiled down to catching a serial killer. Such a waste."

"Do you think that's why he committed suicide? Because he missed something?"

"Detective Ryder is it?"

"Yes."

"Bill would never commit suicide. I can't tell you what happened to him, but I can say for certain he didn't take his own life."

"What makes you say that?"

"Because he was dedicated, stubborn, and driven to the core to find answers. He may have seemed calm on the outside, even condescending at times, but he would do what it took to find the answers. He would never kill himself before learning the truth." She sighed again. "Bill spoke highly of you. He said you were a good detective, and he appreciated your help in the investigation."

Ouch. "We worked hard to close it."

"Detective, would it be possible for you to look into his death? I realize that's a big ask, but I don't want his reputation stained by a lie."

"Alabama is not part of my jurisdiction."

"Bill said you were the kind of detective that didn't let things like that stop you. Please, will you at least investigate it for me, on the side, of course. I've asked his partner, but he believes Bill killed himself and wants to let it go."

If Tommy hadn't been killed in front of me, and someone

had told me to let it go, I'd have sucker punched them. Divorce aside, she still cared for Johnson, and she deserved the truth. "I'll look into it, but I can't make any promises."

We finished the call as I pulled into the stables from Birmingham Highway. An hour later I was back in my Jeep and dialing Bishop on my way home.

He answered with, "No. I'm sitting on my deck enjoying the sweltering heat." Bishop had moved a month prior. He'd opted for a townhouse near mine, but his had a shaded patio with a wood pergola covered with ivy.

"I'm coming over."

"Can't we spend our days off without each other?" His tone was light.

"Johnson killed himself earlier today."

"He what? No, did he?"

"I just got off the phone with Detective Anderson. He must have got my messages to Johnson. I also talked to Johnson's ex-wife, Elizabeth."

"You didn't tell Anderson why you were calling, did you?"

"I mentioned the Natalie Carlson death and said I had some questions about the investigation. He'll get the call from Grimes, too, so he'll know something's up."

"Did Johnson leave a note?"

"Not according to Anderson, but his ex-wife doesn't think he would kill himself, especially without knowing the truth about those murders, and she said he told her he thought he'd missed something."

"Interesting."

"Right? Anderson said he'll keep me posted about the service. We should go."

"That would be the right thing to do."

"Yes, it would. Rob, come on. Do I have to say it?" I pulled into his driveway and shut off my Jeep.

"You're here, aren't you?"

"How'd you guess?"

"I hear your Jeep in my nightmares."

I walked back to his small back yard. "Should I say it?"

"Let me read your mind. Let's see, Johnson killed himself because he killed the men in Alabama regardless of what his ex-wife said."

"It's possible."

"And the girl last night?"

I sat next to him. The sun setting left a pink and purple haze across the sky. "He could have driven out here yesterday, killed her, drove back to Birmingham, felt remorseful, and killed himself."

He leaned his head back on his seat and closed his eyes. "Do you really believe Johnson is a serial killer?"

"It doesn't matter what I believe. It makes sense."

"Murder doesn't always make sense."

I wrapped my long brown hair into a ball and re-clipped it on the back of my head. "I know."

"I liked Johnson. He was a good man, an honorable man. He's not a serial killer. You're grasping at straws."

My cell phone rang. I checked the caller ID. "It's Michels."

Bishop sat up. "He's off shift."

I answered the call and put it on speaker. "What's going on?"

"Chillax, Ryder. Not everything is a crime. Beers at Dukes. Chief's here."

I checked my watch. "I'll be there." I glanced at Bishop.

"Oh, hell. I'll be there, too."

8

Dukes is a restaurant and bar in Hamby frequented by law enforcement where the owner gave anyone with a badge a discount on alcohol along with free food to support our efforts in the community. He always gave me my non-alcoholic drinks for free, too.

I ordered an O'Doul's and sat beside Jimmy. "How'd you get out of the house?"

"Savannah drove home to Macon with Scarlet. She'll be back the day after tomorrow."

"She didn't tell me she was going home. Is everything okay?"

"Yeah, everything's fine. There's some famous photographer in town for a show, and her mother convinced him to photograph Scarlet. It's a last-minute thing."

"Savannah's going to love that."

"Tell me about it."

The bartender slid my drink to me. "Thank you," I said, and then I turned to Jimmy. "You're going to sleep like a baby tonight."

"God, I hope not. Scarlet hasn't slept through the night in ages."

"Wait until she's a teenager," Bishop said. "You'll never sleep again."

Michels arrived a few minutes after us. He sat next to Bishop.

"Where's Ashley?" I asked.

"This is why we didn't tell anyone. All y'all acting like this."

"All us aren't acting like this," Bishop said. He flicked his thumb at me. "She is acting like this."

I grimaced. "Fine, I'll stop. But seriously, I was hoping you'd bring her out with you. She wanted to talk to me at the cookout. Is everything okay?"

"She's got a bug. I heard from her this morning. She said she was staying home from work, and she'd call me later."

"Oh, I hope she feels better," I said. I drummed my fingers on the glossy bar top. It was wood with a smooth glass-like surface.

"What's wrong?" Jimmy asked. "You've had your Chicago scowl on your face since you walked in."

"Have I really?"

He nodded. "I've become very familiar with that face. Something's bugging you."

"Detective Johnson committed suicide earlier today."

Jimmy's eyes widened. "He what? No."

Bishop held his beer to his mouth without taking a sip. "That's what I said."

"Did he leave a note?" Jimmy asked.

"Not according to his partner."

"She's run the gamut of connections to Stuart's victims and the murders in Birmingham," Bishop said. "It's how she gets when she latches onto something."

"First of all, Jimmy expected me to follow up with John-son, and I did." I turned my head toward my partner. "And I'm rarely wrong when I latch onto something."

Michels held up his beer. "I'll drink to that."

"Thanks for the support," I said.

"Your theory's that Johnson offed himself because he's the Birmingham killer?" Jimmy asked.

"And suddenly acquired a conscience," Bishop added.

"That doesn't connect him to the Suwanee case," Jimmy said.

"She surmises he could have driven here, killed the girl, drove home, and killed himself," Bishop said.

"I'm saying it's possible," I said. "And, also, I spoke to his ex-wife. She claims Johnson wouldn't kill himself, and that he said there was something he'd missed on the Stuart case. Let's say it wasn't Johnson. What if he realized Stuart didn't kill the men in Alabama? He wasn't a bad detective. He could have figured it out and someone, maybe the real killer, killed him."

"Where are you on a scale of that's it and it's not?" Jimmy asked.

"Not sure. We need to explore it further. His ex had a lot of good things to say about his character, and that stumps me."

"She's the expert," Bishop said. "And if they're divorced and she's still saying nice things about him, she's probably telling the truth. Bitter women don't speak kindly of their exes."

"I'll drink to that," Michels said. He guzzled his beer down fast and asked the bartender for another.

"Bishop and I want to go to his service."

"Unless something comes up, I'm good with that," Jimmy said. "I'll let you go on our dime. You can represent the depart-ment." He sipped his beer. "You're going to ask about the Stuart investigation, aren't you?"

"It might come up."

Bishop laughed. "Do bears shit in the woods?"

Michels left first, and Jimmy followed, leaving just me and Bishop. He yawned. "I was hoping for an early bedtime tonight."

I paid the tip on the tab, but the bartender refused to let me pay for the drinks. "Come on old man, you need your beauty sleep."

"I'm not going to comment on that."

"Probably wise."

The lot had been full when we arrived, so we both had parked across the street in public parking near the boutiques and specialty stores. As we walked to our vehicles, a familiar face peeked out from under the awning of a closed women's boutique. I recognized him immediately. "Baker."

"What?"

"There." I pointed to the man. "Scott Baker."

Bishop gripped my upper arm lightly. "Rachel, don't."

I yanked my arm away and aimed straight for Baker. Five big steps and I was across the street and within a foot of him. "Got business in town?"

His lips formed into a snarly smile. "Detective Ryder, what a pleasure." He took a puff from his cigarette, dropped it to the ground, and stomped out the end with his shoe. "I didn't know you frequented this area in the evening."

"What're you doing in town, Baker?"

He smirked and said, "Business," and then he winked.

I stepped a few inches from him, and it hit me. Cedar-wood. *Tommy.* I shook off the familiarity of it and focused on Baker. "What kind of business?"

"Detective, I don't think I need to be answering your questions. Our business together is done. I suggest you leave me be."

Bishop stood beside me. "Let's go, Ryder." He tugged on my arm that time and pulled me back.

"Wonderful to see you," Baker said.

"Asshole," I muttered under my breath.

"Me or him?" Bishop asked.

"Both."

He didn't let go of me until we were at my Jeep and outside Baker's earshot. "What the hell did you do that for?"

"Don't you think it's a coincidence, him showing up here like that?"

"I think he does business in the area, so it's plausible to think we might run into him at some point."

"Right after a woman is killed and our names are left at the scene? You don't see a connection?"

"Baker didn't kill the men. Stuart did," Bishop said.

"But Baker's daughter was one of the alleged women one of those men attacked, and he commended Stuart on it. He wanted to thank him. You heard him say that yourself. Hell, he even paid for his legal fees. For all we know, he could have had other conversations with Stuart and found out about the vinyl stickers."

"And what? Murdered a woman then left our names to taunt us?"

"Yes," I said.

"Then he just shows up here to put himself in the hot seat?" He shook his head. "No. Baker may be an a-hole, but he's not stupid."

9

My mind wasn't ready to go home and relax, so I hit each of Stuart's crime scenes again. I didn't get out of my Jeep, just drove by with a sour taste in my mouth for a guy I hated. Buildings on fire. Lives ended. And none of it made a difference. Bad men would still do bad things, and serial killers would still freely walk the earth.

I arrived home to Kyle in his normal position on my couch, legs out and resting on my wood trunk I used as a coffee table.

"Hey," he said. "I was getting worried. Your shift ended a while ago."

"It ended before lunch. Jimmy let us go early."

He tweaked his head to the left. "And you've been?"

"I went to lunch with Savannah, then ran some errands, and then to Dukes. I should have called. I'm sorry."

"It's okay. I figured I'd stick around and make sure you got home okay."

It was nice having someone watching out for me like that, though at times I pushed back. I struggled with the self-imposed claustrophobic emotional pressure it sometimes brought. I took off my boots, cleared the chamber in my SIG then put a fresh bullet into it, and set the gun on the kitchen counter. I walked to my bedroom and took a quick shower.

Kyle walked into the bathroom. "You okay?"

"Bill Johnson killed himself this morning." I rinsed the soap off my body and quickly washed and conditioned my hair as we talked.

"That's awful," Kyle said. "And it makes you think you were right in suspecting him, doesn't it?"

"Kind of. The thing is, I can't stop thinking that he couldn't live with himself for killing the men in Birmingham."

He handed me a clean towel. "I didn't get the impression Johnson was a killer. Besides, if that was the case, then why did he wait this long?"

"That's where I get stuck, but people didn't get that killer impression from Ted Bundy either."

"Valid point."

"Bishop thinks I'm grasping at straws, trying to make something out of nothing."

"That's not your nature. Unless it involves a donut."

I'd walked into the bedroom to get dressed. He followed behind. I turned to him and jabbed my finger into his chest. "I called that donut, and you know it." A while back, Nikki, Hamby's crime scene tech, brought some special edition Dunkin' Donuts to the office. Kyle happened to be there and smiled when I called the chocolate and vanilla crème one, but he ate it anyway.

"Nobody calls donuts unless they're teenagers. Besides, you know the saying, first come, first served."

I let the towel fall and grabbed it before it hit the ground. I pulled it tight and twisted an end. Kyle held up his hands and stepped closer. "You wouldn't flick that at an unarmed man, would you?" His smile was big, and his eyes crinkled at the sides. "Go ahead, make my day."

I tried not to laugh. "Your Clint Eastwood impression sucks." I whipped the towel at him, but he caught it with his right hand, then yanked me toward him. He pressed his clothed body against my skin. "You're going to pay for that." He flipped around, pushed me onto the bed and fell gently on top of me.

I kissed him and said, "Go ahead, make my day."

My Ring doorbell blasted me awake from a deep sleep clouding my brain. It took me a second to recognize the sound. I glanced over at Kyle snoring beside me, his arm draped over his pillow. Did he not hear that? "What the—" I rolled over, latched onto my iPhone, and then tapped on the Ring app. "Michels?" I whispered to myself. "What's he doing here?" I checked the clock. Too late for a casual call, too early to be waking me up for something unimportant. My stomach rolled. I climbed out of bed knowing that was the last good sleep I'd get for a while.

Michels had come up through the ranks at Hamby, starting first as a patrol officer, or beat cop, or slick sleeve, as law enforcement liked to call them. He advanced to the unofficial title of minion for the dicks, what our chief would call an assist on calls. He set his sights on a detective spot, and when he passed the detective exam, received his promotion. He wasn't a newbie any longer, but everyone still referred to him that way because we could. He was an excellent detective, and I knew his being at my door at that time in the morning meant it was urgent.

I opened the door with a nagging uneasiness burning in the pit of my stomach. Michels's red eyes, tousled hair, and well past five-o'clock shadow sent shivers down my spine. He'd all but fallen apart since I saw him last. "Jesus, Michels, it's three in the morning." I gave him a quick once over. His shirt was untucked, and he wasn't wearing socks. Dark, tiny bags hung loosely below his eyes. "You look like hell. What's going on?"

He took a step back and dragged his hand over the top of his short black hair. "Ashley's gone. I think something happened to her."

My body stiffened. "Gone?" I bumped my front door open more with my butt. "What?" I pushed the door with my hand. "Come in so we don't wake up my neighbors."

He stepped inside, bouncy and jittery like he'd had too many coffees and too little sleep. "I'm serious, Ryder. She's gone. It's bad. I know it's bad."

I motioned for him to sit on the couch, and I sat across from him on my newer leather chair. I tucked my legs underneath me and took a deep breath, working hard to stay calm, if not for Michels, for me. Ashley was fine, I told myself. "Slow down and tell me what's going on. Is Ashley hurt? Was she in an accident or something?"

Michels' eyes stared through me as if he was trying to find the right words to tell me the bad news. The shaky stomach from earlier jiggled to life again, burning its way up my esophagus and leaving a bitter taste in my mouth. Michels and I were friends, but not exactly the kind that shared our secrets, even the casual ones. My law enforcement experience taught me what people showed us wasn't always real, and no matter how much we believed we *got* someone, most of the time we didn't. People were capable of things we couldn't predict or imagine, and I'd learned to never forget that. Michels didn't come off as violent, but anything was possible. Had he and Ashley fought earlier that night? Did he lose control?

"Did something happen between you two?"

Kyle walked into the room, his eyes filled with sleep. "Everything okay?"

"It's Ashley," I said. I turned toward Michels and raised my eyebrows as I waited for his answer.

"No, no. Of course not. She wasn't feeling well, remember?"

"I remember."

"I called her when I got home from Dukes, but it went straight to voicemail. I figured she was asleep, so I streamed an episode of Luther and fell asleep. When I woke up a little while later, I felt bad for not staying with her, so I figured I'd go to the twenty-four-hour Walmart, grab her some medicine, then head over and just, you know, be there."

I didn't like where this story was heading.

"Her car was there. I don't have a key, so I called her real quick to see if she would let me in."

Kyle sat next to me, his eyes glued on Michels.

"When she didn't answer, I knocked on the door, but she didn't answer that either. That's when I realized. I knew something was wrong. She's a light sleeper. The birds wake her up. Hell, the neighbor coming home above her wakes her up. She wouldn't just leave me out there knocking. She'd worry I'd wake the neighbors. I had to do something."

I cocked my head to the side. "What did you do?"

"I picked the lock. I had to. I thought she was in danger. Rachel, she wasn't there. Her stuff was, but she wasn't. Something's happened to her."

I rubbed the back of my neck. "Dammit, Michels, you broke into her house? What the hell were you thinking?"

"I was worried something was wrong. I was doing a welfare check."

"You're an off-duty detective, and you entered your girlfriend's apartment illegally. That's not a welfare check. That's a felony."

"I wasn't there with the intent to commit a crime. It's not a felony. Did you hear me? She's gone. Ashley's gone." He paced around the back of my couch, dragging his hand through his short hair. "Gone as in something's happened to her."

I dropped my head to the right. "We need to call Jimmy." I widened my eyes and stared at Kyle as a nudge for support.

"She's right. You unlawfully entered her home. Are you sure you two weren't fighting?"

"I told you, she was sick. We weren't fighting." He swiped his hand down his chin. "You don't understand. Something's not right. I told you, all her stuff was there. Her sunglasses, her keys, her cell phone. And all my calls and texts were right on the screen, unread. She never checked them. She hasn't since sometime after I heard from her yesterday morning."

"Maybe she decided to stay with a friend?"

"She'd stay with me, not a friend. And her car was there. Something's happened to her. I need help. I need to find her."

"Maybe she got antsy and went for a walk? I do that sometimes when I'm not feeling well," Kyle said.

A red flush climbed up Michels's neck and settled on his face. His eyes narrowed as he spoke. "You're not listening to me. I know my girlfriend. Her bed was still made. She left everything there. Please, can you come with me to her place? Just come and check it out and tell me what to do. Please." He balled his fists and pressed them against the sides of his thighs. When he released them, he said, "Maybe I'm wrong. I just need you to come and look, please."

"She can't do that, Michels. You need to call Jimmy."

I blinked. "You know how this works. We need official approval to start a missing persons case, and the fact that you entered her home without her approval? You know that was wrong. We've got to fix what you've done, not make it worse."

"You know if we call Jimmy, he'll put me on the desk. If Ashley's missing, I need to work this. I need to find her."

I studied him carefully. Quick breaths. Clenched fists. Tight jaw. Disheveled clothing, as if he'd had them on too long. He paced back and forth, his head angled down, though he lifted it periodically to make eye contact. I'd never seen him like that. "Let me get dressed," I said. I stood.

Kyle stood with me. "Rach, you can't—"

I mouthed, "I know," then whispered, "I'll make sure this is by the book." I walked into my room and closed the door, then quietly called Jimmy on his cell.

"Ryder." His voice was groggy. "What the hell time is it?"

"Chief, we have a problem."

10

We arrived at Ashley's apartment complex twenty minutes later. I took my Jeep and followed Michels, and Kyle followed me in his vehicle. He couldn't officially be involved in the situation without approval from his boss and mine, but Kyle and Jimmy were friends, and his opinion was always welcomed.

Two patrol officers got there before us, and Jimmy was on his way. He'd told them to wait until he arrived before entering the unit. Michels wasn't thrilled, but he didn't have a say in the matter. I'd called Bishop after Jimmy, and he showed up just as we did.

We stood outside by our vehicles away from the uniformed officers. Michels paced in a panic, his hands rotating between being stuffed into his pockets and dragged over the top of his head. He kept his head down as if he was concentrating. Was he planning his defense?

Would Michels hurt Ashley? I couldn't say. I didn't know their relationship or his history. All missing persons and suspicious deaths required law enforcement to look to the spouse or significant other first. Most crimes such as those are committed by someone close to the victim. I hated that we'd have to question Michels in that capacity, but it was necessary.

Bishop attempted to pull information from Michels. "Are you sure you two didn't fight? Maybe she was upset because you went to Dukes? My ex would get upset about that kind of thing all the time."

Michels exhaled. "How many times do I have to tell you people, we weren't fighting? I mean, yeah, we fight some, but never anything serious, and not now. I am not involved in this, I promise."

"If she's missing, we'll find her," Bishop said. "But you know you'll need to be interviewed."

Michels threw his hands in the air. "I'm the one who's reported her missing."

"You know the drill. We need to eliminate you as a suspect," Bishop said.

Michels hung his head and nodded. "I know, but we need to get out looking for her first." His voice hitched in his throat. "What if she's hurt or, God, even worse?"

Images of the Suwanee victim flashed through my mind. I caught Bishop's eye and flicked my head for him to follow me. Kyle came, too.

Bishop said, "If he's right, and Ashley's missing, I don't think he's involved."

"I don't either," I said. "But what if this has something to do with Natalie Carlson's murder? Ashley pulled me aside at the barbeque to talk about Stuart, but we got the call from Suwanee. I called her back and left her a message. She hasn't returned my call."

"If it could wait, it probably wasn't too important," Bishop said.

"Or maybe she didn't get the chance to follow up."

He raised his eyebrows. "You think Ashley's dead?"

"I know there's a dead girl in Suwanee around the same age with our names tied to the scene, and Ashley wanted to talk about Stuart's case. You do the math."

"Did Suwanee say when their vic's parents saw her last?" Kyle asked.

I nodded. "I got a text from Detective Grimes. She'd gone out with a friend the night before and was supposed to stay the night. They were going to Lake Lanier for the day. So about twenty-four hours."

"That's not what I wanted to hear," Kyle said.

"Neither did I," Bishop added.

"Exactly." I walked back over to Michels with the two of them on my tail. "You said Ashley told you she wasn't feeling well, right? Did you speak with her directly?"

He shook his head. "She sent me a text."

I eyed Bishop. His eyes closed slowly, and he let out a breath.

"Did she ever mention anything about the Stuart case?"

He blinked. "We talked about it, sure. It was all-consuming in the thick of it."

"What about since then?"

"Not really, why?"

"She wanted to talk to me about it."

"What for?" Michels asked.

"That's what I'm asking you."

"I don't know. We talked about work a lot. Don't you and Kyle do that?"

We did, so I had to assume they did, too. Jimmy's department vehicle raced into the spot beside my Jeep. I pointed at Michels. "Keep your cool. You're already in hot water."

Jimmy hurried from the vehicle, his eyes locked on Michels.

"Boiling hot water," I muttered under my breath.

Jimmy wore a pair of jeans and a white Hamby short sleeve polo. He stood inches away from Michels. His temper teetered on crazy, his face so red the little vein across his forehead swelled. "What the hell were you thinking? You know procedure. You should have followed it."

Michels lit up with no regard for who he was talking to. He stuck his face up close to Jimmy's. "Screw procedure." He pointed to the building. "I know my girlfriend, Chief. Something's happened to her." He took a deep breath. "There's no way in hell you'd follow procedure if your wife disappeared."

I cringed. Jimmy wouldn't like having that shoved in his face, because whether he could admit it or not, Michels was right. As my father-like friend and former boss, Lenny Dolatowski once said, *all rational thought goes out the window when someone you love is in jeopardy.* He was right. I'd experienced that myself after Tommy's murder.

Jimmy dropped eye contact with Michels, took a step away from his personal space, and spoke calmly. "We'll go up to the door and have a look, but you need to stay here." He walked back to his vehicle and opened the door. "Get in. And you stay in here until I tell you to come out. Do you understand?"

"But I—"

Jimmy spread his legs out even with his shoulders and placed his hands on his hips. "Don't make me cuff you."

Michels ducked his head and crawled into the back. Jimmy had left his vehicle running, kept the windows up, and the door automatically locked when closed, so Michels was there until someone let him out. Hopefully, he wouldn't convince an officer to do that.

"I'll stick by him," Kyle said. "Make sure he's okay."

"Appreciate it," Jimmy said.

Like most apartment complexes in the area, Ashley's was newer. The entrance was gated, but the system was down, and the gate was left open. I'd made a mental note of that when we'd entered, wondering how long it was down, and if that had anything to do with Ashley.

She lived on the second floor facing the parking lot. The entrances to each unit were in an outside, covered hallway with a stairwell on each end. Because of its location, our end was probably considered the front of the building. The back end butted up to a fenced, wooded lot that connected to a self-storage facility with outdoor garage-style units. We climbed the stairs and walked quietly to her apartment, the first one near the stairway. Garbage cans filled with bags sat beside some of the units, but not Ashley's.

"I hate these kinds of apartments," Bishop whispered. "They should have locked entrances into a hallway. This is just easy access for trouble."

I agreed.

We stood in front of her door and listened carefully. I turned the handle. Michels had left the door unlocked. "It's open."

"Because Michels picked the lock," Bishop said.

"Keep it shut," Jimmy said. "Michels's screwed us under the Fourth Amendment, and this situation doesn't satisfy the exigency exception, so until we get permission from her family, we stay out."

"But what if he's right?" Bishop asked.

"Her parents are local. If they haven't heard from her, we'll get permission and have them file a missing person report." He turned back to the stairs. "Let's go."

11

Given Michels entered Ashley's apartment illegally, Jimmy took lead, if for no other reason than to cover his butt. He sent Bishop, Kyle, and me home. I had no intention of going back to sleep, so I got ready for work. Kyle made egg sandwiches for the two of us.

We stood leaning against the kitchen counter and ate. "You think she's missing?" he asked.

"I don't think Michels would make it up."

"He was genuinely concerned," he said.

"I think so, too, but that doesn't mean she's disappeared. They could have had a fight, and she decided to stay with a friend to get away from him."

"So, you don't believe him about them not having a fight?"

"I can't rule it out. If he hid their relationship for a year, why wouldn't he hide a fight? Especially after just announcing their relationship to everyone."

He cringed.

"The thing that gets me is her wanting to talk about the Stuart case. That and the dead girl in Suwanee? Can't be coincidental."

"It's possible it's not related, but it's important to find out." He finished his egg sandwich and wiped his face with a paper towel. "I'll tell you this, fight or not, if you weren't home in the middle of the night and hadn't answered my calls or texts all day, I'd do exactly what he did." He brushed my hair away from my shoulder. "I couldn't help myself."

I smiled. "That's sweet, but I'd be livid if you broke the law."

"I wouldn't care. You wouldn't go dark without a reason. I'd check all the possible ones first and then do what had to be done."

Had Michels done that too? "Did you know Ashley called in sick?"

He walked the few steps to the sink and washed the pan he'd cooked the eggs in. "No, but we aren't active, so it's not a big deal, and I wouldn't have been notified. If we were on a case, I'd get a call."

"Can you check and see when she called into work?"

"Sure." He dried off the pan and put it away. "I'm heading to Atlanta this morning. I'll let you know."

"Thanks," I said. I pulled my hair back into a ponytail. "I'm going to the office."

"It's not even seven."

"I know, but I want to check something in the Stuart files."

He nodded. "You don't think Johnson killed himself, do you?"

"Not after talking to his ex. It's another piece of the puzzle, and I'm not sure what to do with it. Between us, she asked me to help learn the truth."

He turned toward me. "You can't investigate a suicide in Alabama."

"Not officially."

"You're dipping your foot in a pool that might end up drowning you, Rach. Be careful."

"Always am," I said and headed out the door.

I tapped out a text to Bishop who said he was already enroute to the station with coffee from Dunkin'. I then texted Jimmy and asked if he'd moved forward with the missing person call. He replied that he had. My heart ached for Ashley and her parents.

Jimmy had four parking spots in the department lot marked off for detectives, giving Bishop, Michels and myself a spot and leaving one open for the detective he'd hire in the next few weeks. He was in the process of interviewing but assured us we'd get a say about the final candidates. He wanted to promote from within, and there were three possible hires who'd passed the test. I had a pick in mind, and I'd put my recommendation in for Lauren Levy, a tough cop with common sense and an excellent internal BS monitor.

Michels was happy about the idea. It meant he'd no longer be the newbie, and he'd have a partner. I just hoped he hadn't ruined his career.

I met Bishop in his cubicle. He'd placed the coffee on the front side of his desk, and I snatched it up quickly and took a sip, begging the caffeine to do its job fast. The smooth, warm liquid was magic to my lagging energy. "I'd marry you if you weren't old enough to be my father."

His eyes stayed glued to his computer. "That thought scares me more than death."

I laughed out loud. "Any news on Ashley?"

"Her parents are meeting us at her apartment in an hour."

"Glad I decided to come right in."

He finally glanced up over his reading glasses. "Jimmy called me and told me to come in STAT."

"Really? He didn't call me."

"Because I told him not to. I knew you'd already be on your way."

"It's scary how you do that sometimes."

"You're easily readable, Ryder."

I grimaced. "You really think that?"

He chuckled. "You may have that whole resting bitch face thing going on, but I see through that."

"That's alarming. I need to step up my game."

Jimmy tapped on the cubicle door. "My office. Now."

Bishop shut his computer, and we headed to the other side of the pit.

"There weren't any reports of females matching Ashley's description or with her ID admitted or registered to any hospital. No morgues have her, either," Jimmy said.

Each of us breathed a collective sigh of relief.

"Mary and Glenn Middleton haven't spoken to their daughter since early on the morning of July Fourth. In that conversation she told them she was going to a party at Michels's house, and that they'd planned to tell us they were dating. She was excited about that, but according to her mother, something was bothering her. She said she could tell in her general tone, her mood. When she asked about it, Ashley said it was nothing. They know of no plans after that, and they were not aware she'd called in sick."

"Did her mother press her about what was bothering her?" Bishop asked.

"No."

"Did she mention any friends Ashley may have visited?"

"They're bringing a list. The mother also has her social media login information and will bring that."

I raised a brow. "Interesting."

"Mrs. Middleton said that given Ashley's work, her daughter felt it was important someone had it."

"When did she give it to her?"

"About two weeks ago."

"That was intentional," I said.

"Agreed," Bishop said. "We'll get Nikki there in case we find something."

"She's already on notice," Jimmy said.

"Chief," I said. "Ashley wanted to talk to me about the Stuart case. I'm concerned this is connected."

"What about the case?"

"I don't know. We had just stepped aside at Michels's place to talk when we got the Suwanee call."

"I can't see how it's connected. Stuart is dead."

"Yes, but our names were left with Natalie Carlson's remains."

"Could be a coincidence, but keep looking for a connection. The last thing we need is another whack job out imitating a serial killer."

A sense of relief washed over me. Jimmy had, for the most part, supported my intuition, and more importantly, respected it. I rubbed the back of my neck. "Uh, Chief, what about Michels?"

"For now, he's suspended with pay. Ashley's parents aren't pressing charges, but he needs to cool off, and he's not allowed to go anywhere near this investigation."

"That's got to be killing him," I said.

Jimmy made eye contact, and without a hint of sarcasm in his tone, said, "I don't give a damn about his feelings."

"Understood, sir."

"Let them have a quick look inside the apartment. See if they notice anything out of place. Just through the door, and then ask them to wait outside, and do an extensive search. They can go back inside once Nikki's done processing the scene. We need anything we can find to determine where she's gone so if we decide something nefarious happened, we can hit the ground running. I've got a call out to the Fulton County Sheriff's Office to bring in a dog. We're as prepared as we can be, now go do your thing."

We both nodded and left his office, grabbed our things, and headed back to Ashley's apartment.

12

The Middletons stood outside their vehicle waiting for us. Bishop and I walked over and introduced ourselves as Nikki gathered her things.

"Detective Rachel Ryder. Thank you for meeting us here today."

"Detective Rob Bishop. I'm sorry we're meeting under these circumstances."

Mrs. Middleton clutched her purse to her stomach. She was average height, with short brown hair and loads of gold, understated jewelry. She wore a pair of beige dress pants and a white short-sleeved collarless shirt. I knew where Ashley got her big eyes. "Have you heard anything?"

Memories of Ashley flashed through my mind. She'd been kind when I was irritable and defensive. I'd thanked her, but that suddenly felt insufficient. "Not yet," I said. "But we're going to do everything we can to find her."

She nodded.

Mr. Middleton handed Bishop the key.

An ambulance and two patrol officers arrived. Mrs.

Middleton rocked back and forth on her heels, muttering her daughter's name as tears rolled down her cheeks. Sweat poured from the corners of Mr. Middleton's forehead. His hands were clenched into fists so tight his knuckles were white.

He pointed to the ambulance. "Is that for Ashley?"

"It's simply a precautionary measure," Bishop said. "As you know, Detective Michels entered the unit last night and informed us that Ashley wasn't there, but if she's returned, we want to make sure we can help her if necessary."

"Let them go," Mrs. Middleton said.

"Thank you, ma'am," Bishop said. "We'll be back down as soon as it's clear for you to enter."

"Thank you," Mr. Middleton said.

I grabbed a pair of gloves and snapped them on. At Ashley's apartment, Bishop slid the key into the lock with ease. He turned the handle and pushed the door partially open with a gloved hand. He raised his gun and slowly walked in with me following behind.

"Do you smell that?" Bishop asked.

I breathed in through my nose. "Cedarwood. It's the same smell Michels had on at his party."

"Makes sense," he said. "He was here. It's bound to smell like him."

We worked our way through the small apartment, clearing the living area, the kitchen, the bathroom, and her bedroom, then met back near the door.

I put my gun back into its holster then stepped outside and called down over the stairwell for the Middletons to come up.

The couple walked into the apartment calmly. Mrs. Middleton held a tissue over her mouth. Tears fell from her eyes. Her husband placed his hand gently on the small of her back and whispered something into her ear. Whatever he said stopped her tears.

"Please," I said. "Take a look inside. Please don't touch anything, and just go into the entry area for now. If something looks out of place or wrong, let me know."

While they stepped inside and examined the small area, I took mental snapshots of the apartment. A cream-colored couch butted up against the door's wall, a side table on its right. A box of tissues and a small lamp took up most of the table's space. A matching loveseat formed a small L shape with the couch, with an oblong dark wood coffee table in the middle. On the coffee table was a half-filled glass of water and a few magazines. *Cosmo*, *Good Housekeeping*, and *US*. A large, framed print of the ocean hung above the couch, but other than that, there was little personal décor in the place.

The Middletons stood facing each other and whispered together. Bishop and I stood near the door twiddling our thumbs waiting for them to finish. Mrs. Middleton turned toward us, and Mr. Middleton put his hand on her back again. He smiled. "Everything appears to be in place. We have never been in Ashley's bedroom. Would you like us to glance in there also?"

"Let's wait until we're finished. If you'd like to come back then, that would be okay."

He glanced down at his wife. She shook her head. "No, thank you," he said. "We think it's best we return home. We'd like to be there if Ashley comes by or calls."

"I've left her cell phone passcode with the officer downstairs," Mrs. Middleton said.

"Thank you," I said. "I promise you we'll do everything in our power to find your daughter."

Bishop walked them to the stairwell, and I began examining her apartment.

On the wall behind the door was a small oblong gray table with a drawer. On that Ashley set her keys, cell phone, and purse. Mail stacked in a pile sat on the corner of the table. I flipped through the envelopes, all pre-approved offers for credit cards. Inside the drawer were rubber bands, a few peppermint candies, three black pens, and some notepads.

Bishop returned. "Those poor people."

"I can't imagine." I closed the door and pointed to the table. "Michels was right. Her phone is here." I picked it up, and it came to life. "He's been texting her since early yesterday morning. He called her three times, but she's not seen any of these notifications or the call from me." I pointed to her car keys. "Those are hers." I walked over to the balcony which faced the parking lot. "It's the red Camry three down from yours."

"Let's check out the rest of the place, see what we can find. You take the bedroom. If it turns out Ashley isn't missing, I don't want her embarrassed that a man went through her woman things."

"She'll appreciate that." I kept my eye out for any sign that her disappearance was related to the Suwanee murder.

Her bedroom was small, maybe ten by fourteen max, fitting only a queen-sized bed, a five-drawer chest, and a small nightstand on the right side of the bed near the closet. I checked the chest first. Clothes. A jewelry box sat on top next to a small ceramic bowl filled with rings and earrings. Behind them were three framed photos. I studied the photos. One was of Michels and Ashley, another of her with an older man and woman, probably her grandparents, and the last of Ashley with another girl, both dressed in togas. I snapped photos of the pictures with my cell phone.

The closet was a small walk-in. Ashley used one side for clothing and shoes, which she'd kept mostly in their boxes, and on the other side, along the length of the wall, was a three-shelf bookcase. It was the only area in the entire apartment where she kept personal stuff. Books, papers, photo boxes, and random office supplies. I flipped through the books and boxes but found nothing that would clue us in to Ashley's whereabouts. I moved back to the shoe boxes and opened them. Nothing of interest in them either.

I stood and studied the closet. The bookcase wasn't flush with the wall, but about an inch or so away from it. I moved the photo boxes off the top and examined between it and the wall, and I hit pay dirt. Stuffed behind the bookcase were seven large manilla envelopes. I pulled them out and recognized them immediately. My stomach flipped. Copies of the Stuart investigation files. Why would Ashley have our case files when she no longer worked for the department? Were they the reason she wanted to talk to me about Stuart? I called for Nikki. "Please tag these. Make sure to bring them to the station."

She glanced inside. "How'd she get those?"

"If you're asking me for the correct answer, I don't know, but my guess is Michels gave them to her."

"Dang, he's already in trouble."

I nodded.

"I found a small dark hair on the dresser, too," Nikki said. "It's probably Michels's, but I'll run it and check."

"Good."

She studied the small closet. "Did you notice how she has very little stuff? Nothing but one picture on the wall, and a few I just saw on her dresser."

"I did notice that."

"You know why it's like this, right?"

"Nope. Why?"

"Because she's a crime scene analyst. We deal with so

many physical possessions, we can't handle having too much ourselves."

"You know, that makes a lot of sense. Thank you for telling me. Do you keep copied files from cases too?"

She smiled. "Only the ones I think y'all got wrong."

13

Jimmy called my cell just as we finished our search. "Did you find anything?"

"Nothing that shows she's been abducted or had any kind of altercation. It's like she just walked out without taking anything," I said. "But Jimmy, she had seven envelopes full of copies of the Stuart investigation files."

He groaned. "She's not authorized to have those."

"Yet, she does, and she wanted to talk to me about him."

"Jesus, what the hell is Michels doing?"

"Her having them doesn't mean Michels gave them to her," I said.

"Did you?"

"No."

"This isn't complicated, Ryder." He groaned again.

"Nikki found a hair. She's doing a rapid DNA test and running it through the system. It's probably Michels's, but that doesn't mean—"

He held his palm out. "I know. Fulton County is enroute with a dog. Have you talked to the apartment manager?"

"They're not in until ten, but I did catch a grounds employee. He said the cameras in each of the hallways to the apartments work about half the time. He put a call into the corporation that owns the complex, but we're going to need a warrant."

"I'll get someone to write it up for you. Text me the information but make it quick. We don't want to lose time on this."

"Yes, sir," I said. "Chief, we have her cell phone, but other than the texts and calls from Michels and one from me, it's been wiped. I'll have Bubba see if he can get anything from the carrier."

"I'll get the warrant for that, too." He swore under his breath. "Figure out what the hell is happening, Ryder. I need you hard on this."

"I'm on it."

Bishop and I met back outside. "Should I call Michels?" I asked Bishop.

"No."

"But we need confirmation on where she got the files."

"Let Jimmy make that call," he said.

"This is our investigation."

"No. Jimmy's lead for the time being."

He was right, and it annoyed me.

"It's possible she wanted to disappear."

"No. You saw her at the cookout. She was happy about her and Michels."

"If she was abducted, do you think she'd take the time to lock the door?"

"No, but I bet the person who took her would. It would make it harder for us."

We stood in the parking lot waiting for the K9 unit to arrive. I leaned against our vehicle. "Why would she have those files, and why would she want to talk to me about Stuart?"

"You're committed now, aren't you? You believe her disappearance has something to do with the Stuart case," he said.

"Look at it all. Natalie Carlson. The stickers. Ashley wanting to talk about Stuart. It's connected."

"I know I'm going to regret saying this, but I think you might be right."

The K9 unit arrived, and a tall, well-muscled deputy stepped out of the vehicle. He walked like Kyle, with the purpose of either former military or someone with advanced, specialized training in the field. His shoulders were back, his head was high, and his arms were slightly bent.

Bishop elbowed my arm. "You're drooling."

I touched my lips without even realizing it at first. "You're a jerk."

He laughed silently, but hard enough that his head bobbed up and down.

The deputy walked over with a brown bloodhound whose long ears deserved a good rub. "Major Curtis Morgan," he said. "And this is Magnum."

We introduced ourselves and explained the situation, and then I asked, "Does Magnum have a good track record? The victim worked for our department and is now a crime scene tech with the DEA."

"Yes, ma'am," he said. "Magnum has a ninety-nine percent location rate. Bloodhounds' olfactory bulb has over 300 million receptors, while most dogs only have 200. They're motivated by scent, and Magnum is very persistent." He examined the surrounding area. "I'll be honest, it's more complicated when the scent is in a busy area like this, and the odds of your victim walking off without getting into a vehicle are slim."

"And Magnum can't track the scent if she got in a vehicle," Bishop said.

"Correct. I was told her vehicle is here. I'd like to start there. Do you have something of hers with her scent on it?"

I'd taken the jumper Ashley wore on July Fourth. It was the only item in her laundry basket. I handed it to Major Morgan. "She had this on the day before she went missing."

"Perfect. Which vehicle?"

We walked the short distance to her Camry.

He squatted down to Magnum's level, gripped the leash where it attached to the dog's collar, and held the jumper to Magnum's nose. The dog sniffed it vigorously. "Go get her, boy." He unclipped the leash, and the dog dropped his head and went to work.

He kept his head down, sniffing around her Camry, then moved at a rapid pace toward the apartment. He shot up the stairs as we followed behind him. He stopped at her door, paused, sniffed there for a bit, then put his head back down and headed the opposite direction.

Bishop and I exchanged a look.

The dog followed the scent down the stairs across the small grassy area to the chain-link fence. He stood there barking. Major Morgan told him to stay, then jogged back to his van. He returned with a specialized ladder made for dogs, set it up against the fence, and Magnum climbed up it.

Morgan followed, then Bishop suggested I go next. He made it up and over just as the dog got to the first set of storage garages. Magnum paused again, sniffed around one unit, and quickly discarded it. I made a mental note of the unit number. He followed Ashley's scent to another storage unit, stayed there again and sniffed around, then sniffed off toward the parking lot. I made another mental note of that unit number.

He reached the fence to the parking area, and Morgan hit the button for vehicles to exit the fenced area. Magnum followed the scent to an empty parking space and then stopped. He sat and sighed heavily.

"She got in a vehicle here," Morgan said.

"Great. Just great."

Bishop got on his cell and within five minutes we had patrol out searching the area. Nikki walked the entire scene but found nothing. No prints, no droppings of blood, no clothing scraps. It was like Ashley just casually walked through the woods, climbed the fence, and left.

The manager of the storage facility walked out of the office. "The officer said you wanted to see me?" She was about fifty pounds heavier than her short stature should hold, and from the way she waddled over, it was obvious the weight did a number on her knees and hips.

I showed her my badge and explained the situation. "We're going to need the rental information on those two units."

"I can't give out that information without a warrant."

"We'll get that," Bishop said. He walked away to make the call and walked over a minute later. "Email?"

She gave him her email, and fifteen minutes later the warrant hit her inbox. Ashley's job worked to her benefit. Everyone in law enforcement wanted to see her brought home safely.

"Each unit was rented by the same person. Barry Preston." She printed off copies of the contracts along with his driver's license and handed them to us. "He paid cash for one year each and rented them on June third of this year. Oh, he also got the insurance, and he brought his own locks, but we can snap those off easily."

"Did he rent it from you? Do you remember the man?"

"He did it all online."

"Then how did he pay cash?" I asked.

"We have an arrangement for those who can't come during work hours. They leave the cash in the drop box at the office. The next day we put their contract, unit information, and lock and key in one of the combination-locked wall units over there." She pointed to a wall of small lockers. "And they pick it up."

"Do you have cameras on those units or in the storage area?" I asked.

"Yes, ma'am."

"We'll need copies of the camera footage," I said.

"We can look at the cameras now, if you'd like."

"That would be good," Bishop said.

"It'll take me a minute to get to them."

Bishop and I studied the license. We had no idea who the man was, but I believed it meant something that Magnum went to each locker belonging to him. What did he have to do with Ashley's disappearance? I sent Bubba a photo of the license and asked him to do a search and get back to me. We headed to the units to examine them, telling the manager we'd be back to view the videos.

"I'm required to go with you," she said.

"Not a problem," Bishop said.

The first unit was completely empty.

"We require our renters to clean the units after they empty them. If they don't, they're fined," the manager said. "Looks like this guy did that."

"Or didn't put anything in here to begin with," Bishop said.

"Because he rented it to distract us," I added.

He nodded.

The next unit was the same.

"Definitely a distraction," Bishop said.

The manager pulled up the last few days of video as well as the day the renter would have left the cash and picked up the lock and key.

The recordings were black and white, and very blurry, but we were able to recognize Ashley walking from the area near the wooded lot with someone wearing a dark pullover hoodie with the hood over their head. A man? Maybe a teenager? It was hard to tell.

"She doesn't look like she's being forced," Bishop said.

"Just because she doesn't have a gun pointed at her doesn't mean she's not being forced."

Instead of walking to a vehicle in the secured area of the lot, the person did as we did, pressed the button, and walked through the gate. We expected that based on Magnum's route. They walked over to a black pickup truck with a Chevy emblem on the front backed into the space. We couldn't see the rear of the truck or the plate.

"That's not a Chevy," Bishop said. "It's a Ford."

"How do you know?" I asked.

"The front is a Ford F150 bumper. They changed the emblem."

"Are you sure?"

"Yes."

"I drive an F150, and that's about what my truck looks like," the manager said. "It's parked out front here if you want to take a look."

I did, and then I googled the Chevys, and they were right. It was a Ford.

The video showed Ashely getting into the truck, the man closing the door, then pulling something out of the truck bed and carrying it over to the camera. He tossed it over, and the video went black.

"He did all of that on purpose," Bishop said.

"With a plan," I added.

"Ma'am," Bishop said. "We're going to need those tapes."

"Yes, sir. I'll get them emailed to you."

14

Back at the department, we filled the chief in on what we'd learned, which was only enough to fill a page of a small spiral notepad. "Bubba's running the license and some additional information," Bishop said to Jimmy. "He'll have it in a few minutes."

I reminded Jimmy of the case files. He scrubbed his hand down around his mouth. "Why the hell would she have those?"

"Because she thinks we got something wrong."

"We didn't," Bishop said.

"Why would she think that?" Jimmy asked.

"I asked Nikki if she'd bring any case files home, and she said, *only the ones I think y'all got wrong*."

Jimmy grabbed his cell phone from his desk and pounded out a number. "Get here now." He threw the phone back onto his desk.

I assumed he'd called Michels.

"Are the Alabama files in there, too?" he asked.

"Yes, but I'm not sure if it's all of them," I said. "Either way, it's copies. All double-sided, so there could be some things missing. We'll have to compare them to our files to know for sure."

"What the hell is she doing?" The question was rhetorical. He dialed Nikki's line and asked her to come to his office.

Nikki walked in. "Yes, Chief?"

"Did you tell Detective Ryder that you bring home the files of cases where you think we got something wrong?"

She twisted the ring on her right hand. "Uh, yes, but I was kidding."

"So, you don't bring home files from cases you think we got wrong."

"I haven't personally, but I do know other people in my position who have."

"Is Ashley one of them?"

"I can't say. She didn't mention it to me."

"Thank you," he said.

"Sure thing."

Before she left, Jimmy asked, "You get everything in the system?"

"Not yet, but I'm close."

"Keep us informed."

"Chief," I pointed to Nikki. "May I?"

He flicked his head to the door. "Go. Investigation room, thirty minutes."

I hopped out of my chair and grabbed Nikki's arm lightly as I walked out, closing Jimmy's door behind me. "I am so sorry. I only told him that because it was a logical reason for Ashley to have them. I wasn't intending for him to call you on it."

She chuckled. "It's fine, really. I told you that people in my position do that, and I can't say that I wouldn't, just that I haven't."

We all had copies of both the Georgia murder files and the Birmingham ones, but if Johnson continued to investigate the murders after they'd closed the files, he may have added additional information to his. I put a call in to Detective Anderson. It went straight to voicemail. "Detective Anderson, this is Detective Ryder in Hamby. I'm calling to request any additional documentation Detective Johnson may have added to the Stuart case files. I will get a written request for them, but I wanted to give you a heads up. Thanks."

Michels tapped on my cubicle partition wall. His eyes were red from lack of sleep, but he'd showered and put on a pair of khaki pants and a short-sleeved polo shirt. "Anything?" He wandered into my cubicle. He smelled of cedarwood again.

"Are you wearing cologne?"

"What? No. Have you found anything?"

"You know I can't answer that. You smell like cedarwood."

"It's my body wash. Ashley got it for me. Why are you asking?"

"Tommy wore cedarwood cologne."

"Oh, I didn't know."

"Jimmy wants to talk to you."

"Just tell me what's going on, please."

"Nothing yet. Did you give Ashley copies of the Stuart files?"

He paused before he spoke. "I mean, she—"

"Answer the question, Michels."

"No, I didn't give her copies, but I had the files at my house. My copies. She might have taken those and made copies."

If Michels and Ashley had dated a while, they would have met some of each other's friends. Maybe Barry Preston was

Ashley's friend or even a previous boyfriend. "Do you know Barry?"

"Barry? Barry who? Is that who you think has Ashley? What's his last name?"

I left the rest of the questioning to Jimmy. He was the boss. "You need to go before you make things worse. Jimmy's already on fire about this."

Bubba caught up to me as I headed to the investigation room. "Detective," he said. "Barry Preston died four months ago. The photo on the license you sent me isn't him." He handed me a copy of a license with the same information as the other one but with a different photo.

I studied it. "How did he do this?"

"Probably Photoshop or something like it."

"Can you run the photo and see if you get a hit?"

"I already did. Nothing came up."

"That means our Preston imitator isn't in the system, and that makes it even harder to find him." I opened the investigation room door and set my portfolio on the table. "We can call Preston's family and ask them to take a look at the video from the storage place. See if they recognize the guy. Can you find his next of kin?"

"Already tried. Nothing."

"Damn."

Bishop and Nikki came in together and sat across from Bubba and me. Jimmy came in a few minutes later with Michels behind him. He kept his head down and sat at the opposite end of the table.

Jimmy sat at the head of the table in front of the whiteboards. When Jimmy had become chief, he'd convinced the mayor to update our office with better technology and a working room for investigations. He didn't expect Hamby police would use the room as much as we had. Jimmy set a pad of paper on the table and folded his hands on top of it. "Detective Michels is suspended without pay, however I believe his connection to Ashley is an important tool for our investigation. He will not be involved in the process but will only be available for questions as necessary." He directed his next comment to me and then Bishop. "I already questioned him about her disappearance, and while I feel he is not involved, I will have Bishop and Ryder interview him again."

Jimmy was only doing that to tick off boxes on a suspected bad cop to-do list. If he thought Michels was involved, he wouldn't allow him in the investigation room.

I imagined scenarios of how I'd handle the situation. Kyle had said he would have done what Michels did if I was in danger. Tommy would have, too. I wanted to think I'd follow the law, but in truth, probably not. When someone you love is in danger, it's hard to leave out your emotions. When I killed Tommy's murderer, I rushed over to my dead husband and held him close to my body, crying and begging for him to come back to life. I'd effectively destroyed the crime scene, which put me in hot water, but I'd do it again in a heartbeat. So, no. I wouldn't follow the law.

"What updates do we have?" Jimmy asked.

"We know that the driver's license used for renting the storage units was altered. Barry Preston died four months ago," I said. "Bubba checked for next of kin but there isn't any."

"Did you run the photo in the system?" Jimmy asked Bubba.

He nodded. "I can't find a match."

I handed Michaels my copy of the license, and he examined it carefully. "I don't know this guy," he said. "I haven't seen him before, and Ashley never mentioned the name." He reached over and handed me back the copy.

"I'm going to go through the case files from Ashley's apartment," I said. "I took a quick glance and saw she made some notes on them, so maybe I can figure out what she was doing. If she found something, then we have to assume her disappearance is somehow related."

"Chief," Michels said.

Jimmy's face reddened. Michels was supposed to be an observer, only there for questions. "What?"

"Ashley had a locker at her DEA office. If she was looking into the investigation, she might have left notes there for safety purposes."

Jimmy gave him one nod. "Bishop, get a warrant for the locker and any workspace she has at the DEA. Let us know what you find."

"Yes, sir," Bishop said. "I'll talk with some of the people there, too. See if Ashley said anything to them."

"Sounds good," Jimmy said.

"Can we add the password to her laptop to that?" Bubba asked. He then eyed Michels. "If it was a work laptop, that is."

"It wasn't," Michels said. "And I know the password."

"The parents signed off on everything, so Ryder, you and Bubba go through it."

I nodded.

Jimmy turned to Nikki. "Anything?"

"The door handles were wiped clean. I couldn't even pull a partial. Closet doors, too," she said. "I was able to get Ashley's prints in the usual spots, and a single print off the toilet seat, but that belonged to Detective Michels."

"What about her vehicle?"

"We brought that to the impound lot. It's still there," I said.

"But a cursory look didn't give us anything. In fact, all that's in there is repair paperwork and her insurance and tag information."

"Did you look in the trunk?"

"Spare, a jack, and an emergency kit."

"I did run prints on her car," Nikki said. "Wiped clean also, at least on the handles and trunk, but I need to get inside."

Michels cleared his throat and then his lips formed a thin line. I had no idea what he thought, but I was glad he'd kept his mouth shut. Jimmy was in no mood for back talk, especially from Michels.

"Any word on the cameras from the complex? Jimmy asked.

"They were blacked out," Nikki said. "Didn't you see?"

The eyes around the table all widened.

"Did you talk to the manager?" I asked.

She shook her head. "No, but that's what she'll tell you. I took photos of the cameras while I was there." She pulled the photos from her growing file. "I can make copies of everything once we're done here. Something about the cameras looked strange, so I zoomed in. Each camera, and there are just the two, had a small piece of black duct tape over it. It was almost perfectly cut to match the size of the lens."

"That couldn't have been done at night," Bishop said.

"Agreed," I said. "Someone went there earlier and set up. Probably while we were at Michels's. I lived in an apartment once. The pool was packed on the Fourth of July, so it's reasonable to think this guy could have dressed like a grounds employee working on the cameras."

Jimmy sighed. "Ryder and Bishop have lead on this now. I want constant updates, but I can't be active in the investigation. I've got a budget due to City Council in three days, and I need to get it finished. Our BOLO hit, and we've already got reporters calling. When they show up here, and they will, I want Ryder to be the face, but not unless we have something solid to report." He jabbed his finger toward me. "Last thing we need is a pile of reporters screwing with our investigation. You talk to me before you talk to them. Understand?"

"Completely."

He stood. "Let's get moving. If something breaks, I want to hear about it yesterday." He pointed at Michels. "You speak when spoken to, or you're out of here." He walked out of the room and slammed the door behind him.

We all sat quietly for a moment until Bubba said, "Budget time always screws with him."

"Ain't that the truth," Bishop said.

I whispered into Bishop's ear. "We have to interrogate Michels."

He nodded. "For the record."

I nodded. "Michels, we need to interview you. Meet us in the interrogation room in ten." I stood and darted out the door before he could argue. My cell phone rang. "Ryder."

"Detective," Jessica Walters said. "You didn't tell me your former crime scene tech was missing. Is that why you asked me about the numbers? Do you think we've got a copycat on our hands?"

"No comment," I said.

"Do you think Ashley Middleton is dead? And if so, do you think the person who killed the Suwanee woman has her?"

I rubbed my tired eyes. "Listen, I'll talk with you, but I need some time."

"May I have a quote at least? I'm going live at noon."

Of course, you are. "Ashley Middleton went missing on July fifth. We are actively searching for her. We have a tip line set up. You can get the number there, and we will release a person of interest photo, but that's all I've got."

"I can work with that. Thank you."

I hit end, walked into my cubby, and tossed my phone onto my desk. "She's going to be a pain in my ass. I can feel it."

"You were supposed to clear it with Jimmy before you talked to the media," Bishop said.

I tapped out a quick text and gave him the details. "Ready?"

"Give me ten. I need that warrant for Ashley's locker."

"See you there."

15

Michels sat across from us with his arms folded over his chest. He'd brought a water, but it sat unopened.

I dimmed the lights. Bright lights gave off heat, and small, hot, well-lit rooms made suspects uncomfortable. I didn't want Michels uncomfortable.

Bishop and I sat with our portfolios open and got down to business. We weren't using the good cop/bad cop technique. Michels knew the drill, and he wouldn't fall for any of the games we played with suspects.

I checked the light on the camera to make sure it was on and recording, then I smiled at him. "Can we all agree this is uncomfortable?"

He didn't flinch.

"Michels, tell me exactly what happened from the time you last saw Ashley."

"I haven't done anything." He dragged his hand through his hair. "Jesus, Ryder, you know me. You know I wouldn't hurt her."

What I knew was that love and money drove people to do

things they never believed possible. Michels was human. As an officer, I couldn't assume his reactions in a heated situation with someone he loved. Cleared or not, this was for the record. We needed to do it right. "You know how this has to roll."

"Someone took her."

"When did you see her last?"

He ran his hand through his hair and stared at the camera on the ceiling in the corner of the room. "The Fourth of July. Technically it was the fifth. She left my house at around two a.m. She was going to stay the night, but she said she wanted to sleep in her own bed."

"Did you two have an argument?" Bishop asked. "Is that why she didn't stay the night?"

"I've already told you, we weren't fighting. She was just tired, and she doesn't like my bed. She went home. I sent her a good morning text the next morning. She responded and said she wasn't feeling well and was going to call in sick to work. I joked that those margaritas I'd made were too strong for her. She sent a laughing face emoji, told me she loved me, and that was it. You have her phone. You can see that."

"And you didn't hear from her after that?"

"Again, no. And before you ask, I called her three times. I left a voicemail on the last call telling her I was worried. You'll also see several texts from me."

"You didn't seem concerned at Dukes," I said.

"I wasn't then. The last call was after we left. That's when I got nervous. I went home, sent her a few more texts, then decided to drive by her apartment and check on her."

"Why?" Bishop asked.

"Why? Because I thought maybe she was unconscious or something. It was a wellness check."

"We won't go over that again," I said. "What time did you

go by her apartment, and what did you do when you got there?"

"I got there at around 2:30. I looked in her window, but I couldn't see much because the blinds were closed."

"Her apartment is on the second floor," Bishop said.

"I used binoculars."

I shivered. That was a stalker-like move, and not a point in the innocent column for him. "You carry binoculars in your vehicle?"

"No. I brought them with me."

"The door was locked when you arrived," Bishop said. "How did you get into the apartment?"

"I told you. I picked the lock."

"What about the dead bolt?"

"It obviously wasn't locked." He took a deep breath and exhaled. "After that, I saw her phone and keys on the table, and I knew something was up. I checked her bedroom, but the bed was made like she hadn't even slept in it."

"Would she make her bed if she was sick?" I asked.

"Yes. She believes in that whole make your bed daily stuff for productivity, but I know what you're thinking. I know she came home from my place because we texted the next morning, and her clothes were in her hamper."

"I wasn't thinking that," I said. "We used those clothes with the dog. What I was thinking was that maybe she was abducted early that morning after she undressed."

"But she texted me."

"No, you received a text from her phone. That doesn't mean she sent it."

"The phone was at her apartment." He paused and then dropped an F-bomb. "You think whoever abducted her was there with her for a while, don't you?"

"I think it's possible, but it's also possible he came that morning."

"We have her on video with the Preston imposter in the morning, so we know she was there, we just don't know how long her abductor was with her," I said. "Michels, has Ashley mentioned anything about old friends coming to town, someone bothering her at the grocery store? Anything that might make her feel uncomfortable?"

"No. I'd be all over it if someone made her feel uncomfortable."

"What about the Stuart investigation? She said nothing to you?"

"Again, we talked about it during the investigation."

"She doesn't work for us," Bishop said.

Michels dropped his head back and sighed. "Come on, really?" He looked me in the eye. "You talk to Kyle all the time."

My eyes shifted to Bishop. He nodded. I focused back on Michels. "Do you remember what was said about the investigation?"

"That was six months ago."

Bishop slammed his hand on the table. "Think!"

Michels flinched. "I told you, I can't remember. You think this has to do with that investigation? Why?" His eyes were wide and his skin pale. "That call you got on the fourth, the girl. Why were you called?"

"Because there were vinyl stickers with our names near the victim," Bishop said.

Michels sank back into his chair. "If this is related to the Stuart murders, that means she knew something, and the killer found out," he said.

"This is just a theory," I said. "I'm going to go through her notes and compare them to our files. I'll figure out what she was thinking, but I need you to try to remember every conversation you two had about the investigation. Can you do that?"

He nodded. "I didn't do anything to Ashley," he said, his eyes pinned on Bishop. "You know that."

"This is how things work," Bishop responded.

16

Michels and Bubba unlocked Ashley's personal laptop, but it was wiped clean and set back to factory settings. There was no email account attached to it, no downloaded music, nothing.

"Why would she do that?" Bubba asked.

I scrolled through the laptop checking for myself. "If she did, which we can't say for sure, it was because she had something on there she didn't want anyone else to find."

"Or," Michels said. "Someone else found it and reset the laptop to factory settings so no one could get it."

"Bubba, can you recover anything?"

"I can try, but this has Windows 10. If a quick reset was done, I might be able to get something, but if it was a complete delete, those files are unrecoverable."

"Give it a shot and let's hope it was a quick reset," I said. "What about her cell phone? Was there anything else on it?"

"Just the text messages from Michels and some calls from the two of you, but her email and photos were wiped clean."

"Someone did that," I said. "But they left Michels and my texts and calls."

"Or those came after the phone was wiped."

"That's odd."

Michels sighed. "I did not do that. I wasn't trying to cover my ass."

"I didn't say that you were."

"It doesn't matter. I want you to see my Ring recordings. You'll see the times when my car left and when I came home. If you compare that to when I came to your place, you'll see I didn't have enough time to do any of this."

"Michels, stop. We only asked you the questions we did because we had to. It's procedure, something you'd better learn to follow if you want to keep your job."

"Doesn't matter." He motioned for my laptop.

I slid it over to him. "This isn't necessary at the moment."

"But it might be later, so better do it now."

He pulled up his Ring videos through his online account. "There, this is when I got back from Dukes, and here is when I left. Then I come home hours later. What time did I get to your house?"

"Around 3:15."

"Then you know I wasn't involved."

"Get me copies of these for the file please," I said.

He nodded.

"Let me get back to the laptop," Bubba said. "Be back in a few." He left the room.

Michels sat across the conference table from me. I eyed him with a raised brow. "You want to see the files, don't you?"

"I want to help."

"You know you can't do that. You're suspended."

"But I worked the Stuart investigation with you. I might find something you missed."

I shook my head. "Jimmy will flip, and we can't afford to waste time dealing with his anger." I waved my hand toward the corner of the room. "Sit over there. If I have a question, I'll ask. Okay?"

He moved his chair to the corner of the room without another word.

Five minutes later the manager from Ashley's apartment complex emailed the tapes.

Nikki was right. I called the manager to let her know the deal with the black tape because she'd written she was baffled as to why the cameras were 'down'. She informed me she'd fix the problem immediately.

Unfortunately, it was too late for Ashley.

Three hours later Bishop walked in with a printed version of the warrant for Ashley's locker. "Took over two hours to get approval for this thing, and then the judge's clerk failed to email it."

"I called and talked to a few agents and staff to let them know what's going on and that I'd be there. They didn't know anything about any case she might have been looking into. Everyone said Ashley was quiet about her personal life." I had Ashley's files spread out across the table. He picked up one with a yellow sticky note on it. "Taking notes?"

"Trying to figure out her theory."

"Anything on her laptop?" he asked.

"Nope. Wiped clean. Bubba attempted to recover at least some of the files, but he couldn't. I called Kyle. He's at the DEA district office, so he'll help you with the locker."

"Sounds good. I was going to bring one of the patrol officers with me. Maybe Levy?"

"Sounds like a plan."

His eyes flicked to the empty chair where Michels had been for the last few hours. "Wasn't Michels in here with you?"

"I sent him for Subway. It was so pathetic, him just sitting there helpless. I felt bad for him."

"Understood." Bishop pressed his thumbs into his temples and sighed. "It's been at least twenty-four hours since she went missing. What are the odds of her being alive?"

"If this is a copycat, slim. Once I'm finished here, I'm going to follow up with Anderson about Johnson's memorial service, and then I'll call Detective Grimes for an update. I'd like to get face time with the girl's parents. I believe Natalie Carlson and Ashley are connected, and we need to figure out how."

"I'd like to be there, too," he said.

"Of course. Let me know what you find in her locker."

He walked out, and I got back to reviewing Ashley's files.

It had been four hours since I'd sat down with the files. Too focused on the task at hand, I hadn't called Grimes or Anderson. Jimmy stopped by and asked for a follow up.

"Of the seven envelopes we took from her apartment, I've gone through two." I handed him a copy of my typed notes from the first body at the fire. "She highlighted things in different colors. All coordinating within all the documents in these two files, so, they're probably the same in the next five."

He scanned the paper. "Yellow for setting?"

I nodded. "Blue for description of each victim, pink for the victim's identity. Light orange for the stickers, and then these numbers." I handed him another sheet. "I'm not sure what they mean yet, and I've only found them in two of the victim's notes."

"You're tracking everything I assume?"

"Yes."

"Good job. If anyone can figure out what she was doing, it'll be you." He squeezed my shoulder. "Get something to eat."

"Michels got me Subway a while ago, so I'm good." I took a shot at Michels helping with the investigation in a more formal capacity. "He's intimately connected to our investigation, Jimmy. I think his help could be beneficial. He could lead us to Ashley."

"Sounds like you think he's a suspect."

"I'm not saying that. I think he can be a valuable asset."

He shook his head. "Can't do it. He should be out of a job, and you know that. He broke the law."

"I would have done the same."

"Don't. We need you here."

"I'm just saying I would have, too. Like Michels asked, what if it was Savannah? Would you have followed procedure?"

"It wasn't Savannah, and it doesn't matter what you or I would have done. What matters is what Michels did." He exhaled. "I sent him home and told him to come back tomorrow at noon. If you need him before then, let him know."

"I will."

My cell phone rang as he closed the door behind him. I recognized Bishop's ringtone. "What'd you find?"

"An envelope with a bunch of photos in it," he said.

"Well, don't leave me hanging. Photos of what? Something related to Stuart?"

"Ashley and some girls at a toga party."

"Wait. I've got a photo of Ashley and another girl from a picture frame on her dresser. They were dressed in togas."

"Be there in fifteen."

"I'm still in the investigation room."

Twenty minutes later Bishop tossed the envelope onto the

only open space on the table. "It's a little awkward for me to look at these." He handed me a pair of latex gloves. "They haven't been processed yet."

"Let's get them to Nikki first. I'd rather not blur any fingerprints that might be on them."

He picked up the envelope in his own gloved hand, said, "On it," and left.

I dialed Detective Anderson's number. He answered on the second ring. "Anderson."

"Detective, it's Detective Ryder in Georgia. I'm calling to follow up on Detective Johnson's memorial service. Is there a date yet?"

"Yes," he said. "I'm sorry I haven't returned your call from earlier. The service is scheduled for July eleventh at two p.m."

"Thanks. My partner Detective Bishop and I will be attending to represent our department."

"I'm sure Johnson would appreciate that. See you then." He disconnected the call.

"That was a little abrupt," I said out loud to myself.

Bishop returned. "Nikki's gone home for the night. I can call her in?"

I shook my head. "It's getting late." I leaned back in the chair and stretched my arms over my head. "I'm getting a flat butt from sitting in this chair all day. Let's go home, get some rest, and then regroup in the morning." I organized the items on the table and put them with the others to bring home.

"Sounds like a plan," he said.

17

Kyle sat on my couch watching the Braves vs. Cubs game. I set my things on the dining room table and followed the same process with my weapons I followed every night. "Who's winning?"

He didn't break eye contact with the TV. "Braves are up by two."

"Go, Braves," I said without any enthusiasm. That got his attention, though it wasn't my intent. He raised an eyebrow. "Go, Cubbies," I said. I just wasn't a Braves fan.

He smiled. "Any progress on Ashley?"

"Not really."

"I talked with my team. She hadn't said anything about the Stuart investigation to anyone, and she sent an email saying she wouldn't be in. She didn't say whether she was sick or not."

"Do you have the email?"

He walked over to the table near my front door and picked up his laptop bag. He removed several papers and handed them to me. "I made five copies for your team."

"Thanks," I said as I read the email. "This is from her laptop."

"I'm not sure."

"No. I mean, it doesn't say it's from her cell phone. Usually when you send an email from a cell phone, it says it's sent from one."

"That's something you can add or remove from settings."

"Right." I chewed on my bottom lip then grabbed my phone from the dining room table and called Michels.

He picked up before the first ring finished. "What's going on? Did you find her? Is she okay?"

"We haven't found her yet, Michels. I'm sorry."

He sighed.

"Has Ashley ever emailed you?" I asked.

"Yeah, a lot. Why?"

"Can you differentiate whether a text comes from a phone or her laptop?"

"Let me check." A minute later, he said, "Yeah, she's got sent from my mobile on them."

"Great. Thanks."

"Is that it? What's this about?"

"I'm not sure yet. I'll see you tomorrow." I hung up before he could ask any more questions. "This is from her laptop. She has a notation on her phone email."

"What does that mean?"

"Her computer was wiped clean. She sent it that morning at six o'clock, so either she or someone else wiped her computer clean after the email. That means whoever took her did it after six a.m." I walked into the kitchen and poured myself some iced tea. I wasn't a fan of the stuff when I first moved to Georgia, but Bishop had forced it on me a few months after we became partners, and, shortly after, it had become my new favorite drink. I'd even learned to make it.

Thankfully, it just required sunshine to cook it, not the oven. "I'm going to take a shower," I said.

"Okay," he replied, his eyes still glued to the game.

I gave Louie a quick glance, but he was too busy swimming through his little castle to notice. "Did you feed Louie?" I asked as I walked to my bedroom.

"Yup," Kyle said.

I took a quick shower, towel dried my long brown hair, brushed it, then twisted it into a bun and secured it with a large butterfly clip. I slipped on a pair of Kyle's boxer shorts I'd washed for him the week before. They were too big for me, but they were comfortable, and that's what mattered. To show my loyalty to my hometown, I put on one of Tommy's Chicago Cub shirts. I stared at myself in my full-length mirror. Was it sacrilegious to wear my deceased husband's shirt with my boyfriend's underwear? Guilt nudged at my heart, and I dropped the boxers and switched them for a pair of my sweats.

I spread out the file I'd been reviewing at the office on my dining room table then opened my portfolio with my notes. "Blue for description of each victim, pink for the victim's identity, light orange for the stickers."

"Can you repeat that?" Kyle said from the great room.

"Talking to myself," I responded.

It was after ten. I watched Kyle cheering on the Braves. Kyle and Louie doing their thing, comfortable in their skin—and scales—while I worked. It was comfy, and it filled my heart in a way I never believed would be possible after Tommy's death.

Kyle turned to me and smiled. "Do you need help with that? I can turn off the game."

"It's okay," I said. "Go, Cubs."

He shook his head, and as he turned back to the television, said, "A house divided."

I gathered the papers with the stickers first. Why would she keep track of the stickers? What did that mean and how was it connected to the stickers from Natalie Carlson's murder?

Detective Grimes had emailed copies of his report to both me and Bishop. I powered up my laptop and opened the email, then scrolled down to the photo of Natalie her parents had provided. It was a full body picture. Natalie Carlson's body was trim. She would be considered petite. Something about her clicked in my brain. She was familiar. Was it the crime scene or something else? Long, light blond hair, big blue eyes, and full lips. Sure, she shared traits with probably half the women in the South, but I recognized something. I just couldn't put my finger on it.

Something nudged the back of my mind. I closed my eyes and focused on it, but it wouldn't come. My eyes grew heavier as I read the files over again. Kyle tapped me on the shoulder, and I shot awake. "I'm up," I said with a groggy voice. I wiped away the bit of saliva pooling at the corner of my mouth.

He rotated my chair so I could get up easily. "It's late. You fell asleep on the files, Rach. Let's go to bed."

I was only half awake. I rubbed my eyes. "Who won?"

"They're not finished."

"Are you going to watch it?"

"No. I'm going to sleep with you."

He helped me up, wrapped his arm around me and guided me to the bedroom. It was a sweet gesture. "I love how you take care of me."

He smiled.

Ashley wrapped her arm around Natalie and smiled for the picture. "Take another one!" She and Natalie laughed. They wore matching togas that sat above the knee. A large cloth with gold trim was tucked into a gold belt at their waists, the other side flipped over one shoulder and clasped to the other end with a plastic gold band. Two girls behind them moved out of the picture frame and walked over to Chip Stuart.

I sat up quickly, sweat dripping from my temples. I scanned the room, but it took a few seconds for me to realize I'd been dreaming. I stared over at Kyle who was sound asleep. It was just a dream, I told myself. Chip Stuart was dead. He wasn't going to any toga parties. And then that little nudge in the back of my mind showed itself.

The girl in the photo with Ashley was Natalie Carlson. Her hair was a different color, and she had on glasses in the photo, but it was her.

18

I couldn't sleep, but I didn't want to call Bishop or Grimes. It was a few minutes before five in the morning. Too early. I quietly put on a pair of jeans and a light blue, short-sleeved Hamby PD polo.

As I tiptoed to the bathroom, Kyle said, "What time is it?"

I turned to him sitting up in bed, his short hair unchanged, sleepiness apparent in his eyes. "It's early. I can't sleep, but don't let that stop you."

He stretched and then climbed out of bed. He slipped into a pair of jeans from the chair on his side of the bed and walked to the bathroom. I stepped out and let him do his business, putting my socks on in the process.

"Are you going to the station?" he asked.

"Yeah. I figured I'd get a head start."

"Can I at least make you breakfast?"

The realization that Ashley and Natalie probably knew each other kept my heart rate at cardio level and my stomach in knots. I had no desire to eat. "I need to get in. I want to check the photos Nikki's supposed to work on."

"Something come to you during the night?"

"I had a dream I was at a toga party with Ashley and Natalie Carlson."

"The girl murdered in Suwanee?"

I nodded. "I think they knew each other. I just need to look at the photos to make sure."

"Do you want some help?"

I put on my second boot. "It's okay. You have your own job. You need to sleep for that." I smiled up at him. "Come over again tonight?"

"I practically live here as it is," he said. His eyes widened. "I'm not saying I—"

I cut him off. "I ask you to stay a lot. It's a natural response." I stood and kissed him. "I've got to go."

———

I hit Dunkin' Donuts for a large coffee with cream on my way to work. It was half-past five, and the woman at the drive-thru said I was their first customer, so my coffee was free. I handed her a five and told her thank you, then headed to work.

I stopped at Nikki's lab and removed the envelope of photos from her desk. I left her a note to let her know I had them since Bishop had left a request form for a fingerprint check. He'd put them in a large plastic evidence bag, so I wasn't worried about contamination at that point. I took them to the investigation room, put on my gloves and carefully flipped through the photos.

There were twenty-four, all from what looked like an older cell phone camera. The pictures were fuzzy, though they were clear enough to see one thing.

Ashley and Natalie weren't strangers.

I pulled up the image of the photo I'd taken at Ashley's apartment. It wasn't a match to any in the file, but it was obvious they were from the same event. I stared at the other girls in the background, but it was just too fuzzy to see them clearly. I scanned through the rest of the photos to see if I could recognize anyone.

And I did. Claire Baker.

I didn't care what time it was, I called Bishop.

"I'm up already," he said upon answering. "What—"

I cut him off. "Ashley knew Natalie Carlson and I think she knew Claire Baker. Claire Baker, Rob. We need to bring Scott Baker in."

"Hold up," he said with a mouth full of something. He spit. Must have been brushing his teeth. "Give me thirty. Don't do anything before I get there."

"Hurry," I said and hit end on my cell. I stared at the photos.

Claire Baker, the daughter of Scott Baker, was an alleged assault victim of one of the Birmingham victims, Daniel Travis. He was a twenty-two-year-old college graduate who had just started a job with a supply chain company. He was found shot in the head outside an abandoned building off Fifth Avenue South in Birmingham. The number one vinyl sticker was found in his left hand.

Why hadn't Ashley mentioned that she knew Claire? Was this part of the reason she felt we got the wrong guy, or was it something else? I pulled up the other female alleged assault victims and compared them the best I could to the photos from Ashley's locker. There were no other matches.

The names of the alleged female victims were never made public, but they were in the files, and Ashley would have easily found them. Did this mean she knew Daniel Travis? If so, why hadn't she told us during the investigation? I dialed Michels.

"Hello," he said, his voice tired but awake. "What's going on?"

"Did Ashley ever mention she knew Claire Baker?"

"No. Why would she?"

"What about Daniel Travis?"

"Daniel Travis? Wasn't he the first victim in Birmingham?"

"Yes. Did she tell you she knew him?"

"No. Why are you asking me these questions?"

"Because she has photos of herself with Natalie Carlson, and Claire Baker is in the background."

"I'm coming in," he said, and he hung up.

Bishop arrived with two Dunkin' coffees. I'd already downed the one I had and refilled it with a double Keurig pod and one barely expired creamer from the kitchen. I put it into the garbage can and sipped from the one Bishop brought. I was beginning to feel the effects of lack of sleep, and I needed the caffeine to keep me going. "God, I love you."

"You're not the first, and you won't be the last." He chuckled then turned serious. "What've you got?"

I showed him the photos, then showed him the ones of Natalie Carlson and Claire Baker.

"Okay," he said taking a seat beside me. "It's obvious she knows Natalie. They're arm in arm in that photo, and it was framed on her dresser, but Claire's a different story. She's just in the background. That doesn't prove they knew each other."

"They were at the same party."

Bishop put on a pair of gloves and carefully went through the photos until he got to one with a big keg. "It's a frat party. There could be girls from anywhere at that party. It doesn't prove they were friends or even acquaintances."

He was right. "But we need to talk to Claire to find out," I said.

"Before we talk to her father," he said.

"He's in town when a girl at a party with his daughter is murdered. Add the stickers and his time with Stuart, and he's a clear suspect. Stuart could have told him about the stickers, Rob."

"I agree, but why would Baker murder a young woman? The whole reason he wanted to thank Stuart, why he paid his lawyer fees, was because his daughter was attacked by one of his victims. It's a stretch to think he would kill a woman that age."

"Maybe Natalie and Claire had been friends, and she didn't believe Claire when she told her she was attacked."

"Did Claire tell her?"

"We don't know yet, but it's possible."

"True, but it's still a stretch that her father would murder the girl for that."

"Maybe it's something else then," I said. "We don't know how many girls these guys assaulted or attempted to assault. Maybe Natalie was attacked by Travis, too, and Claire wanted them to go to the police together, but Natalie wouldn't."

He sipped his coffee. "We need to have a face-to-face with Natalie's parents."

19

Michels walked into the investigation room. I held up the photo of Ashley and Natalie on my phone and shoved it into his face. "Why didn't you tell me Ashley knew Natalie Carlson?" The cedarwood scent distracted me for a moment, but I refocused.

His eyes widened, and he examined the photo. "I...I didn't know. I swear."

"This picture was on her dresser, Michels."

He took my phone from my hand and studied the photo further. "No. No, this wasn't on her dresser. I know the frame. It had a photo of the two of us at Pelican Pete's on Lake Lanier. We were just there a few weeks ago. She got a print of it and put it in that frame. I swear I've never seen this photo."

"That photo was behind this one," I said. "When was the last time you saw this frame?"

"I...like a few days ago, and we were in it. That picture wasn't."

"Did she mention changing it?"

He shook his head. "No, she loved the photo of us. She wouldn't have changed it."

"Did Ashley ever mention Natalie or Claire Baker?"

"Claire Baker? No. I mean, she talked about the investigation, but she never said she knew her. What's going on?"

I showed him the photos from her locker. "There," I said pointing to Claire Baker. "They were at the same party."

"In Alabama? She had a lot of friends there. She went to school there for a year but switched to stay in state her sophomore year."

"And you're sure she never mentioned knowing Claire?" Bishop asked.

"No. It's a big school, and it's got a large population of Greeks. You know, fraternities and sororities. There could have been girls from anywhere on campus at this party or even GDI's. It doesn't mean Ashley knew them all."

GDIs. *God damn independents*, those who weren't part of the Greek system.

"Bishop," I said. "Set up a meeting with Grimes for eleven. Ask him to bring Natalie Carlson's parents. I'm going to call Ashley's parents and have them look at the photos, but I need Nikki to process them first." I checked my watch. "I'm calling her in now."

"I'm on it," he said.

Nikki returned the photos to me within minutes. "The frame and the photos were wiped clean."

"Even the picture itself? Wouldn't that damage the photo?"

"Not if someone used a cloth and was careful."

"Then someone put the photo there on purpose," she said.

She shrugged. "I can't determine that from the evidence, but maybe." She eyed me staring at the photos. "You don't think it was Michels, do you?"

"No, but I'm missing something, and I can't figure out what."

She stood there for a second, then finally asked, "Anything else?"

I peered up at her. "Oh, no. Thank you. May I keep these? I'd like to take a clearer photo of them with my cell."

"Sure. Just put them back in the evidence bag and get them back to me."

"I will. Thank you, Nikki." As she opened the investigation room door, I said, "Nikki?"

She turned around, "Yes, Detective?"

"Promise me something. If you're ever suspicious about something regarding an investigation, whether open or closed, you'll come to me. Don't try to figure it out on your own."

"I promise," she said and left the room.

I hunted Michels down in the kitchen. He'd just finished making a cup of coffee, his back to me. His shoulders slumped inward, and his head hung heavily, as if the weariness growing inside of him added weight to his entire body. I coughed.

He turned around. "Hey, want a cup?"

"I'm good, but thanks. I'm calling the Middletons now. I'd like you in there, but I don't want you to say anything, okay?"

His shoulders pushed back. "Yes, please. Thanks, Ryder."

Back in the investigation room, I dialed their number. Mrs. Middleton answered, but it sounded like we were on speaker. I put Mr. and Mrs. Middleton on speaker on my end, too, and asked them about Natalie Carlson.

"The girl murdered in Suwanee?" Mrs. Middleton asked. "We heard about her, but we didn't know her."

Natalie's photo was all over the news, but that didn't mean

the Middletons were watching or that they'd recognize her if they were. They'd been in the throes of searching for their daughter, and, based on my experience with other missing persons cases, attention was paid only to the task at hand. Finding their loved one. TV wasn't a priority. "Have you seen any photos of Natalie Carlson?" I asked.

"We haven't paid attention to anything but finding our Ashley. I can't bear to turn on the TV, especially to see a girl close to Ashley's age dead."

"I'm going to email you a photo of Natalie. I need you to see if you recognize her. Okay?"

"Yes." She gave me her email.

I sent it from my phone. "It should arrive any second."

"It's here," she said. "Hold on." She was quiet for a moment and then gasped. "Oh, no! That's Reni!"

"Reni?"

"Yes, that's Ashley's friend from high school. Reni Carlson."

I checked Natalie's full name. A chill ran down my spine. "Rene was her middle name."

"Well, I only knew her as Reni. That's what all the girls called her." Her breath hitched. "Could Ashley be—oh, no? No. No. No. Please Detective, you need to find my Ashley." She sobbed across the line.

Mr. Middleton spoke. "Detective, find our daughter."

"We're doing the best we can, sir, but I need some questions answered. Do you think you and your wife can do that? The more information we have, the better chance we have of finding Ashley."

"Yes," he said. Mrs. Middleton sniffled. "Yes, I...we can."

"You said Ashley and Reni were friends in high school. Were they good friends?"

Mrs. Middleton cleared her throat and took a deep breath. "They were in cheerleading together. Ashley was a competitive cheerleader for Twisters from elementary school until she graduated from high school. Reni was a few years younger than her, but she was a little thing, and a fantastic tumbler, so she was used as a fly on the advanced team with Ashley. They became friends, I can't say if they were good friends or not, but I think they lost touch when Ashley went to college."

"Has Ashley mentioned Natalie, I mean, Reni recently?"

"I don't think so," she said. "Honey, has she talked to you about her?"

Mr. Middleton said, "No, not that I can recall. Do you know what happened to Reni?"

I couldn't tell them what I suspected for a variety of reasons, but mostly, I didn't want them to panic more. They needed hope, not despair. "The Forsyth County Sheriff is still investigating."

"But you think they're connected? My daughter's disappearance, and Reni's murder?" he asked.

"We're not sure. In doing the search at Ashley's apartment we found photos with Ashley and Natalie Carlson together. We're exploring every angle we can, and this is one of them."

"I don't understand what's happening," Mrs. Middleton said.

"We're working to figure that out," I said. "I'm going to send you a few more photos. Can you text me and let me know if you recognize any of the girls in them?"

"Yes, of course."

"Okay, I'll send them now," I said. "Thank you." I took photos of the toga party images and sent them to Mrs. Middleton.

"They're here," she said.

A few seconds passed. "No, I don't recognize anyone in those photos. Just Ashley and Reni, I mean, but no one else."

Mr. Middleton said, "I don't either."

"Okay, thank you. I'll be in touch with an update soon, okay?"

"Yes, please find our daughter," Mr. Middleton said and then ended the call.

Michels turned away as he covered his mouth, then turned back around and said, "Reni." He dragged his hand down his face. "She told me about her before the Stuart murders, but she never called her Natalie. Only Reni."

"What did she say?" I asked.

"Same as Mrs. Middleton said. They cheered together, but they'd lost touch after freshman year in college."

"She never mentioned them going to a party together?"

"Ashley was a freshman when she went to Alabama. Reni was still in high school."

"Doesn't mean Reni didn't go to visit."

"Yeah, but Ashley never mentioned it." He pushed his legs against the table. "You won't find my prints on the frame. I never touched it."

"The frame and photos were wiped clean."

"Shit," he said. "So, someone put the photo in the frame for a reason." He paced the room. "To walk us into the connection between Ash and Reni."

I nodded.

Bishop walked into the room. "Got the meeting. We need to leave in five."

"Natalie Carlson, the girl in the photo with Ashley is known as Reni to the Middletons. She didn't attend Alabama when Ashley was there. They were in cheerleading together in high school, but Ashley is older than Natalie, I mean Reni. Also," I showed him the photo. "This photo was placed over one of Michels and Ashley at Lake Lanier from a few weeks ago. The photo is behind the one of the girls."

"And Ashley wouldn't have done that," Michels said.

Bishop eyed me, and I nodded. "Whoever took Ashley is Natalie Carlson's killer."

20

We arrived at the South District unit of the Forsyth County Sheriff's Office a few minutes late. Traffic from the intersection of Peachtree Parkway and Atlanta Highway to Ronald Reagan Boulevard was insane. The backup to get onto 400 southbound came from both the north and south sides of Atlanta Highway, and no one was interested in giving anyone the courtesy of letting them cross lanes to bypass the cluster.

"This traffic is worse than Chicago. At least there you have the tension release from honking your horn."

Bishop tapped his horn and smirked at me.

"You're doing it wrong. You smash your hand onto the horn and hold it there for a good ten seconds, then throw your hands up in the air and yell some profanities. Doesn't usually work, but it feels good."

"That doesn't sound like a release of tension to me."

"That's because you're from here. It's slower here." I took a deep breath and changed the subject. "If we had any doubt the two girls were connected, we don't now."

"I know."

"What's the common denominator?"

"That's what we have to find out."

"We don't even know if Ashley's still alive," I said.

"We treat this like she is. Until we have—God forbid—a body, we move forward searching. We'll find her, Rachel."

I wasn't as convinced as he was.

———

We updated Grimes on what we'd learned and then headed to meet the Carlsons.

Mr. and Mrs. Carlson could barely hold it together. They sat side by side in a small conference room. Mr. Carlson held his wife's hand on the tabletop. Deputy Grimes sat at the head of the table. Bishop and I sat across from the Carlsons and introduced ourselves.

Mr. Carlson tilted his head. "Why are you here?"

I opened my portfolio and slid the picture in an evidence bag across the table. "Do you recognize the girl with your daughter?"

Mrs. Carlson nodded. "That's one of the girls she cheered with. Al...Ashley, I think."

I smiled. "Yes, Ashley Middleton. Ashley was reported missing on the morning of July fifth, less than twelve hours after your daughter's body was discovered."

Mrs. Carlson gasped. Mr. Carlson studied the photo and then quickly looked away. His eyes were wet. He was a wreck, and understandably so.

"Are they connected somehow?" Mrs. Carlson asked.

"We believe so, and we're trying to determine how. Did you know Ashley?"

"Only from cheerleading," Mrs. Carlson said. "She was always so nice to Natalie, and I know they were friends."

"Did a lot of people call your daughter Reni?" I asked.

She nodded. "She didn't like Natalie, so when she was in second grade, she asked the teacher to call her Rene, her middle name. The teacher misunderstood, and she called her Reni. It just stuck. We've always called her Natalie though. It was my grandmother's name."

"Did your daughter go to college?" Bishop asked.

Mr. Carlson beamed with pride. "Yes, she went to Alabama, where I went."

"Ashley was a student there her freshman year. We assume they either ran into each other at a party or planned to get together," Bishop said.

"Oh, I remember that. Natalie was there for a cheerleading event. The girls were spending the weekend with the Alabama cheerleaders. Their instructor from Twisters is an alumnus. I think I recall Natalie saying she saw Ashley there."

I pointed to a girl in another photo. "Do you know this girl?"

They both scrutinized the photo but ultimately said no.

I took a deep breath before speaking. "I know this is an uncomfortable question, but we have to ask it. Was your daughter ever sexually assaulted?"

Mr. Carlson's nostrils flared and the veins in his neck thickened to triple the size. He breathed through gritted teeth, but he didn't say a word. Mrs. Carlson tugged at her long dark hair as she rocked back and forth in her chair. Neither of them answered, but they didn't have to. Their body language said it all.

"Was it reported?" I asked.

Mrs. Carlson shook her head and tears streamed down her face. "We wanted her to report it, but she wouldn't. She said it would make her life miserable, that he'd blame her, and she'd have to leave school."

"So, this was at Alabama?" Bishop asked.

Mr. Carlson nodded.

"Did she ever tell you the name of the boy who assaulted her?" I asked.

"She refused," he said. "She was worried I'd kill him."

"But she told you she was assaulted?" I asked.

"She was raped," Mrs. Carlson said. Tears streamed down her cheeks. Deputy Grimes handed her a box of tissues. She pulled one out and wiped her cheeks and then her nose. "And we only found out when she miscarried. The bastard got her pregnant. She was eighteen years old. Just a baby herself." She shook her head and then sobbed into her hands.

Her husband's jaw was tight. "She wouldn't tell us anything. She just wanted to move on, to forget everything. I tried to convince her otherwise, but I couldn't."

I had Bubba send me photos of the three Alabama male victims and the three Hamby male victims to see if they recognized any of them, but they did not. They questioned us repeatedly about what was going on, and we did our best to appease them. Once they left, we caught up with Grimes, reiterated what we'd learned, and promised to stay in touch with new information.

Bishop pulled into the Starbucks drive thru. The hot air from his open window melted the little eyeliner I'd drawn on my eyelids that morning. I was sticky instantly. "Dear God, this humidity is awful."

"Does that mean you want an iced coffee?"

I shook my head. "Get me one of those frappie things."

"What kind?"

"The cold kind."

"They're all cold. What flavor?"

"I don't know. Just get one that will stop me from melting."

"Are you thinking one of our victims or the Alabama victims raped Natalie?"

"Yes," I said.

"So, how can we find out? They're all dead."

"We need to call all the parents of the male victims and have them look at the photos. They might recognize her."

"So, you think one of them said, *hey check out the girl I raped*?" he said.

"No, but we need to check."

He handed me a cold, chocolate laden drink with whipped cream piled on top of it. My tastebuds were in heaven. It was too bad my head couldn't get out of hell.

"Let's ask Jimmy if someone else can make those calls. We have a lot to do."

21

Back at the office, I put a call in to Claire Baker, but it went straight to voicemail. I asked her to call me as soon as she got the message. I doubted she would, but I'd continue to call back if I didn't hear from her. She wasn't my biggest fan and given the run-in I'd just had with her father, she probably liked me less than before.

We pulled everyone into the investigation room, Jimmy, Michels, Nikki, and Bubba, and caught them up once everyone was sitting.

Jimmy shook his head, but not in disbelief. It was more of a frustrated, *what the hell is going on* shake.

"At least we have confirmation that it's connected to the Stuart investigation," Nikki said. "So, what happens now?"

"We need someone to call each of the male victims' families and get them the photos to see if they recognize either Natalie or Ashley," Bishop said.

"I can do it," Michels said.

"No," Jimmy said through his teeth. "You're on probation. You shouldn't even be in this room."

"Chief, we need help. We can't do it all ourselves," Bishop said. "It's just a few calls."

Jimmy breathed through his nose. "Fine, but just the calls."

"Thank you," Michels said.

"Michels, did you ever mention any of the female assault victims' names to Ashley?"

He shook his head. "No."

Jimmy glared at him.

Michels held up his hands. "I swear, I never mentioned any of their names." He turned to me. "Do you think Ashley was assaulted?"

"I think Ashley saw the files at your house, discovered that Claire Baker was one of the allegedly assaulted women, whether she personally knew her or not, and decided to dig deeper."

"And then what? The killer's dead. The cases are closed," he said.

"The Hamby killer is dead. I think Ashley discovered Stuart didn't kill the Alabama victims, and she found out who did."

The air in the room stilled. No one said a thing, and for a moment, nobody even moved. My words hung like a slow burning match waiting to be dropped into a bucket of gasoline. None of us wanted what I said to be true, but from the silence in the room, I could tell they agreed with me. Ashley learned the truth, and whoever killed the men in Alabama got wind of it. Jimmy tapped his pencil on the table. Nikki stared down at her files, eyed me, then went back to the files again. Bishop pressed his lips together and tipped his head back. Bubba stared at the wall. It was Michels who finally broke the silence.

He ran his hand through his short hair and went back to

his pacing routine. "He killed Reni Carlson so he could leave your names on the scene. He knew you'd figure it out because of the vinyl letters. He wants us to know he's got Ashley." He dragged his hand down his face. "Jesus, we've got to find her. He's going to kill her."

"Michels," Jimmy said softly. Michels didn't respond. He just kept pacing, his mind locked with the fear of Ashley's demise, I was sure. "Michels," Jimmy said again.

Michels stopped. "She's not dead, Chief. She can't be dead."

"We're doing everything we can," Bishop said. "We'll find her."

One way or another.

"We need to bring in Scott Baker," I told Bishop. "It's looking more and more like Natalie Carlson was connected to his daughter, Claire."

"We will," he said.

———

Nikki and Bubba were charged with keeping Michels busy while Jimmy, Bishop, and I figured out what the hell to do. A few things were missing from the Alabama files when I went through everything, so I asked if Michels could give them a pass and confirm what was missing. Jimmy approved it, and Nikki and Bubba got him set up in a conference room where he wouldn't be distracted by us. He fought it, wanting to stick around and help us, but even if he wasn't on suspension, Jimmy wouldn't have allowed it. He was too close to the case, too emotional.

Jimmy stared at the wall, his eyes sullen. Bishop flipped through his files and skimmed page after page. I wasn't sure what he was looking for, if anything, but his face was much like Jimmy's. Defeated and afraid.

"We need to bring in Scott Baker," I said. I'd keep saying it on repeat until it happened. He was involved. I knew it.

"We need evidence," Jimmy said.

"He's clearly a person of interest. You know that."

"What I know is he'll lawyer up and we'll never get anything out of him. He's not stupid, Ryder. He knows how to play the game."

"All the more reason to think it's him."

"Not yet," he said.

"I'll be right back," I said and rushed out of the room. I jogged to the private women's only bathroom down the hall and locked the door behind me. It was a three-stall bathroom, but I didn't care. I stared at a closed stall door as tears streamed from my eyes. I caught my breath, but I couldn't maintain my composure. If Ashley was dead, it was my fault. Stuart's confession, the rhyme? He wanted me to know he wasn't guilty of all the murders. I understood that then, but I did nothing. Nothing! I clenched my fists and gritted my teeth. I should have fought it, not let Johnson close the damn case. I should have insisted. I blinked back tears, then drew back my left arm and, with all the strength I had, punched the door.

"I knew!" *Punch.* "I should have done something!" *Punch. Punch. Punch. Punch.*

The bathroom door opened, but I couldn't stop. My heart raced. My hand throbbed, but I didn't care. Pain mattered. A girl was dead and another was missing, and it was my fault. I didn't take action when I should have. I deserved to hurt. They didn't.

Jimmy stepped close. "Rachel, stop." But I kept going, punching the stall door each time it swung back at me. My hand was bloody and swollen, but I didn't care.

"Rachel!" Bishop stepped behind me and grabbed my arm. "Stop!" Jimmy stood on my left. The two men gently guided me away from the stall door. I couldn't breathe, my chest heavy with emotion. I bent at my waist to catch my breath. Blood drops covered the floor. My hand throbbed as blood continued to drip on the floor.

"Get the paramedics," Bishop yelled.

I turned to him, my eyes filled with tears. "It's my fault."

He wrapped his arms around me, and I cried into his shoulder, blood still seeping from my injured hand. "It's not your fault," he whispered over and over.

Bishop said I must have had an angel watching over me. I only broke one knuckle, but the others were swollen and jammed. It would be a few weeks before that hand would function normally again. He said I was lucky it wasn't my dominant hand, but I didn't feel lucky.

We left the emergency room without saying much. What was there to say? It would be a miracle if Ashley was still alive. The killer had left our names there to show her death was on us, and then switched out the photo in Ashley's apartment to tell us he had her. If she wasn't already dead, he wasn't going to let her live.

"I'm taking you home," Bishop said as he closed the passenger side door. He walked to his side and climbed into the car. "No arguments."

I wasn't sure I had any argument left in me.

22

The doctor had given me a shot of something that made me drowsy and numbed the throbbing pain in my hand, but it didn't last. I unwrapped the gauze and examined my knuckles. They were swollen and a variety of colors, mostly varying shades of purple. I moved them, and a pain so fierce shot down my hand and up my arm. It brought tears to my eyes. I crawled off the couch, peeped at Louie who was oblivious to my pain, and thanked him for his support as I went to my bathroom to grab some Ibuprofen. I swallowed back four of them, dry, and shook my head afterwards, hating the taste of the stuff. I was exhausted, but my mind raced. I picked up my cell and called Lenny Dolatowski.

Lenny had been my rock after Tommy died. Not only was he my boss when I first suited up for patrol in Chicago, but he was my best friend Jenny's father, and a father figure who lived in the duplex attached to my parent's place. I wasn't close with my parents. Growing up they were more about rules and obedience than love and emotions, but Lenny was never short on a bear hug, or good advice over a steaming pot of bigos stew. We became even closer after Jenny was killed, and he was family regardless of genetics. Lenny also had a way of seeing what I couldn't.

He'd followed the Stuart investigation from day one, keeping me in line from afar with his logical approach and keen ability to cut through my emotions blocking me from discovering the truth. I couldn't imagine my life without him.

He picked up on the third ring. "Rach, hold on." He grunted and coughed then mumbled something as he covered the phone. "Okay, I'm back. What's going on?"

"I could ask you the same question."

"Oh, nothing. My niece is over. We made stew."

"Wish I was there for a bowl, but I'll let you go. I don't want to interrupt your time with Chrissy."

"No, no. Let's catch up. Chrissy's just leaving. Give me a minute." He put the phone down and a lump formed in my throat as he and Chrissy said goodbye. I missed Lenny, and just hearing his, *come on by any time, sweetheart*, made me want to jump in the car and drive to Chicago. "Okay, she's gone. It's late. Are you okay?"

"I was wrong about Chip Stuart, and now, because of me, a girl was murdered, and Ashley, our former tech, has disappeared."

"Why do you think you were wrong?"

"Remember the riddle I told you Stuart said?"

"I remember he said one, but I don't recall it."

I'll never forget it. *"One, two, three, you can't pin on me. Seven, eight, nine, I'll add to my crimes. Four, five, six, add to the mix."*

"You think he didn't commit the first three murders?"

"He told me he didn't. Why didn't I believe him?"

"Serial killers are professional liars, Rachel. You know that. If we took everything they said as fact, we'd never solve any murders."

"No," I said. "It's not like that. He was dying when he told me. What did he have to lose?"

"He said it to screw with your head. That's what they do." He coughed again. His cough was worse each time I talked to him. "Listen, hon. You can't let a dead man take away your confidence. That was a solid catch. Weren't those first three murders in Alabama?"

"Yeah, and before you say it, I know it wasn't my jurisdiction, but I should have pushed."

"What's the detective from there say?"

"Nothing. He committed suicide a few nights ago."

"You don't think it was suicide, though, do you?"

"How'd you guess?"

"Your voice goes up an octave when you think something's crap."

I laughed. "You know me so well."

"What makes you think these recent situations are tied to the murders?"

I explained everything to Lenny without interruption. He sighed when I finished. "That's concerning."

"Ya think?"

"Do you have any persons of interest?"

"Scott Baker. The guy that paid for Stuart's initial attorney. He's the father of a previous victim, but Jimmy's not ready to go there. He wants more proof."

"Then you have to dig deeper into Ashley's life and the girl that was killed, what was her name again?"

"Natalie."

"Natalie's life. The proof is there. You're just not looking hard enough."

My cell beeped through with another call. I checked the caller ID. It was Michels. "Len, hold on a sec. I've got to take this."

"I'll let you go. Rachel, this isn't your fault, and I know you're going to find Ashley alive. If she was going to be killed, you'd have found her body already."

"Thanks. I'm trying to think on those terms too."

I clicked over to Michels. "Michels, what's up?"

"How're you feeling?"

"Stupid, embarrassed, like an idiot. Want me to continue?"

"You care about Ashley. I appreciate that."

I wanted to apologize for not getting it right, for not staying a few minutes more at his party to let Ashley tell me what she wanted to say, for wasting time following procedure when he came to my home two nights before. But I didn't. It wouldn't change anything. I'd failed, and I had to make things right. "Thanks for checking on me—"

"That's not what I'm doing. I mean, yeah, I wanted to make sure you're okay, but I found something."

I perked up. "What?"

"Can I come over?"

"Does Jimmy know what you found?"

"I'm not at the station, but I need to show you."

"You can't bring the files, Michels. You're on suspension."

"No, I know that. Just—" He paused. "Can I come by?"

"Come on over."

He laid out two envelopes. "Remember the picture of Ash and me? The one from Pelican Pete's?" He set down another envelope. "Ashley gave these to her friend that took the picture. She works there." He handed me a folded piece of paper. "Read it."

I opened the paper and read the short note.

. . .

If something happens to me, please make sure these envelopes get to Detectives Justin Michels and Rachel Ryder with the Hamby Police Department. You can reach Justin at 770-555-3769. Do not give these to anyone else, especially not another police officer. Please, Staci. This is important.

Ashley

He exhaled. "She gave them to her friend to keep safe."

"When did you get these?"

"About an hour ago. Staci found out about Ash and called me. We met halfway between Hamby and Buford, and she gave them to me." He handed me an envelope. "Open this one first."

Inside the first envelope were photos like the ones from the toga party picture in Ashley's frame. "More photos?"

"Open the second envelope," he said.

I did, and I immediately found the writing familiar. "Who?" I said looking up at Michels. He motioned for me to keep reading. It was a photocopy of a photo on regular print paper from a toga party and a list of names written along the side. Each name had an arrow pointing to a woman in the photo. I scanned it and stopped at Natalie Carlson. I looked him in the eye. "Natalie Carlson is on this list."

"So is Ashley."

"Hold on," I said. I grabbed my case files off my dining room table, where I left them every time I came home, and came back to the couch. I opened a specific folder and showed it to Michels. "Look at the script."

He studied it. "Who wrote that?"

"Detective Johnson."

Michels's head flinched back slightly. "How the—was Ashley working with Johnson?"

I reviewed the list of names again. "I'm trying to figure out how she would have gotten the list otherwise."

"I know you've thought Johnson killed the guys in Birmingham, but why would she get this from him if he was the killer?"

"I don't think he is anymore," I said. There were a few ways to think about it. Ashley could have somehow figured out Johnson was the Birmingham killer and pretended she didn't know to get information from him, or they were working together. I no longer picked Johnson for the murders, not even slightly. His wife made it clear he was obsessed with the case, but not in that way. I trusted her.

And Claire Baker was at that same party.

"Okay," he said. "I don't see Johnson for it either. It doesn't make sense. Say this is a hit list for the Birmingham killer. We know Stuart had a very specific reason for his murders. Justice, right?"

I nodded.

"What kind of justice would Johnson or anyone else be serving on these girls? Is it a new theory? New set of crimes? This looks like we've got a list of possible victims we need to get protected stat."

He was right. "If I had any doubt Johnson wasn't our guy, I don't anymore," I said.

"If this is a hit list, then he would have finished, not killed himself."

"Then it means he and Ashley were working together."

I scanned the names again. "I think so, and I think you're right. Somehow, they figured out what was coming, and narrowed down the next victims to these women."

"But how?" he asked.

"I don't know, but first things first, we need to bring in Scott Baker."

"You think the chief will let you now?"

I nodded and waved one of the photos. "Yes. Natalie Carlson was allegedly raped in college. What if it was the same guy who assaulted Claire Baker?"

"Can we answer that question?"

"Her parents don't know. She wouldn't tell them because she didn't want to go to the police."

His eyes focused on Louie's castle. "Baker could be getting justice for his daughter."

"Right," I said. "If the same guy that assaulted Claire Baker assaulted Natalie Carlson first, and she didn't report it."

"Damn."

I took a photo of the list and handed it back to him. "Get this to Bishop. Make sure the chief knows about it, too, and tell them our theory. Have them get Baker in for an interview. I want to be there, so someone needs to tell me when it is."

"What about the Birmingham PD? Some of the girls live in Alabama," he said.

"Have Bishop get it to Anderson. He needs to know there may be another murder."

It was nine o'clock, only eight in Birmingham. I called Elizabeth Johnson.

"Have you learned anything?" she asked.

"I'm working on it. I do have some questions if you're up to answering them."

"Of course."

"Did your husband—"

"Ex-husband," she corrected.

"Ex-husband, sorry. Did he ever mention a woman named Ashley?"

Her end of the line was quiet for a moment, and then she said, "Not that I can recall."

"What about any of these women?" I read off the list of four women from the photo.

"I don't think so. May I ask why you're asking?"

"Natalie Carlson was murdered on July fourth, and Ashley Middleton disappeared on the fifth."

She gasped. "He was right then, wasn't he? He thought he missed something, and he did. The killing wasn't done."

"Ashley Middleton is a DEA crime tech. She worked for the Hamby Police Department. We found copies of the investigation files in her home. We think she was working with your ex on the investigation."

The tone in her voice was strong, determined. "And you think whoever they believed was the killer found out and killed my husband."

"And abducted Ashley."

"Oh, my God, this is terrible. Do you have any idea who it might be?"

"I have a few theories," I said. "Did he mention Scott Baker?"

Her end of the line went quiet again, then she said, "I remember that name. Didn't he pay for Chip Stuart's attorney?"

"That and a few other things. Did he say anything else about Baker?"

"Um, I don't think so. Have you talked to Detective Anderson about this?" she asked.

"Not yet. We have someone getting him the list."

"He called me earlier today. He's very upset over Bill's death. He believes he committed suicide. He was agitated when I told him I didn't. He blamed me. He said Bill told him he wanted to get back together, and I said no, but that never happened. Bill would never say that. Why would the detective say those things?"

"I don't know, but I'm going to do my best to find out."

"Thank you. As I said before, Bill did not take his own life. That wasn't who he was."

23

My cell phone alarm beeped at four-thirty in the morning. I leaned over to shut it off but ended up hitting snooze instead. Five minutes later, it went off again. I grabbed the phone and turned off the alarm, and then I sat up and rubbed the tired out of my eyes.

"You think you should be going in today?" Kyle asked. He'd come over after I'd crashed.

I didn't want to tell him the alarm was for an early riding lesson. "They're bringing in Scott Baker for questioning. I need to be there." I unwrapped my hand to check my knuckles. Riding would be hard with one hand, but I needed to go. My knuckles had turned a darker purple overnight, but the pain hadn't lessened. I walked into the bathroom and dropped four ibuprofens into my mouth and swallowed them back dry. My throat was already dry, and the pills stuck in my throat. I coughed, but they didn't come up. I grabbed the cup on the counter, filled it and swallowed back the water as hard and fast as I could. It worked.

"Rach," Kyle said. He gently put my hand in his and scrutinized it with a worried look. "This is bad. You need to relax today."

"Ashley is missing, and I think Scott Baker knows where she is. I can't stay home."

"Bishop told me how upset you were yesterday." He put his hands on my shoulders and looked me straight in the eyes. Concern flashed over his face. "This isn't your fault. You know that, right?"

I swallowed back a lump in my throat and swept my fingers over my eyes to clear the tears. "I missed something. Stuart didn't murder those men in Alabama. He tried to tell me that, but I didn't listen. Now we've got another victim and a missing friend. She's my friend, Kyle. She's your friend, too. I need to fix this. I have to find her."

He pulled me close, and I buried my head into his chest. It was firm and strong, and for the first time in a long time, I felt like I was home.

He rubbed my back softly. "This isn't your fault."

I couldn't stop the tears from coming. I kept my head pressed against his chest and took deep breaths to keep myself from losing it again. "I think it's Baker. I think I've figured some of it out."

"Rachel." He stepped back and put his hands on my shoulders again, but that time, he kept his elbows bent so I was closer. "You're the best detective I've ever met, and I've worked with a lot of them. You will figure this out." He kissed the top of my head. "But right now, you need a shower. I'll cook up some breakfast while you're at it, okay?"

I took a deep breath and nodded, and then I briefly closed my eyes and released the breath as a shudder from deep within my bones coursed through my body. It was time. Kyle was special. He supported me, helped me take myself less seriously, and whether I could admit it to Savannah or not, something big was happening between us. He should know, and I needed to be honest. If we didn't have honesty, we had nothing. I scratched my arms, surprised at how nervous I was. "I have to tell you something."

He smiled down at me. "What? You don't like my breakfast burritos?"

I smiled. "I love your breakfast burritos."

"Thank God. That would have been a deal breaker."

My breath hitched. "This is important. I haven't exactly been honest with you about something."

He furrowed his brow. "You haven't been honest with me?" He was genuinely concerned. "You can tell me anything, you know that."

Would he wind up eating those words? I pressed my lips together and stepped back toward my bathroom counter, then leaned against it for support both physically and emotionally. "I should have told you this months ago, and I didn't. I wanted to, and I planned to, but I didn't know how. I didn't want you to be upset or feel like what we have together doesn't mean something to me, because it does. I just—"

He took a step toward me and tilted his head to the side. He didn't say anything at first, instead looking me in the eye with an expression I wasn't sure I recognized. "How about you just say it, and we'll figure it out from there?"

My heart raced. On the surface it all sounded so silly. Riding lessons. So what? Except it was more than that. It was a commitment I'd made to the man I expected to spend the rest of my life with. The man who had been taken from me far too soon. The man I still loved and still missed. The meaning behind those riding lessons could end things with Kyle. I swallowed back the lump in my throat. I didn't want to lose him.

"It's okay," he said. "Just say it."

Every muscle in my body tensed. He was so patient and

kind, and I was going to say something that could change that. *Get over it. Just say it.* "I've been taking riding lessons. Because of Tommy and my promise. I know we're together now, but it didn't feel right, letting it go. It doesn't mean I don't—" I wasn't sure how to express feelings I couldn't quite grasp myself. I placed my palm over my mouth and my fingers over my nose and shook my head.

His pursed lips formed a wide, toothy grin so big his eyes smiled along with it. "Riding lessons? Is that it?"

"I don't want you to be mad or think I'm betraying you, because I'm not. It's a promise and I need to keep it."

Kyle leaned his head to the right. "Mad?" He shrugged though he was still smiling. "Why would I be mad at you for keeping a promise you made to Tommy?"

"Because I'm with...we're together now. We're a couple."

"Rachel, Tommy was your husband. You loved him and that love doesn't go away because he's gone. I expect you to keep your promise. Your word is your word, and I know you well enough to know you stand by it. To be honest, I thought about asking when you were going to start taking them, but I didn't want to push you."

Relief washed over me. My heart stopped pounding, and the anxiety disappeared. I exhaled and relaxed. "Really?"

He rubbed his forehead. "Do you really think I'm the kind of guy that would be upset because you're keeping your word to someone you love?"

Tears fell from my eyes again. Damn, I hated crying, and I especially hated crying in front of people. "Yes. No. I don't know. I was afraid it would upset you. Tommy's gone. I know that, and I was worried you'd think I haven't moved on."

He wiped my tears with his thumb and stepped close to me again, lifting my chin to look me in the eye. "I'm not a replacement for Tommy, and I don't want to be. You can still carry love for him in your heart and let me in, too. There's plenty of room for us both, okay?"

The lump once in my throat forced its way back up again. I swallowed. "Okay."

He kissed me on the forehead. "I don't want you to feel you have to keep things from me. This isn't a drive-thru relationship. I'm in this for the long haul, and whatever bridge needs to be crossed, I want to cross it together."

I nodded. "I do, too."

"Okay." He smiled. "Now, how about breakfast burritos?"

"Can you make mine to go? I want to get to work."

I ate and drove, a skill I'd yet to master. Cheesy eggs dropped onto my pants, and I chided myself for not bringing a napkin. I put another call in to Claire Baker. It rang once and then went to voicemail. She'd sent me there on purpose. I didn't know whether she had my cell phone in her contacts, or if she sent any unknown calls straight to voicemail. I left her a message. "Claire, this is Detective Rachel Ryder in Hamby. I need to talk to you as soon as possible. Thanks."

I wasn't about to tell her we were going to interview her father about murdering a possible friend of hers and kidnapping Ashley.

Bishop met me in my cubby. "It's a weak thread you're working with here, partner."

"It's the only thread we've got. Baker wanted retribution for his daughter's assault. He praised Stuart for his murders. If Natalie Carlson was attacked by Daniel Travis before Claire, Scott Baker could be enacting his own justice for that."

"Because if Carlson reported the assault, Travis couldn't have attacked Claire."

"Right."

"But Travis could have been out on bail. We can't say what he would or wouldn't have done," he said.

"You're thinking like a cop. Think like a father. How would you feel if Emma were attacked, and it could have been prevented?"

Bishop cringed at the mention of his daughter. He'd been divorced a while, and Emma was getting ready to start graduate school at Georgia Tech after finishing her bachelor's degree a few months before. Bishop lit up every time he talked about her, but not in reference to a sexual assault. "I'd want to kill the guy."

"What about the girl who didn't report it?"

He shook his head. "That's different."

"Maybe to you, but what if it isn't to Baker? He's been arrogant and smarmy from the first time we met him. I wouldn't put this past him. Also, when we first interviewed him about the murders, he said something like..." I scanned through the files. "This. He said this. *If I killed Travis, I would have just shot him in the head. I wouldn't waste my time on the rest of this shit. I'm not afraid to go to prison.*"

"Natalie Carlson wasn't shot."

"No, but her crime scene wasn't as clean as Stuart's scenes were."

He nodded. "I'll get him in."

24

Bishop had arranged to meet Baker at a local coffee shop under the guise of follow-up questions to finalize the files on Chip Stuart. I wanted to go, but Jimmy axed that idea for fear I'd end up on the news for assault. He had a point. He also wanted everything to appear casual and keep Baker from being suspicious.

Bishop returned to the office alone.

"Where's Baker?" I asked.

"He didn't show."

The hairs on my arms stood. I jumped from the chair in the investigation room. "He knows, Bishop. He knows we think he's involved. He's running. We need a BOLO on him."

"Already done."

Jimmy stormed in. His face was red, and his hands were clenched into fists so tight his knuckles were white. "You lost him?" It wasn't exactly a question.

"Chief," Bishop said. "He didn't show."

Jimmy ran his hand over his cropped hair. "Call Birmingham. See if they've had any interaction with him since the investigation closed."

I retrieved the phone number and called Detective Anderson. He picked up on the second ring. "Anderson."

"This is Detective Ryder with Hamby PD. Mind if I put you on speaker?"

"No problem, ma'am."

I hit the speaker button. "I have Detective Bishop and Chief Abernathy in the room with me."

"Gentlemen," he said. "What can I help you with?"

Bishop spoke first. "Did you receive the email I sent you earlier this morning?"

"Yes, I did. I've already got calls out to the victims, but I'm not sure why this is important."

"We can explain that in a moment," I said. "Right now, we have a question regarding Scott Baker. He was the father of Claire Baker who was attacked by Daniel Travis."

"I don't remember the name but go ahead."

"Has your department had any interaction with him since the investigation closed?"

"Give me a moment." He put us on hold.

"He's an odd one," Bishop whispered.

"If by odd you mean condescending, I agree."

Bishop rolled his eyes. He always assumed I believed all male law enforcement was condescending. I probably did, but that wasn't my point then.

Anderson returned to the line. "Detective, Mr. Baker is no longer a resident of Alabama. In fact, if you were to check for yourself instead of calling me, you'd see he's a current resident of Alpharetta, Georgia. I believe that's close to your town, correct?"

Bishop and I made eye contact. He raised a brow and mouthed, "He moved?"

"We are aware of his move," I lied. "I'm asking if he's had any run-ins with your department."

"Unless he was arrested, we wouldn't have noted anything in our system, so, to the best of my knowledge, no, there has been no interaction with Mr. Baker."

"Thank you," I said.

"May I ask why you're asking?"

I regarded Jimmy. He shook his head. "We like to keep an eye on people who support serial killers, and he paid for Chip Stuart's attorney."

"I understand. And regarding the assault victims?"

I looked over at Bishop again. I wasn't exactly sure what he said in the email.

"One of the victims here was threatened, and we've learned the women on that list may be at risk, too."

"I'll make sure we have people on them. You'll keep me updated?"

"Yes," Bishop said.

"Will I still see you at the memorial?"

"Yes, we'll be there," I said. I killed the call. "Baker moved to Georgia?"

"Alpharetta," Bishop said.

"Why the hell didn't we know this?" Jimmy asked.

"It's my fault," I said. "I'm the one that wanted to move on him. I should have covered all bases."

"Then do it now," he said. "We've got a missing woman. If Baker's involved, I want his head served to me on a silver platter." He turned around and slammed the door behind him as he walked out.

Bishop and I stared at each other. "He's upset about Ashley," I said.

"I'll get Baker's address and get over there."

"Take someone with you," I said.

"On it," he said and left the room.

I wrote Baker's name on a whiteboard and detailed everything we'd learned about him and his interest and involvement in the previous murders. Underneath it, I wrote what we believed to be his reason for killing Natalie Carlson would be. *Justice*. I drew a circle around it.

Bubba burst into the room. "Oh, good, you're here. At three o'clock this morning we got a tip line call saying Ashley was sighted at a gas station in Tampa. I called Tampa PD, and they got the video from the station. They sent it to your email just now."

I stepped around to my laptop and flipped it on. I tapped a pencil on the table while the damn thing took forever to load. Finally, I typed in my login information and went straight to my department email. It was the first email listed.

I clicked on it, bypassed what they'd written, and went straight to the link. Bubba and I eyed the screen. I held my breath, praying to a god I didn't believe in that it was Ashley, and she was okay. But when the woman walked across the camera's view, my chest heaved and deflated. I sighed. "Damn."

Bubba's shoulders sank. "I really wanted it to be her."

"Me, too," I said as I clicked back to the email. "I can see why they thought it might be, but that doesn't help."

"No." Bubba's usually clean-shaven, baby face showed early signs of a five o'clock shadow, something he'd never had. He rubbed his finger and thumb across his jaw. His eyes closed, and he sighed. "She's dead, isn't she?"

"We don't know."

He nodded. "No, she's dead. It's been too long. Women who are missing this long are rarely found alive." He rubbed his scruff again, looked up at the ceiling and then closed his eyes. "*Om Namo Narayanaya*," he said. He repeated it several times.

I had no idea what that meant, but it gave me a sense of

peace. I waited until he opened his eyes and said, "That was beautiful." Bubba's family came from India. He was raised in the Hindu religion, but he never mentioned much about it.

"It's a funeral prayer. Lord Narayanaya is the supreme god. Bowing to him offers peace to the dead."

"I didn't know you practiced Hinduism. Is that the correct way to say it?"

He nodded. "Yes, and I don't really practice it, but it felt right, saying the prayer for Ashley."

"Bubba, we're going to find her. I promise you that." What I didn't say was that the odds were high we wouldn't find her alive.

"She's my friend," he said. "Please, find her alive."

25

Bishop brought in Scott Baker about an hour later. I met them in the interrogation room. There was a glass of water in front of Baker. We'd kicked up the temperature in the room and flipped on all the lights. We needed him to talk.

A civilian wouldn't peg Baker as a possible serial killer, but then again, no one that interacted with Ted Bundy had, either. Baker stood at about six feet, dressed for success in a dark suit and crisp, white shirt underneath. His hair, salt and pepper and wavy in that George Clooney kind of way, was probably attractive to women of all ages. Except me. I saw nothing attractive in Baker.

He sat in the metal chair with his legs crossed and a smarmy smile set like stone in his face. "Detective, as always, it's a pleasure."

I pulled out a chair across from him and sat. "At least for one of us."

Bishop stood behind me and coughed.

"I'm sorry I missed my appointment with Detective Bishop, but I was delayed by a long-winded client on a Zoom call. I would have sent a text, but I don't have his number."

"Right," I said. "Detective Bishop explained to you why we brought you in today, correct?"

"In part. I'm assuming I'm not under arrest."

"Not yet. We have some questions regarding Natalie Carlson and Ashley Middleton," I said.

He smirked. "Questions I am not legally required to answer, nor could I with anything other than what I've seen on the news." He waved his hand and shot me a condescending look. "But go ahead."

I returned his imitation smile. "Where did you spend July Fourth?"

He picked up the glass and sipped the water. *Perfect.* Baker wasn't as smart as he believed. "At Thunder on the Mountain."

"Thunder on the Mountain?" Bishop asked.

"It's the Alabama Fourth of July celebration. This year it was at Red Mountain and Vulcan Park. Google it if you don't believe me."

"Approximately what time were you there?" I asked.

"We got there early to secure a spot. So, ten o'clock I believe, and before you ask, we left when the fireworks ended, but it took us two hours to get out of the park."

"We," I said. "Who were you with?"

"A lady friend." He set both feet on the floor, put his palms on the table and then formed his index fingers into a steeple. Smiling, he asked, "Am I a person of interest in your investigations?"

I studied him. He kept eye contact with either me or Bishop. His shoulders were straight not slouched. He never looked away or down. All signs he wasn't lying, but I still didn't believe him. Baker was manipulative, and as a sales executive, he would know how to work people, how to present himself with confidence even if he didn't feel it.

"We're doing our due diligence," Bishop said. "What's the name of the woman you were with?"

He leaned back in the chair, folded his hands together and placed them on his lap. He smirked again. "It was our first date. I'm not willing to drag her into your unwarranted accusations at this time, but thank you for asking."

I hated the guy and had to speak through gritted teeth. "We're just having a conversation, Mr. Baker."

"Oh, I'm aware of what we're doing." He winked.

I gripped the sides of my seat to push myself up, but Bishop put his hand on my shoulder and squeezed. His message was clear. *Stay calm.* "Let me tell you what we know." I leaned forward and stared into Baker's eyes. "We know that Natalie Carlson was murdered on July Fourth. We know that the victim attended college with your daughter." I removed the photos from the file and placed them in a line horizontally. I didn't bother pointing out the victim. "We know that Natalie Carlson was allegedly raped prior to your daughter's alleged assault." I paused to give him a moment to process my use of the word alleged. His nostrils flared, and a flicker of anger passed through his eyes, but he caught it, and his face went blank. I continued. "We know that you were understandably angry about Claire's alleged assault, and you wanted justice. In that desire, you supported the efforts of the serial killer Chip Stuart."

His jaw tensed. "It was not alleged, Detective. My daughter was sexually assaulted."

"Yet she didn't report it to the police."

He narrowed his eyes at me. "The system does not favor young women."

"That makes you angry, doesn't it?" I asked.

"It should make *you* angry, Detective."

Bishop spoke next. "I can understand your feelings, Mr.

Baker. I have a daughter close to Claire's age, and if we experienced what you experienced, I'd want justice, too, and I'd want someone to pay."

"Travis did pay," I said. "With his life."

Bishop walked to the right side of the table and gripped the back of the chair. "No." He shook his head. "That wouldn't be enough. I'd want to know if he attacked anyone else and if it was reported." He walked over to Baker and leaned his body against the table, just inches away from the man. "And if I found out there were other victims before my daughter, I'd want them to pay as well."

Baker stared at the door, then his eyes flicked to the camera in the corner of the room. He stood. "I don't need to sit here and be verbally assaulted with your passive aggressive accusations."

I smiled. We'd shook him, and a sense of accomplishment washed over me. "Have a—"

He cut me off. "This conversation is over." He smiled and removed a card from his wallet. "In the future, should you have any additional questions, or any reason at all to speak with me, please contact my attorney." He walked over to the door. Bishop doubled his steps that direction and opened the door for him. When he was outside the room, Baker gave us a half shrug and asked, "I wonder, have you considered speaking with Niles Wentworth about this?"

Bishop rolled his eyes and then made eye contact with me. "I'll escort him out."

I waited a few seconds to make sure they were out of the hall before I left the interrogation room for the investigation room. I was afraid I'd tackle Baker to the ground and beat his attitude out of him. He was our guy. Every bone in my body hummed with that realization. We just needed evidence to prove it.

I called Bubba from the department line.

"IT Department," he said.

I didn't bother saying my name. He recognized my voice. "Bubba, can you find out if a Fourth of July event in Birmingham had cameras?"

"I can try. Which event?"

"Thunder on the Mountain."

"Detective, that's the biggest Fourth of July event in Alabama. It draws thousands of people. Even if they have video, if you're looking for someone specific, it'll be impossible to find them."

"Nothing's impossible," I said.

"There could be personal videos online too. I can check for those, but it'll take some time. Do you want me to go through them? I'll need to know what you're looking for."

"Scott Baker."

Bubba sighed. "I'll do my best."

26

Jimmy stood near the whiteboards. His white Hamby PD polo was wrinkled. He caught me staring and glanced down at his shirt then attempted to smooth it out. He gave up quickly and said, "We can't charge a guy because he's an asshole."

"His alibi is bull," Bishop said.

"I can't find him in any video," Bubba said. "There are just too many people in the crowd."

"It was worth a shot," I said. "But it does play in our favor."

"If we bring him in again because he won't give us the name of his date," Jimmy said. "We'll never get anything out of him."

"Agree," I said. "But we have his prints." I glanced at Nikki.

She nodded. "He left them on his water glass. I sent them to Forsyth County. I'll check back with them when we're through here."

"If we can attach them to anything related to the crimes, we can get an arrest," I said.

"That's a lot of ifs," Jimmy said.

"It's all we've got right now."

Bishop spoke. "What I don't get is why he would move away from his daughter?"

"Job maybe?" Bubba suggested. "He's not with the same company he was six months ago."

"Revenge," I said. "It's convenient to live where you kill. We need eyes on him. There are other girls on that list. If he's our guy, we can catch him."

"We don't have the manpower for that. With Michels out, we're down a detective, and we're already down one as it is." He exhaled.

"Bring Michels back. He can watch him," I said.

He folded his arms across his chest. "That's not happening."

"Chief," Bishop said. "We need someone on Baker. What about Lauren Levy? She's applied for the detective job already. Test her out."

"I'm not comfortable putting a woman on Baker," he said. "If he's got Ashley, I'm not sure she can handle him."

"She can." I furrowed my brow. He knew that, so why even bring that up? "I've shot with her on range, and I've sparred with her on the mat at training in Jasper. She knows her stuff."

He exhaled. "She's on day shift. I can drop her from rotation and put her on Baker, but I want her in constant contact with us, and I want check-ins by patrol."

"He's in Alpharetta. It won't be our patrol," Bishop said.

"I'll set that up," I said.

"Do it," Jimmy said and charged out of the room.

I gathered my things and followed.

Lauren Levy had signed on with the department about five months earlier. She came from the City of Atlanta Police

Department where she'd worked patrol for six years. She was taller than me by at least two inches, putting her at five-foot-seven, and she spent more time at the gym than I did. She was skilled in Krav Maga, a military defense program developed in Israel. I was familiar with the program, but that was about it. Levy knew it well. A few months back we'd attended advanced training at the academy unit near Macon, and I'd cheered when she blocked a punch and kneed a man in the groin, then dropped him to the floor. His right leg weighed more than Levy. The girl was tough.

Levy didn't give off the cop vibe, nor did she look like one, and those combined with her other skills, were her secret weapon. Her straight blond hair hung just past her shoulders, giving her a feminine look to balance her fit body. She wore her hair down when she came to work, but somehow it was up in a bun every time I bumped into her during the day. It was a smart move. Buns weren't easy to grab and pull. Ponytails were.

Jimmy worked fast. Levy walked into the kitchen a few minutes after me. "Detective Ryder, the chief told me about the assignment. He said you and Detective Bishop are lead. I'm ready now."

Bishop met us in the kitchen. He smiled at Levy. "Word travels fast."

"Jimmy told her," I said. "Let's get moving."

We filled Levy in on everything about Baker's personality, his stature, and his desire for revenge. We explained his manipulative tendencies and ordered extreme caution if confronted.

"I've got a change of clothes in my locker so I can get started right away. Any idea where he would be right now?"

"No," Bishop said.

She nodded. "I'll start with his residence."

"Constant updates," Bishop hollered as she left the kitchen.

"Yes, sir," she responded.

"I like her," I said.

Bishop nodded. "She could kick Baker's ass."

"Let's hope she doesn't have to." I stirred some cream into my coffee. My cell phone rang, and I checked the caller ID. "It's Michels." I hit accept and put him on speaker. "Michels."

"What's going on? Did you arrest Baker?"

"We don't have the evidence to arrest him, but we've got someone on him."

"Who?" he asked.

"Lauren Levy."

"Okay," he said. "She's good. She won't let him get away with anything."

"Did you get the information to Detective Anderson in Birmingham?"

"No. I got a call from Jimmy first thing telling me to stay home and stay out of it. He handed it over to someone else."

"And yet you're calling me."

"As the boyfriend of a missing woman, yes." He paused. "Ryder, come on. I'm going crazy here. Every bad scenario is going through my mind."

My heart broke for Michels. "We'll do our best to keep you updated, but if you can put any of the pieces together, call me or Bishop, okay?"

He exhaled. "Okay."

I attempted to type out an email to Detective Anderson, but his name didn't show up in the *to* line. "I don't have his full contact info on my phone." I headed toward my cubby with Bishop by my side. "Why do you think Baker tossed out Wentworth's name?"

He sat in front of my desk. "He knows he was a person of

interest in the Stuart investigation. It's distraction." He rubbed the scruff on his chin. "Or deflection."

"Wentworth did approach Chastain, his daughter's alleged attacker, in a bar," I said.

"And he had two arrests for assault twenty-five years ago, but the charges for each were dropped. He could have figured out that Chastain assaulted Natalie Carlson before his daughter and just lost it."

I nodded.

I found Anderson's email and sent the names to him. My gut told me to forward it onto the chief at the department also, so I found his email and sent it to him too. "But we don't know who assaulted Natalie Carlson, and Marissa Wentworth was in Alabama. Chastain was here in Atlanta."

"We need to have a talk with Wentworth anyway," Bishop said.

"Let's go."

27

I found Wentworth's work address in a file. "CarMax on Highway Nine in Roswell. You drive."

Bishop took Highway Nine instead of Georgia 400. Traffic was jammed from McFarland, through downtown Alpharetta, and into Roswell. We sat through four red lights for two strip malls and two more to get through McFarland. "I hate traffic here," I said.

"It could be worse. I don't think Wentworth is our guy."

"His daughter Marissa wasn't in any of the photos in Ashley's things. I don't have a good feeling about this."

"Meaning?"

"Baker brought him up for a reason. It can't be good."

He pulled into the CarMax parking lot. "I agree. Let me take the lead on this."

I saluted him. "You got it, sir."

He rolled his eyes.

A car salesperson hit us up right when we stepped out of the vehicle. Could he not see the government license plate? "Good afternoon, y'all looking for a car today?"

Bishop showed him his badge clipped to his pants. "We're looking for Niles Wentworth."

It wasn't even noon, but I was sweating like I'd been in the sun all day.

"Wentworth? He's off today." He crooked his head to the left. "Everything okay?"

"Do you know where he lives?" Bishop asked.

"Sure, but I'm not supposed to give out employee information like that. You need to talk to the manager inside."

The manager was a younger man with slicked back, black hair and acne scars on his face. He weighed more than his clothes could handle, and he reeked of body odor. I gave him a pass on the body odor because of the weather.

"I'm not supposed to give out employee information," he said. "But if this is important, I guess I can."

"It's important," Bishop said. "But that's all we can say at this time."

"Got it." He wiped the sweat off his forehead with the back of his hand. When he wrote down Wentworth's address, some of the sweat on his arm dripped onto the paper. "Here you go. I'm sure you could have found it yourself, anyway."

"Yes," I said.

Wentworth lived in Poplar Ridge, a small community of older townhomes in an area near the mostly updated downtown. It was odd seeing the antiquated rows of townhomes sitting in the middle of new, modern communities. The homes' muted colors blended to make the units appear bigger than they were. Wentworth's was four down in the first set on the left. We parked a few spaces away, then walked up to the plum-colored door. It was slightly ajar.

Bishop stepped in front of me and removed his weapon from his belt. I removed mine, too. I stepped to his right. He moved to the left, tapped the front door with his right foot, and peeked inside. He counted to three with the fingers of his free hand. "Niles Wentworth? Detectives Bishop and Ryder from Hamby PD. If you're home, please answer."

I counted down five seconds, and Bishop spoke again. "Mr. Wentworth? If you're here, I need you to let us know."

Still nothing. Bishop made eye contact. I moved behind him as he entered the townhome with his weapon out in front of him.

The steps to the second floor were right inside the entrance. There was a black shoe on a step about halfway up. Bishop turned his head and flicked it toward the stairs. I nodded.

The cedarwood scent hit me immediately.

On the left was the kitchen. It was empty, but in disarray. Broken dishes cluttered the floor. The refrigerator door hung open and partially off the frame.

"Clear," I whispered.

"Shit," Bishop said.

We stepped farther toward the living and dining area. A fireplace and mantle highlighted the room on the right against the corner wall. On its left was the back door. The dining room was on the left, but there was a half wall dividing the rooms. Niles Wentworth lay on the floor with one shoe missing and a bullet in the middle of his head. His mouth and eyes were frozen wide open in fear, the last emotion he'd felt before he died. Bishop crouched down and carefully checked the man's wrist for a pulse. He looked at me and shook his head.

"Can you smell cedarwood on him?"

"Are you kidding me? The guy's blood is all over the wall. I can't smell anything but that, and I'm not going to get close enough to find out if he dabbed some cologne on this morning."

"It's light, but I can smell it. Bishop, it's the same scent Baker wore."

"I don't know how you can smell anything other than blood."

I sighed. "I'll call it in," I said.

We answered every necessary question with Alpharetta's first responders. When their detective, a tall, thin man with a mustache that hung a little too far over his top lip, arrived, we rattled off the same answers to his similar questions.

His eyes widened with sudden recognition. "That's right," he said, pointing at me. "You're that Chicago detective. Did a number on Hamby's government a few years back." He smiled. "Nice work."

I wasn't sure how to respond to that. The number I did on Hamby's government was solving a complicated, devastating murder that broke open a disgusting situation I preferred not to think about. "We'd like to be kept updated on this investigation."

"I understand, but I'm going to need a little more than *we're working on an investigation your vic might be connected to*, ma'am." His *ma'am* was both condescending and arrogant at the same time.

I despised detectives with attitude, especially when they'd just unsuccessfully patted me on the back, metaphorically speaking. "We have a missing woman. I'm sure you're aware of the case?" He pressed his lips together and furrowed his brow. Ashley's disappearance was all over local media. His job at pretending to give it some thought was pathetic and a waste of our time. I didn't bother waiting for an answer. "Detective." I chose not to use his name, which he'd given us earlier. "We're working with a ticking clock here. We need whatever prints you get. If you're apprehensive about sharing, I'm happy to put in a call to my chief and make sure he connects with yours." I dug into my pocket for my card. "If you have any additional information, give me a call."

As we walked away, Bishop said, "What a tool."

"That's not our biggest issue."

"I know. Either Baker's psychic, or he just killed Wentworth."

28

We met with Jimmy in his office.

"He's got an alibi," Jimmy said. "Baker's alibi is solid. Alpharetta confirmed he was on a Zoom call, and then he was here. Like Bishop said, Wentworth's body was still warm, so he wasn't even in rigor when you found him. He hadn't been dead more than three hours, and Dr. Barron doesn't even think it was that long."

"He didn't just bring up Wentworth to screw with us," Bishop said. "He knew we'd take the bait and find him dead."

Jimmy rocked back in his chair. "It's out of our hands, anyway."

I chewed on a fingernail. Jimmy eyed me and raised an eyebrow, so I dropped the hand and stuffed it under my leg. "It's not just him. He's not working alone."

Bishop and Jimmy stared at me. Bishop spoke first. "Go on."

I stood and walked small laps horizontally behind the chairs where I'd sat, swinging my injured hand into the back of one and swearing. The bruising hadn't lightened. "He knew Wentworth was dead because he's got a partner."

Bishop stared at the rough outline of Baker's morning activities on the whiteboard. "We don't have enough of anything to go on."

"Let's go back and work through our timeline. There's something there. We'll find it."

Forty-five minutes later we were fully caffeinated and reviewing the information with Bubba.

"Is Nikki coming?" I asked.

"She's finishing something and will be in," Bubba said.

"Anything more on those videos?" Bishop asked.

Bubba shook his head. "I gave up. There were too many people at the event. My grandmother would say I was looking for a needle in a haystack."

"I would have said that," Bishop said. "God, I'm old."

My cell phone rang. I glanced at it then at Bishop. "It's Levy." I tapped the icon and put her on speaker. "What do you have?"

"I had him but lost him." She spoke quickly. "I'm in Suwanee. Traffic is bad, and there was an accident. I couldn't get through."

I closed my eyes and exhaled. "Did you see if he turned?"

"He did, but the road's blocked. I can't get through."

"Can you hop over the median or anything?" Bishop asked.

"No. A vehicle t-boned another one in an intersection, and a third hit the t-boned vehicle. Fire and paramedics just arrived and blocked off everything."

"Do what you can," Bishop said.

"I'm sorry," Levy said.

"It's not your fault," he said.

"Keep us posted," I said and disconnected the call. I

walked over to a whiteboard and started from the beginning. "Ashley wanted to talk to me about Stuart. Natalie Carlson is murdered. We got the call about our names being at the scene of a murder. Ashley disappears. Johnson allegedly commits suicide. We find items that conclude Ashley had information about the Stuart investigation." My cell phone dinged with an email. I glanced down at it. "It's from Anderson." I read the email. "He's putting patrol watch on the girls in Alabama. He'll be in touch."

Bishop nodded.

Just as we started to dig into our notes, the department phone rang. I hit the speaker button.

"Detective Ryder, this is Hamilton in dispatch. We have a call from Detective Grimes. May I send it to you?"

"Yes, thanks."

"Detective Ryder," Grimes said. "We have another body."

The sun burned down on us. The summer breeze failed to appear, replaced instead by an invisible wall of humidity so thick I could taste it. I'd changed my clothes at the department, choosing a black short-sleeved shirt and a pair of dark jeans.

Grimes handed us each a Tyvek suit.

Bishop held up his palms. "It's a hundred and two with the heat index. I'm not wearing that."

Grimes raised his eyebrows. "It's procedure."

Bishop and I traded eye rolls. "It's not ours," I said.

"If you want to be involved, then you need to wear them."

We begrudgingly stepped into the white saunas.

"Another golf community," Bishop said.

"How do you know it's the same guy?" I asked. Dread clanked through my gut like a ball in a pinball machine.

"I've been doing this a long time," he said.

I recognized her face instantly. My eyes trailed from the young woman lying in the grass to Bishop. We didn't speak. We didn't have to. It was clear the dead girl was one of the girls in Ashley's photos. And she was from Alabama.

"How long?" Bishop asked.

"She's cold," Grimes said. He crouched down and gently lifted her left arm. It hung limp in his fingers. "And already out of rigor."

"So, more than thirty-six hours," I said. "Or she was refrigerated to cool her faster."

"I can't say for sure, but that's a reasonable assumption."

The heat rising in my Tyvek suit wasn't just from the weather. "Son of a bitch."

"I'll get with Levy," Bishop said and stepped away from the scene.

I asked Grimes a few more questions before filling him in on Baker. "No note or stickers?"

"No. But everything else is the same. The manner of death, the positioning. It's like whoever did this was copying his last murder."

"Except he'd killed her earlier and waited until now to leave her," I said. "Any ID?"

"Elana Mills. Lives in Alabama. I've got someone from there delivering the death notice."

He called out a BOLO for Scott Baker.

Bishop returned with an update from Levy. "The last time Levy had eyes on him, he was heading into Gwinnett County."

Grimes made sure patrols were in Levy's area on the hunt for Baker. "I'll have our men process the scene and get you a report," he said.

"Three murders, none in Hamby," Bishop said.

I rubbed the sides of my jaw. "On purpose."

"Because he doesn't want us investigating."

"And he taunts us because he knows we can't do anything." I chewed my nail. "Elana Mills was on the list I got to Anderson."

"Probably couldn't find her."

"Because she was already dead," I said.

"We need a timeframe for Baker's moves. This doesn't fit what we know so far."

"We'll figure it out," I said.

"We'd better do that soon." Bishop's shoulders stiffened. His body twisted slowly toward me. "He's got Ashley."

29

It was Levy who apprehended Baker. She'd called it luck, finding his vehicle at a RaceTrac, but I argued it was an excellent eye and even better detective work.

"He wouldn't come peacefully," she said as a Forsyth County paramedic dabbed a cold cloth on the lump growing below her left eye. She snatched the cloth from his hands, then apologized. "May I do it myself?"

The paramedic nodded and skirted out of the room.

She and I made eye contact. She shrugged, and I laughed. "I bet you scare a lot of men," I said.

"Probably why I don't go on many dates."

I glanced back at the clock. It still ticked in slow motion. "How long should this take?"

"Am I supposed to answer that?" she asked.

"No."

"Good to know."

"He didn't say anything about the victim?"

"Like I said when I got here. He didn't really have the opportunity. He saw me, pushed an older woman in front of him to the ground, jumped over her, and ran toward the door.

I rushed him, threw myself onto his back and knocked him down. We wrestled, and he got in one good punch before I rolled him onto his back and cuffed him."

"You forgot breaking his wrist in the process."

"He fought me. The guy's carrying a lot of anger."

"It would appear."

Bishop and Grimes walked back into the room. "He's ready."

"Thank God," I said as I stood.

"Is his wrist actually broken?" Levy asked.

"Hairline fracture. He'll survive," Grimes said.

Levy glanced at Bishop, the senior in our department. "It's on tape. The cashier told me."

"I wouldn't worry," he said.

"He's in interrogation room two," Grimes said. He flicked his head toward the door as he eyed me. "You want to start?"

"Hell, yes, I do." My cell phone rang, and I removed it from my back pocket. I eyeballed Bishop and said, "It's Nikki." I clicked speaker when I answered. "Please give me something good."

"The hair I found at Ashley's? It's Baker's."

Baker sat handcuffed to a metal chair, his head dropped toward the tabletop. He didn't speak when we entered. I sat down across from him. Bishop stood behind me. Grimes closed the door and sat to my left.

I kept my voice composed even though the bomb inside my stomach threatened to explode. "Where's Ashley?"

He lifted his head and glared at me, the cords in his neck tight and thick. "I don't know." He dropped his head again. "Probably dead."

Bishop took two steps toward the table and stopped.

My voice cracked. "Where is she?"

"I killed Natalie Carlson, but I did not kill the other girl."

Grimes leaned forward. "Why?" he asked. "Why—"

I silenced him by clearing my throat. "Your hair was found at Ashley's home." I struggled to keep my words steady. "Where is she?"

He kept his head down and lifted his eyes toward me. A single crease formed between them. "I told you, I don't know."

Bishop slammed his hands on the table and kept them there. He leaned toward Baker. "We have you at her apartment. Where the hell is she?"

He kept his face exactly as before. "I don't know."

A knock on the door sent Bishop upright. Grimes stood and opened it. A young woman whispered something to him. The door clicked closed. Grimes sat back down and folded his arms over his chest. "We have your hair at our second crime scene."

"I didn't kill that girl."

"Where's Ashley?" Bishop repeated.

"I told you I killed Natalie Carlson. That's all I have to say." He narrowed his eyes on me.

I stared at my swollen hand. It throbbed from the blood rushing through my veins. He hadn't asked for an attorney. He confessed to killing Natalie Carlson. He wanted us to know that. Why would he confess to one murder and not another? Why would he tell us he didn't know where Ashley was? Was he only willing to cleanse his soul of one sin or had he truly not committed three? "Elana Mills," I said. "Elana Mills is the second murdered girl. Say her name."

He shook his head.

"Where's Ashley?" I asked again.

Sweat poured from his temples. His neck remained corded tightly. "I don't know. I didn't take her."

I smacked the table with my good hand. "Then where the hell is she?"

"I don't know!" He screamed. "She wasn't part of the deal, all right? Neither was Elana Mills." He dropped his head and cried. Through his sobs he said, "This wasn't how it was supposed to be."

I flicked my eyes toward Grimes and then turned toward Bishop. He stared down at me but didn't flinch. Deal? What the hell was he talking about?

Baker flipped his head back up. His eyes were red, and snot dripped from his nose. "Claire. I did this for Claire."

"What deal? What wasn't supposed to be this way?" I asked. When he didn't speak quickly, I said, "Start talking, damn it!"

He kept repeating *I did this for Claire. I did this for Claire.* He finally stopped and scooted his chair back.

Bishop whipped his legs over the table and landed feet first on the floor beside Baker. "Don't move."

My entire body tensed. I bolted from my chair and pounded my fist into the table as I yelled, "Tell us who you're working with, dammit!"

Baker twisted his head toward Bishop. "I'm sorry." He smacked his head down on the edge of the table. Bam! Blood spurted from his forehead. It was like a scene from a movie. The criminal moves swiftly, taking the cop by surprise. The table butting didn't register in Bishop or me fast enough. Baker did it again, and finally, on the third smack, Bishop yanked his body back by the collar of his shirt. Baker stared through me, his eyes barely opened. "The mastermind," he said before passing out.

30

The Sheriff called the paramedics to transport Baker to Northside Forsyth Hospital a few miles from downtown Cumming.

Back at the Forsyth County Sheriff's Office, while we waited for an update on his condition—something we both assumed was a grade three concussion given that he'd passed out—we struggled through the little he'd said.

I kicked one of the chairs in the conference room. "I knew he wasn't working alone. We should have done something sooner."

"There wasn't anything we could do," Bishop said. "All we have are the files and her notes. The videos from Ashley's apartment complex were a bust. We found nothing to indicate she didn't just up and leave. Johnson is dead. Then Baker appears out of nowhere, and young women start dying." He exhaled then swore bitterly.

I dropped into the hard chair and pressed two fingers into the bridge of my nose. "What does the mastermind even mean? Is someone—" I stood so quickly the chair fell behind me. "The chatrooms!" I reached for my phone across the table and called Bubba.

He picked up on the second ring. "Is he talking?"

I squinted. "Not yet. Can you please go back through the chatroom stuff from the Stuart investigation? I'm looking for anyone that calls themself the mastermind."

He tapped so hard on his computer that the sound echoed through the phone. "I feel like that sounds familiar. Let me see what I can find, and I'll get back to you."

"Thanks." I disconnected. "Whoever this mastermind is, he somehow connected Stuart and Baker to the male victims and then convinced them to get justice for their crimes."

"Except Baker killed a young woman," Bishop said.

I nodded. "Yes, because she was assaulted by Daniel Travis. If she'd reported it, Claire might not have been assaulted."

"We don't know who assaulted Natalie Carlson."

"No, but somehow the mastermind does." I walked circles around the table as scenarios darted through my brain. How had the mastermind person found out about Natalie? What was his connection? Had he known the victims? We needed answers. "Somehow this mastermind found out about these assaults, and he wanted justice. Only, he didn't want to commit the murders. He just wanted to make sure they happened."

"Okay, but how did he find out?"

"I don't know, but he must have. Let's table that for a second. So, this person finds out, decides he wants justice—"

"Because?"

I chewed on one of my few decent nails left. "Let me think on that. Anyway, he wants justice, but he doesn't want or can't do it himself."

"And he what? Goes into the chatrooms where there just

happens to be relatives of two assaulted victims? That's a big reach, Ryder."

I passed Bishop standing in the corner of the small room. "I know. I'm not saying that. He could have been in the chatroom first. He does a little research, learns there's a pattern, then manipulates Stuart into the murders. *One, two, three, you can't pin on me. Seven, eight, nine, I'll add to my crimes. Four, five, six, add to the mix.* He somehow connects with Baker and brings him into the fold."

"Whoever did this has some bad ass detective skills," Bishop said.

I froze. Detective skills. I flipped around and pointed to Bishop. "Who's the common denominator in all this?"

"From the start or recently?"

"Both."

I chewed on the thought blossoming in my brain. "Bad ass detective skills."

"Johnson, but he's dead."

"But you know who's not?"

His eyes lit up. "Anderson."

31

Jimmy walked into the Forsyth County Sheriff's large office dressed in full uniform. His professional appearance spoke to his position, but his narrowed eyes and locked jaw gave away his anger. He shook Sheriff Rodney's hand. "Thank you for allowing us to assist."

Levy and Grimes sat next to each other at Rodney's small conference table. Bishop and I took seats across from them, while Jimmy and the sheriff sat at opposite heads.

"Chief," I said to Jimmy. "We really need to get to Birmingham. We need eyes on Anderson right away."

"Anderson's been MIA since July first."

I blinked. "What? No. I've talked to him, and we've emailed."

"According to his chief he's had his calls forwarded."

"Son of a bitch."

Jimmy nodded. "His chief has stopped that and forwarded his email to his address. He's got eyes out for him."

"But they haven't seen him?"

He shook his head. "The chief sent two men to Anderson's home, but he's not there."

"Because he's here?" Bishop said.

"The memorial is coming up. He'll be at that," I said.

"Not if he knows we're onto him," Grimes said. He took a sip from a can of Diet Coke he'd brought into the room. "Baker's still unconscious. They're worried about intracranial pressure, but if he makes it, which right now, the doctor's won't say yay or nay to, he could have language difficulty, amnesia, or some form of brain damage."

"Jesus," Jimmy said. "He had to hit the table hard."

"Our IT department found nothing on a mastermind in the chatrooms Chip Stuart frequented," Jimmy said. "We'll need to figure out their connection quickly."

"We need Baker to talk," Bishop said. "And quick."

"Right now, he's the only solid connection we have to Anderson. If Baker can't tell us Anderson's the mastermind, we've got nothing," Grimes said.

"Then we'll have to find something," I said.

Bishop took his department vehicle home, and I asked Levy for a ride back to the station to pick up my Jeep.

"Sure," she said. "I live near there, anyway."

Her GPS took us a back route to the station. "I'll just take 400," she said.

"They're doing construction between exits twelve and eleven. It's one lane until tomorrow morning's rush hour."

"Got it." She started the route and followed the first three turns.

The GPS put us on a gravel side road neither of us knew. The gravel had just been added making the road so bumpy it jarred my butt in her hard seat. Wooded lots dotted with For Sale signs framed the side of the makeshift road. Just another area being sucked away from nature and brought into the concrete fold. Metro Atlanta became more and more like Chicago with every heartbeat.

A pickup truck pulled up behind us, its headlights blinding Levy through the rearview mirror. "What's up with this asshole?" She veered toward the right side of the road and the pickup barreled past. "Dumbass."

"Not our jurisdiction," I said.

Dust clouded her windshield. Wiper spray shot out of tiny holes at the base of the hood and with the help of the wipers, cleared our view.

I glanced at the GPS. "Just about another mile, and we'll be on a real road again."

"So much for the fastest route."

"It doesn't take into account the type of road," I said.

"I wouldn't call this a road." She flipped on her bright lights and peered through her windshield with squinted eyes. "Is that a—shit!"

I squinted through her window. Something moved in the road up ahead just out of her bright lights' reach. "It looks like a—" I gasped then instinctively reached for the steering wheel and yanked it hard to the right. "He's got a gun!"

Multiple bullets hit the vehicle. Levy swung the wheel left and right but couldn't dodge them. The front window shattered, and glass flew everywhere. The back passenger side tire blew and we careened down the ledge on the road's side.

The car smashed against rock after rock, jerking me back and forth in my seatbelt. Sharp, searing pain penetrated my right arm as it slammed into the door. My head hit the side window. Something loud popped. Levy screamed. Her body fell to my side, the upper strap of her seatbelt hanging above her. "Levy!" I screamed. "Levy!" I searched the seat for my bag as panic burst throughout my body and rushed through my veins. Smash! The car flipped again and crashed onto the ground with a jarring thud. A second later it flipped once more and rolled out of control toward a group of thick trees. I reached for the steering wheel, but Levy's limp body was in the way. Blood soaked the side of her body. "Levy!" I yelled again. She fell into me as the car tumbled.

I caught a glance out my shattered passenger window and saw the patch of trees we were headed toward. "Shit!" I found the strap of my purse under Levy. I stretched the seatbelt, laid as much of my upper body over her as I could, and braced for impact with my purse firmly secured over my arm and under her so I could call 911 after impact. If I survived. I screamed as we hit the trees.

My head throbbed. I tried to move, but I was stuck. I nudged my shoulder up and to the side to figure out what was on top of me. I was trapped between the seat and the dashboard with Levy a motionless lump underneath me. I tasted blood. "Levy," I screamed. "Answer me!" My body pulsed with pain. I opened my eyes, but even the dark hurt. The radio blared. I worked my right arm out from between the dashboard and the console. It scraped against the dashboard, drawing blood as I yanked on it. I jimmied the key in the ignition, but it wouldn't budge. "Turn, damn it!" Finally, it rotated, and the car shut off.

Levy groaned. Thank God, she was alive. I jerked my other arm again, gritting my teeth and inhaling through them as my skin ripped. I pulled and tugged but my arm wouldn't budge. "Levy? Levy, can you hear me?"

She groaned again.

"Levy, you're going to be okay. I'll get help. Just keep breathing, damn it. Keep breathing."

She groaned once more. Her body grew soft underneath me. "Don't you die!" I carefully jiggled my left arm from between Levy and the back of the seat. I swore from the pain. Tears filled my eyes.

I gritted my teeth and wiggled my hand back and forth, cursing as the pain worsened, but the pressure on each side slowly loosened and I was able to dislodge it. I wouldn't look at it. I didn't want to know how bad it was. I stretched it as far as I could to feel around for Levy's phone. She'd had it on her legs before the man shot at us. Afraid I would hurt her, I gently pushed myself up, getting stuck by the smashed-in dashboard. I forced my hand under me and moved it toward Levy's left leg, wincing from the pain, but hitting something hard and thin. "I got it!" I moved two fingers on top of the phone and drew it out from between us up through where her head and my side met. My chest was tight. I forced out a small breath, sucking in air as much as I could. I could smell gas. We didn't have much time. I jiggled the phone to wake it up and just started hitting it with my finger until finally, the sweet voice of a 911 operator let me breathe again.

"911, what's your emergency?"

"This is Detective Rachel Ryder with..." I swallowed back blood. "Hamby. I'm... we've been... someone shot at us. We went off the road. I... I don't know where. We're injured, and I smell gas."

"Okay, Detective, I've acquired your location and am sending help. How many people are with you?"

"Officer Lauren Levy. She's in bad shape." A wave of tiredness swept over me. I couldn't keep my eyes open. "She's..."

Everything went black.

32

Everything on my body hurt. My head throbbed to the rhythm of my heartbeat. Rubbing alcohol filtered into my nostrils. I coughed and tasted blood. Machines beeped and hummed around me. The hospital. I was in the hospital. I could barely move my arms.

"Rachel?"

My eyes fluttered open. Kyle stood over me, his eyes wet and red. I cleared my throat. "Levy," I whispered.

"She's in bad shape, but she'll be okay." He lifted my left hand, and I winced.

"Ow," was about all I could muster.

"You're pretty beat up, but nothing's broken."

I'd closed my eyes but opened them again. "Someone shot at us."

"I know. Just get some rest, okay?"

I tried to sit up, but I was so tired, I could barely move. Kyle stopped me as I struggled. "You're on some serious pain meds right now. Just sleep. I'll be here when you wake up."

"My cell phone."

"Bishop's getting another one. I'll make sure everything's on it and leave it on your dresser at home."

"Can you bring it to me?"

He shook his head. "You need to rest."

"Okay," I said, and then I rested my head back on the pillow and was asleep in seconds.

The barn doors swung open, and Tommy walked out wearing a tight pair of jeans, a fitted white t-shirt, and a Cubs baseball cap. I loved that look on him. He strutted out with a pure black horse on lead.

God, he looked good.

He tugged on the strap. "Come on big fella, we're going for a ride."

I smiled up at them as I grabbed two grocery bags from the trunk of my car. "If you'll give me a sec to put this stuff away, I'll ride along." I pushed the door closed with my hip, and a bag tipped over. A tomato fell out and rolled to him.

He picked it up and smiled. Then he dropped the lead and took two big steps toward me, his face just millimeters away from mine. I could smell his cologne. Cedarwood. "No, Rach. It's okay. Ride with Kyle."

I jolted awake. "Wait!" I whispered, but the dream was over.

Kyle's eyes burned into mine. "It's okay. It was only a dream." He smiled and rubbed my hair from my forehead.

But was it? Was it only a dream? *It's okay?* It's okay.

"You want some water?" he asked.

"Sure."

The doctor woke me later. I had no idea if I'd slept for five minutes or five hours. "How're you doing, Ms. Ryder?"

I straightened up in the bed, ignoring the spasm in my back and the pounding in my head. "What time is it? When can I go home?"

He stared down at his clipboard and pushed his glasses up closer to the bridge of his nose.

The beeps coming from one of the machines sped up. He eyed the monitor then went back to his clipboard. "Mr. Olsen said you're a tough one. Grew up in Chicago?"

I nodded. "Tougher than I look."

"Internally, everything looks good." He glanced at me again. "For someone who got tackled by the Chicago Bears. When the Fridge played." He smiled. "I'm a Chicagoan. Born and raised. Big Bears fan."

"Irving Park area," I said. "Miss the food." It hurt to breathe, but I wasn't going to tell him that.

"Ah, the food."

"When can I go home?"

"I understand you're a detective."

"Yes."

"Morning news reported two police officers were shot at in their car. The driver lost control, the car went off the road and down a hill. It stopped when it crashed into a cluster of trees."

I closed my eyes and took a breath. "I heard."

He glanced at me over his glasses. "You think those officers would want to find the person who almost killed them?"

There was no point in lying. "Yes."

"After they healed?"

The machine beeped faster. "Probably sooner."

He eyed the machine and set his clipboard on my tray table. "Ms. Ryder. You and the driver narrowly escaped death. You're not a cat. You don't have nine lives."

"Neither do murder victims."

He shook his head softly. "I'm told you're good at your job."

"Then you'll let me do it?"

"If I release you, you're not going to go home and rest, are you?"

"I'll rest. I promise."

"Your friend told me you'd say that."

"Which friend?"

He pointed to the door. Bishop peeked inside and waved.

The doctor raised his eyebrows and tilted his head. "Told me not to trust you, too."

I furrowed my brow and then smiled. "He's a Falcons fan. Talk about untrustworthy."

The doctor sighed. "I'll release you, but I'm not thrilled about it. Rest, alternate ibuprofen, and acetaminophen. Please. You're going to be sore. Tomorrow more so than today, so take it easy." He nodded once. "I don't want to see you back here, you hear?"

I nodded.

He turned to leave.

"Doc?"

"Yes?"

"After the car hit the trees, I tasted blood."

"You bit your tongue." He shook his head and walked out saying, "Can't believe it didn't need stitches."

Bishop closed the door behind him. "You look like hell."

I didn't bother responding to that. "Is Baker conscious?"

He shook his head. "Not yet. Your phone is at your place. The iPhone guy said you had three thousand photos in the cloud. Took forever to transfer it all over to the new one."

"Baker's faking it. We need to make him talk." I tried to push myself up. "Let me get dressed—where are my clothes? Where's Kyle?"

"He's not faking it. He's in a coma. That door is closed for now." He didn't give me a chance to speak. "Kyle's on his way back. He went to your place to get you clothes."

"Can you ask him to bring that phone?"

"Already did." He changed the subject. "Levy wants to see you before you leave."

"Kyle said she's in bad shape."

"The shot hit just above her heart. Went through the seat." He exhaled. "She was lucky."

"It was Anderson."

"We don't know that."

"You might not, but I do."

"It was dark. Levy said the shooter was just outside of her bright lights' reach. She didn't get a good look at the guy. I'm betting you didn't either."

"I don't care. It was him."

Bishop sighed. "I'll find out if he owns a pickup."

"Thank you."

He pinched the bridge of his nose. "I'll be in touch later. Do me a favor. Try not to get yourself killed, okay?"

"Yes, sir."

Kyle returned a few minutes after Bishop left. "You have a visitor."

Michels walked in behind him. He'd showered and dressed in a pair of shorts and a t-shirt.

Kyle set a bag with a pair of Levi jeans, a white V-neck t-shirt, my boots and other necessary clothing items on the bed. "Toothbrush is in there, too."

"Thanks. I'm going to need help with my clothes."

"I know."

Michels stepped close to the bed. "The other girl."

I nodded.

He gripped the metal bed rail, closed his eyes, and breathed in and out. Kyle squeezed his shoulder. I moved my left hand toward his, and just moving it sent sharp pains through my arm.

Michels loomed over me. "Tell me what's going on. Please."

I summed up most everything, leaving out a few details so he wouldn't lose his shit, and ended with Baker's insistence that he hadn't taken Ashley.

"The mastermind? What the hell does that mean?"

Kyle hitched himself up and sat on the edge of my bed.

"It means there's more than one killer, and they're working for someone," I said.

Kyle sucked in a breath and let it out with a trail of f-bombs. "And this... this mastermind has Ashley?"

"Baker said Ashley wasn't part of the plan, but plans change."

Michels yanked his hands off the railing and turned toward the window. He swore again then flipped back and faced me. "You know who the mastermind is, don't you?"

I swallowed. "I have a theory."

His eyes widened. He stepped closer to the bed again. "Who?"

Kyle placed his hand on Michels's shoulder again. "You know she can't tell you that."

Michels whipped around. "The hell she can't! My girlfriend is missing, and she knows who has her. We need to find him!" He turned toward me again. "Tell me. I'll find the bastard myself."

Savannah charged in, dropped her large pink makeup case on the floor, and grabbed Michels by the arm. She yanked so hard he whirled around, lost his balance, and fell to the floor nearly dragging Savannah down too. She dug her high-heeled sandals into the floor and squatted next to him. "Back off, Michels."

Kyle and I exchanged wide-eyed, jaw-dropped looks. Savannah. The debutante bad ass.

Michels dragged his index finger and thumb across his eyes and squeezed the bridge of his nose.

"We're going to find her," I said. "I promise."

33

Savannah cleared the men out of the room after Kyle promised to keep Michels under control. She stood at the side of the bed, studied my face, and sighed. "You definitely won't be posing for any selfies any time soon."

"I don't take selfies."

"Well, don't start now."

"It's not that bad, is it?"

She pressed her lips together. Her perfectly set eyebrows nearly touched her hairline.

I grimaced. "Really?" I touched my face with my right hand. "Kyle didn't say anything." I jerked my head toward her makeup case and groaned. "Ow. My neck hurts. You got a mirror in that thing?"

"I've got everything in that thing, but trust me, the last thing you need is a mirror." She opened the case, its back facing me, and picked through it as she periodically squinted at me. "You can't work looking like this."

"Yes, I can."

"Okay, you can, but you'll distract everyone working with

you. Let me just work a little Savannah sorcery. A few touches and you'll be strutting down the catwalk."

"No."

She grimaced. "No?"

"My face can't be that bad, and even if it is, I don't care." I winced when I grabbed the railing with my right hand. The machine beeped faster again. I took a deep breath. "This sucks."

Savannah gasped. "Sweet baby Jesus! Your back!"

"What's wrong with my back?" Other than the facts that my skin burned and my muscles ached.

"It's purple."

"It's just a bruise."

"No, your entire back is purple. I'm calling the nurse." She pressed the button before I could stop her. Normally I was faster than Savannah, but she one-upped me with her pain-free body.

A nurse walked in as I attempted to push myself out of bed. She rushed over and dropped a few papers onto the tray table. "Oh, no you don't." She held my arm. Pain shot through it, but I didn't let her know. "The doctor told me he's releasing you. The man is crazy. You're a hot mess."

Savannah piped in. "That she is."

"He's the boss though, right?"

The nurse made a tsk sound as she wrapped the cheap, white hospital gown around my back. "Two men told me about the accident. You're not fine."

"Think about that," Savannah said.

I grabbed the bag of clothing Kyle brought and winced in pain. "Kyle was going to help me with this."

I asked the nurse when I'd be released.

She took the papers from the tray table and waved them in the air. "I'll get the wheelchair."

"Oh, I don't—"

She wiggled her finger at me. "It's required."

"May I see the other officer before I leave?"

She nodded. "Room 225. I'll take you there on our way out."

Savannah helped me get dressed. "You're going after him, aren't you?"

"Jimmy told you?"

"Yes."

"Yes, I am."

She slipped the t-shirt over my head. "Why can't you let the others handle it?"

I didn't have an answer for that. I flinched when she bent my left arm into the sleeve, but the pain didn't stop me from getting dressed so I could get out of there.

Kyle left with Michels. I assured him I was fine, and not to worry. He didn't believe me but left at my request anyway. Levy was asleep when Savannah and I walked into her room. Someone had brushed her hair away from her face, highlighting the purple bruising along her chin, and her deep black and purple eyes. Bandages covered her right shoulder.

She opened her eyes slowly. "Hey." Her voice was groggy. "You look like hell."

I laughed and my chest hurt. "Have you seen yourself?"

She shrugged her good shoulder and winced. "I'm here for a while."

"Good. You need to rest."

Tears filled her eyes. "Did I blow my shot at detective?"

Savannah stepped forward. "After your hard work, Jimmy's

probably out printing up new business cards for you right now."

Savannah was the best.

Levy reached for my hand. If she could hold it, I could handle the pain. She stared into my eyes. Her tears slid down her face. Mine did, too. Damn it. "Ryder, you go get that bastard."

Savannah dropped me off and left me—under caution of extreme duress—alone in my apartment. The only way she would leave was with a promise that I'd live long enough to see Scarlet get married. I wouldn't miss that social event for anything.

I texted Kyle. *I'm home.*

I'm with Michels. I'll drop him at home and head there.

Stay with him.

Don't leave.

I responded with a heart emoji. That way I didn't have to lie to him.

I dropped fish pellets into Louie's condo. "Hey buddy. It's nice to see a friendly fish face."

He cared only about the pellets.

I undressed in front of my full-length mirror. Pulling my shirt over my head stretched abused and sore muscles across my back. That dashboard packed a serious punch. My face resembled a loser in a boxing match, but it wasn't nearly as bad as Levy's. I counted twenty-three scrapes, cuts, and contusions over the parts of my body I could see. They hurt when I moved. I'd put my pain level at a six. Once I downed four ibuprofen, it would drop to a four.

I carefully unwrapped the bandages around my left hand

and held it up to the mirror, slowly turning it from side to side. My wrist let me know it wasn't pleased.

I turned on the shower, let the water heat up to a toasty, burn-the-pain-off temperature, and stepped in. The moment the water seared my skin, my pain level shot up to a ten but lowered once my body adjusted. Washing my hair wasn't easy, but I pushed through the pain. I let the water wash over me for longer than normal, thinking through a plan of attack. We had to take out Anderson before another girl died. There were more on that list, and if he'd come after me and Levy, which I believed he had, he knew we were onto him. That was a reactive move out of desperation and lack of control. Desperate people made mistakes.

What he likely didn't know was that we had his hit list and could anticipate his next move.

And that's how we'd take him down.

34

Ninety minutes later, I parked my Jeep in my designated spot and hobbled into the department. I skirted everyone I could knowing I'd be busted for coming in instead of resting. Patrol officers eyed me as I tiptoed into the pit kitchen and grabbed a cup of coffee. Officer Landry, an old school, Southern good ol' boy who'd been stuck in a low-level patrol position since day one and wasn't my biggest fan, stood next to me at the counter. He stirred half a bottle of French vanilla creamer into his coffee as he glared at me. "Ryder."

I gave him a toothy, big smile. It made my cheeks hurt. "Hey, Landry. How's it going?"

He eyed me up and down, his lips curled into a snarl. "You look like shit. Might could use a day or two off and let the rest of us do the work."

"Thanks for the offer, but how 'bout you stick to parking tickets and directing church traffic, okay?" I held up my coffee cup, said, "Cheers," and strutted out into the pit to the best of my ability. His disapproval wasn't my problem.

I'd made it to my cubby without a peep from anyone and was immediately busted. Jimmy leaned his butt against my desk with his arms crossed over his chest. Bishop sat in my chair, his feet up on my desk with one foot crossed over the other. They both eyed the door.

Oh, boy. "Oh, hey."

Bishop chuckled. "Surprised?"

"Not even a little."

Jimmy gave me a once over. "The hell, Ryder? You shouldn't even be out of the hospital."

I snarled at Bishop and shook my thumb behind me. He lifted his feet off my desk, stretched like he'd just woke up, and took his time standing. He'd never make it in Hollywood. I sat and removed my laptop from my bag, forgoing any additional small talk. "He's in town. There are two more women on that list. One lives in Alabama, and the other's in Roswell. We need to get moving."

"We know," Bishop said. "We already have eyes on the girl in Alabama, and the one here is in protective custody."

"Where?"

"Holiday Inn Express off Windward," Jimmy said.

"Do we know who assaulted her?"

Bishop nodded. "Jacob Ramsey. Our first."

I exhaled. "Okay. We need to keep these girls safe, but we also need to find Ashley."

"We aren't one hundred percent sure it's Anderson," Jimmy said.

"I am. And I think Ashley and Johnson were, too. I've just got to figure out how they knew."

"We scoured through those files daily throughout the investigation, and in the past few days. What could they see that we couldn't?"

"I don't know, but we have an eye similar to Ashley's, and we need to use it."

"Nikki," Jimmy said.

I nodded. "We need her to go through the Stuart files. She might see something we missed."

"But Ashley knew the female victims. She knew what she was looking for," Bishop said.

I shook my head. "She found something that identified the killer. Let's give Nikki a shot at doing the same."

I eyed Jimmy. He flicked his head toward my department landline. I phoned Nikki and asked her to meet us in the conference room.

Nikki stared wide-eyed at me. "Wow. You look awful."

I shrugged. "Pretty much how I feel, too."

She eyed the towers of files. "I'm going to need a box of Joe for this."

"I'll send a patrol to Dunkin' right away," Jimmy said.

She pulled out a chair and sat, and then she flipped her head around. "May I also have a few legal pads and some pencils?"

Bishop nodded and left. Jimmy went to get patrol on the coffee.

I sat next to Nikki. "You're going to do great."

She shook her head at the piles of files and stuttered. "I... I'm not a detective. I'm a tech. How...I don't even know what you want me to find."

"I don't know either, but Ashley saw something, and your mind works like hers. You know crime scenes as well as she does, Nik. Maybe something from the scenes or the evidence stood out to her and will to you, too."

"You're a good detective. Wouldn't you have found it?"

"I haven't."

She sighed. "I'm not sure I will, either."

"It's worth a shot though, right?"

"You really think it's Anderson?"

I nodded.

"And you think he tried to kill you and Levy." It wasn't a question.

"I do."

"Then if there's something here, I'll find it."

I patted her forearm and smiled. "You've got this."

I headed back to Jimmy's office. With Nikki in the investigation room, we'd have to use the small conference room off the pit to discuss next steps. As I stepped into the pit, I heard Jimmy yell from his office. "I said no!"

The entire pit full of law enforcement personnel stopped what they were doing to listen.

"I need this, Chief!" Michels responded.

"Oh, shit," I said. I rushed my battered and beaten self toward Jimmy's office.

From the red faces and jabbing fingers between them, it was obvious the argument was in full swing. Bishop shot me a glance and shook his head. Too bad I wasn't good at listening. I shut the office door. "Chief, Michels. The whole department can hear you."

Michels flipped around, his eyes slits and his mouth pursed. "Tell him to take me off suspension, Ryder. Please."

He wore a pair of beige pants and a white Hamby PD short-sleeved polo. He'd strapped his equipment belt to his side, but since Jimmy had taken his weapon and badge, it was empty. "It's not my place," I said. "But knock off the yelling." I flicked my thumb over my shoulder. "It looks bad to everyone out there."

Jimmy narrowed his eyes at me. "You're pushing it, Detective."

I held my hands up. "I'm just saying."

He walked around his desk, grabbed a small booklet from a bookcase, and handed it to Michels. "You want off suspension?" He shoved the booklet at him. "Study this and take the test. If you pass, you're off suspension." He jabbed his finger at Michels's chest. "But there's no way in hell you're working this case."

I leaned toward the booklet to see what it was, but Michels's hand covered the title. He moved it and stared, then raised his eyes to the chief. "You're kidding, right?"

Jimmy shook his head. "Twenty-four hours. If you fail, you're out until I say." He walked back around his desk, leaned his hands on it, and said, "Go."

Michels opened the door and walked out muttering something I couldn't understand under his breath.

"Close the door," Jimmy said.

I pushed the door closed with my fingers. Neither Bishop nor I talked. We both just sat, waiting for Jimmy's face to return to its normal color and his breath to stop seething out between gritted teeth. I'd seen him mad before, but not to that level. I was torn between impressed and alarmed.

He sat and dragged his hand down his face. "Nikki all set?"

I nodded.

"Let's hope she finds something quick. If you're right, and Anderson's our guy, and he's the one that came for you, then Ashley, if she's even still alive, is in more danger than ever."

"She's still alive," I said. She had to be. I'd been prepared to discuss my plan, but a thought nudged the corner of my mind. "Does Anderson have a daughter?"

"I'm not sure," Bishop said.

Jimmy picked up his department phone, checked a number in his cell, and dialed it. "Let's find out."

"Abernathy," Birmingham Chief Thompson said. "Any update on Anderson?"

Jimmy didn't tell him about the incident on the back road. "Not yet. Got a question for you."

"Go ahead."

"Does Anderson have any children?"

It took a good ten seconds for Thompson to respond, and when he did, he sighed. "Not anymore. His daughter committed suicide seven years ago."

"Do you know why?" Jimmy asked.

"She was raped."

I eyeballed the chief. "I'm on it."

35

The reporter Jessica Walters stepped into the conference room. Her long hair was tied back in a tight ponytail at the base of her neck, and she wore enough makeup to rival Savannah's college beauty pageant photos. Her pastel pink dress fit like a glove. I couldn't imagine having to dress like that for work every day, but she did it well.

She smiled at them and then blanched at me. "Is what happened to you why I'm here?"

I smiled. "Take a seat. Chief Abernathy will fill you in."

Both men all but climbed across the table and tripped over themselves to pull out her chair. Walters caught my eye, and we exchanged smiles. That stuff probably happened to her a lot. It never happened to me. Thank God for that.

She removed her phone from her bag and set it on the table. "May I record this?"

"No," I said.

She showed me her screen and then turned the phone over. "I assume I can't take notes either?"

"This isn't the exclusive I promised, but it's an opportunity, and you will get that exclusive if this works."

She pursed her lips. "Keep talking."

Jimmy took over. He must have gathered his thoughts. I was surprised he could speak without drooling. "We have a suspect in the disappearance of Ashley Middleton and the murders of Natalie Carlson and Elana Mills."

She sat straighter in her chair. "They're connected?"

He nodded. "And we believe this person also murdered Niles Wentworth."

Her eyes widened, and her fake eyelashes touched her perfectly shaped brows. "I just reported on that. Last I knew, there were no suspects. Who is yours?"

"We can't say just yet," he said.

"Understood." She crossed her legs. "Is this connected to the Stuart murders?"

Jimmy nodded.

Walters looked at me. "What do you want me to do?"

I laid out the plan in detail. After I finished, she said, "I'll get my team here right away."

Walters was the first reporter given access to the pit. We'd considered other locations for the interview but went with the pit due to its staff only regulation. Anderson would know that, and anything to poke the bear worked in our favor.

I checked on Nikki before heading to the women's locker room to grab Walters. "How's it going?"

She glanced at me and frowned. "Not good."

I patted her shoulder. "Keep the faith."

She leaned back and sighed. "My eyes are crossing, I'm exhausted, and I'm halfway through the box of Dunkin' coffee."

"Take a break. We're holding an interview in the pit. Jessica Walters."

That woke her up. "Seriously?"

I nodded. "Want to watch?"

She stood. "Hell, yeah, I do, but I need to focus on this."

"I appreciate that."

I walked to the locker room. Two women crowded around Walters. One brushed powder on her face while the other puffed out the hair on the crown of her head. I examined myself in the mirror and sighed. My face had worsened since leaving the hospital, and it was as painful as it looked. Swollen, bruised, and scraped. I'd look fantastic on screen.

"I could make that disappear," the makeup woman said.

I eyed her staring at me in the mirror. "It's okay. I'm not really a makeup kind of girl."

"I think it's necessary," Walters said. "We want the viewers, and your suspect, focused on the content, not your face."

I exhaled. She had a point.

"It's not personal, but whatever happened to you will be a distraction. They'll want to know about that and not care about our content."

"It won't take long," the makeup woman said. "And I'll be careful. It looks painful."

"It's not too bad," I lied. I examined Walters in all her on-screen perfection.

"Let's do it."

I tapped out a text to Kyle. *Going on TV in thirty. At the station.*

You're supposed to be home. Resting.

Resting is for the weak. Come watch.

In Atlanta. Won't make it. When will it air?

It's live, but I'm sure they'll have it online, too.

Good luck.

Thanks.

"You ready?" The makeup person asked. "I'm Glenda, and I'm your good witch of the South."

"She'll make magic out of those bruises," Walters said.

"Is your name really Glenda?" I asked the makeup artist.

She giggled. "Katarina, but you can call me Kat."

Twenty minutes later my bruising disappeared. "Wow." I blinked and touched my face. Pain shot through my arm, but I ignored it. I rotated my face from side to side. "You can't see any of them."

"She's the best in the business," Walters said.

Savannah would flip when she saw the interview. I adjusted my t-shirt. Walters's style and beauty put her at the top of the attractiveness scale, and I balanced it.

Walters smiled at me. "Let's make this happen."

The chief cleared out the pit, leaving just me, the camera man, Walters, Bishop, and himself for the interview. Bubba watched from behind the camera. The mayor would throw a tantrum when he found out, but none of us cared. We had a serial killer to find.

"I contacted Grimes and Sheriff Rodney," Jimmy said. "They're on board."

Did it matter? We were doing this for all of them, but Ashley's disappearance was our case, and we made decisions accordingly.

He tossed me a Hamby PD jacket. "Put this on. It'll cover your arms." He smiled. "Savannah's going to be all over that makeup."

"I know."

"Let's do this," Walters said. She focused on the camera. Jimmy, Bishop, and I stood to her side. "This is Jessica Walters.

I'm here at the Hamby Police Department with breaking news." She stepped back, and as we'd been instructed, we all turned toward her. "This is Chief James Abernathy. Chief Abernathy," she said. "Can you give me an update on the disappearance of Ashley Middleton?"

He nodded. "We have identified a suspect in the disappearance of our former crime scene tech. However, at this time, we cannot reveal his name."

"Have you located Ms. Middleton?"

Jimmy's Adam's apple bobbed up and down. "This investigation is complicated, but we have discovered information we believe will lead us to Miss Middleton."

"Can you tell me anything about the suspect?"

Jimmy stared into the camera lens just as Walters told him to. "Yes, ma'am. Through our investigation we have learned our suspect is seeking justice for the suicide of his daughter seven years ago."

"And how was Miss Middleton involved?"

"We believe she discovered his motive and something that led her to him."

"Do you know what that is?" she asked.

"I'm not at liberty to say."

She nodded. "What happens now?"

"I'll refer to detectives Ryder and Bishop for that."

We stepped forward as Jimmy dropped back. Walters turned her body toward us but kept her face toward the camera. "Detectives?"

Bishop coughed. I'd kept my hands behind my back, and I balled them into fists. I waited for my line, the kicker for the interview. I glanced up at the clock across the room, and barely heard a thing Bishop said over the tick-tock, tick-tock vibrating through my head.

"Detective Ryder, would you like to add anything?"

Jimmy touched my hand behind me. I jerked to attention. "Oh, yes." I focused on the camera as if I was talking directly to Anderson. "Just that our suspect is not the mastermind he thinks he is."

She nodded once and turned toward the camera. "We'll keep you updated with this breaking news. Jessica Walters. WXID, Atlanta."

The camera clicked from green to red. "Looks great," the camera man said.

"You really think using a trigger word is going to break this guy?" Walters asked me.

"I'm banking on it."

Savannah called me five times within five minutes after the interview. I didn't have time to answer, so I sent her a text as I walked to the locker room to wash off the makeup. *Can't talk. Doing bad ass cop stuff.*

Nikki stopped me at the door. "Detective." She took a deep breath and spoke fast. "I found something."

36

I stared at the images on the paper. "How would she get ahold of them?"

"I wasn't sure she did." She handed me a copied page from our evidence room log sheet. "Until I saw she signed to view evidence on Sunday, July third."

I blinked. "She's not authorized for that."

She shrugged. "I don't have an answer for that, but if I hadn't gone down and pulled the sign-in sheets, I wouldn't have known for sure." Nikki laid out three papers. "The Alabama tech didn't think to pull them off, and unfortunately, neither did I." She sucked in a breath and slouched. "I could have stopped five murders and two abductions."

I understood her pain. "Nikki, this isn't your fault."

Tears pooled in her eyes. "Ashley figured it out. I should have, too. How could I miss such a minor detail?"

It wasn't minor. It was a long shot to pull fingerprints from underneath a vinyl sticker. Why hadn't Ashley left the information in her files? Had she left it somewhere in her apartment? Was it taken when she was abducted? "Listen, this isn't on you, okay? I've been a detective a long time. I should have known to check those. It's my job. It's Bishop's job. Do not blame yourself." I stretched my arm to pull the landline toward me and winced. "Damn."

"Here," she said. "I'll get it." She dragged the phone toward me.

I called for Jimmy and Bishop. "And get Michels," I said to Jimmy. "It's important."

I'd yet to wash off the makeup, but there was no time for that.

Jimmy examined the evidence room log and his nostrils flared. "Who worked the room that day?" He glared at Michels. "Did you know about this?"

Michels shook his head and held up his palms. "I swear to God I didn't know, Chief."

The chief ran a hand over his head and groaned. "Son of a bitch! Why didn't she come to us?"

I pressed my lips together and stared up at the ceiling. She tried. "She was going to tell me at the party, but we got the call from Forsyth County."

Michels had been leaning against the wall. He pushed off with his back, dragged his hand down his chin and paced back and forth, muttering f-bombs. "She should have told me. Why the hell didn't she tell me?"

Nikki wiped tears from her eyes. "It's my fault. I should have checked the paper behind the stickers."

Bishop finally stopped us. "We don't have time for pity parties. We need to bring Anderson down."

He was right. "Ashley must have recognized one of the male victims. It sparked her interest, and she asked Michels questions," I said.

Jimmy glowered at Michels. "Which he wasn't authorized to answer."

I nodded. "She somehow got ahold of the files and made copies. When she realized she knew some of the alleged assault victims, she must have dug deeper. We all know Stuart's weak but real alibis checked out for the Alabama murders three and a half years ago, and Ashley could read that in the files. She calls Johnson and I don't know, gets him to send her his files. Somehow, she decides to pull the vinyl letters from the paper and—" I smacked my good hand on the tabletop and held back the cuss words ripping through my head. "Anderson found out. That's why Elana Mills didn't have any vinyl numbers or letters with her body."

"And he killed Johnson to keep him from busting him," Bishop said.

"And then he takes Ashley," Michels said. He dropped his head and cried.

"I think she's still alive," I said. "If she wasn't, he'd want us to know. He'd make a presentation of it. That's his MO."

"Then we just royally pissed off a serial killer with that news piece," Bishop said.

"No. We just told a serial killer one of his minions talked," I said. "But he doesn't know what exactly he told us."

"We'd have a BOLO out for him if he did," Jimmy said. "He knows procedure. He's in hiding or on the run."

I shook my head. "He's got a radio. He thinks we don't know it's him, or his ego is so huge he can't see the truth," I said. "Alabama has copies of our files from the Stuart investigation. If he read those, which I guarantee he did, he saw my notes on Stuart's riddle. He knows I think someone else killed the Alabama men." I tapped a pencil against the edge of the table. *One, two, three, you can't pin on me. Seven, eight, nine, I'll add to my crimes. Four, five, six, add to the mix.* "The riddle must have bothered Johnson, too, and that's why he kept digging."

Nikki's head flipped back and forth between each of us like we were pro tennis players. *Hit. Return. Hit. Return.* She sucked in a breath. "So, wait. If Ashley told him about the stickers, what else does she know that would keep her alive?"

That was the million-dollar question.

Jimmy got on a call with Sheriff Rodney, Detective Grimes, and Chief Thompson, and updated them on what we knew. He requested another check for any Jane Does in the Birmingham area. When he hung up the phone, he said, "Anderson's MIA is an official leave of absence, but they consider him MIA since he hasn't been seen. Birmingham procedure allows two weeks when a partner or family member dies. Thompson said most don't take the whole time, especially in partner deaths, but..."

"But Anderson's doing it so he can finish what he started," Bishop said.

Jimmy pointed to me and Bishop. "The memorial is tomorrow afternoon. You two need to be there."

I nodded. "If Anderson wants to keep up his game, he'll have to show up."

Jimmy nodded. "And we need to do the same."

Jessica Walters texted me. I glanced up from my phone. "It's Walters."

Call me ASAP.

I dialed her cell. "Let's see how our corrupt cop responded to our interview."

She picked up on the first ring. I put her on speaker. "You

were right. He couriered a note to the station. And don't worry. I opened it wearing gloves."

My heart pounded. "What did he say?"

"Four, five, six, he'll add to the list. What do you think that means?"

I made eye contact with Bishop. "I know exactly what it means."

"He read the files," Michels said. "We already knew that. But why would he give that away? The rhyme was never made public. He knows that."

"Because he's a cocky SOB," Bishop said.

"He wants us to know there's another murder coming," Jimmy said.

Michels dragged his hand down his face. "Ashley."

"We don't know that," I said.

Nikki cleared her throat. "Um, maybe I'm wrong, but if he mentioned the rhyme, he knows you know he's the mastermind. So, what's the point of going to the memorial? Won't you just arrest him?"

I studied the whiteboards and played back my memory reel from the Stuart murders and recent events. I shook my head. "He'll go. He just won't let us see him."

Bubba walked in and took a seat.

"If Baker's been killing for Anderson, how have they connected?" Michels asked.

"Maybe Baker wiped his phone clean?" Bishop said.

Bubba shook his head. "Chief got me a warrant for the provider. There's been no additional activity on the line, and all comments or accounts regarding a mastermind in the chatrooms are from four years ago."

"Anderson knows it's too risky to use their cells. They have burners." I walked over to the investigation files spread out on the side table. "Three and a half years ago the first murders happened. My guess is Anderson committed those. It took him three years of research and planning, as well as finding someone to commit the next three. Stuart. Then Baker walks into the picture and significantly cuts the time between that round and the next." I searched through one of the folders and held up a paper. "Because Stuart told Baker what he was doing and how to get in touch with the mastermind."

"Because Baker wanted revenge," Bishop said.

I nodded. "Anderson already had the names. He just needed someone to do his dirty work."

"Why not commit the murders himself?" Michels asked. "If he'd already killed three men in Alabama, why farm out the next six?"

"Sport?" Bishop suggested.

"He studied the Birmingham department. He knew he could get away with the first three. He couldn't still work, watch us, and then kill here. And he needed someone else to take the fall, if need be," I said.

Jimmy nodded. "Which is why he farmed out the next three to Baker."

"That doesn't make sense," Michels said.

Nikki agreed. "His prints are on the notes here."

"Stuart confessed, and I believe him," I said. "But that doesn't mean Anderson didn't put his twist on any of the murders."

"The meticulous crime scenes," Bishop said. "Those were his doing. Either Stuart wasn't interested in the details, or Anderson didn't trust him to do it how he wanted. So, he just let him do the kills, and he did the rest."

"Which would explain why Anderson wasn't the one in

the video at the storage place. He had someone else abduct Ashley," Jimmy said.

"No," Michels said. "I saw the guy in that video. Ashley could have taken him. She's tough."

"Not if he had a gun," Bishop said.

Michels disagreed. "Anderson was there. The other guy was a decoy. Just like Stuart."

"He's right," I said. "And if Anderson threatened someone Ashley cared about, she would go with him willingly."

Michels head dropped as his shoulders sagged. "Me."

"Or her parents," I added.

"Baker's scenes weren't meticulous," he said.

"There was no time," I said. "Anderson found out what Johnson and Ashley knew. Taking Ashley wasn't planned. He had to go back to Alabama, kill Johnson, then return and grab her."

"I don't understand," Bubba said. "Why didn't he go after the person who raped his daughter? Why these people?"

"Because he never found out who it was," Jimmy said. "And he's on a killing spree to make up for that."

37

With another murder expected and less than twenty-four hours until Johnson's memorial, the next hours were crucial. We needed to make sure Anderson didn't learn that Baker was in a coma instead of out just waiting to do his dirty work. Each girl had been placed under protective watch at locations Anderson wouldn't know. Thompson made sure of that in Birmingham. The problem was finding a way to let Anderson know the girls were out of reach.

"Our only shot is the scanner," Bishop said. He bit into a taco from the bags of food Bubba had picked up. "We have to bank on him listening."

"I agree," Michels said.

"We need that burner phone," I said.

"We had five people go through Baker's vehicle and his place," Bishop said as he chewed. "They couldn't find the phone anywhere."

"It's somewhere. Baker's not stupid," I said. I unwrapped a taco, but I couldn't eat it. My stomach had tied itself into a knot even a Boy Scout couldn't untangle. "He wouldn't leave it lying around." I re-wrapped the taco and stood. "I'm going to his place."

Nikki jumped out of her seat. "May I come?"

I eyed Jimmy. He nodded. "Go for it."

"Give me five, and I'll come," Bishop said. He wiped a piece of cheese from his chin stubble.

"We don't have five," I said. "We've got this."

Baker lived in an apartment in the newly renovated downtown Alpharetta area, just a few blocks down from the action. Since we had his keys and had already executed a warrant with the apartment manager, we let them know we were back and headed inside.

Nikki stood inside the unit with her hands on her hips. She studied the place carefully. "At least it's not one of the big houses in Hamby. We'd need the whole department to go through that."

"Been there, done that."

"Where should we start?"

"It's not going to be hiding in plain sight. If they communicated by phone, then it would need to be easily accessible, just not visible."

"But wouldn't all those places have been looked at already?" she asked.

"Maybe. Maybe not." I sighed. "Let's start here."

We each took an end of Baker's leather couch and dragged it away from the wall. Nothing. There was so little furniture in the room, and none of it had been tampered with, so we made it through it all in under two minutes.

"This guy didn't cook," Nikki said. "He has one pot and

one pan. No pasta strainer. Who can live without a pasta strainer?"

"Someone who can afford to eat out whenever he wants."

I went through every cabinet, stuck my hand behind the refrigerator and the drawer of the oven. "This is empty, too."

"That's where I put my cookie sheets," she said.

"Guess Baker doesn't like cookies."

Nikki moved a chair from the small dining room table into the kitchen, climbed up on it, and then ran her head across the tops of the cabinets. "Holy shit," she said near the fridge. "I think I found it." She stretched back behind the cabinet above the stove and grunted. "I can't reach it."

"Let me try," I said. I wasn't much taller, but it was worth a shot. "If I can't, we'll find something I can step on." I climbed up onto the counter and searched the area where she'd looked.

"Do you see it?" The excitement in her voice was obvious.

"Dang, Nik. You're good." I reached in and removed what we'd come for from the space between the cabinet and the wall. I held it out to show Nikki and then hopped off the counter. "Seven messages from WhatsApp."

She grabbed her phone and tapped on the screen. "I'll let them know."

"It's passcode protected," Bubba said. He flipped the older iPhone around. "It's the seven, so it's GSM compatible, but I'll need the password to access it."

"What does GSM compatible mean?" Bishop asked.

Bubba adjusted his position in his seat. A smile crept across his face as he set the phone on the investigation room table. "This is my jam." He rubbed his hands together. "A

GSM network is the old, outdated and almost defunct two and three G networks offered by all the major carriers, Verizon, T-Mobile, you get the picture?"

We collectively nodded.

"Aren't those slower networks?" Jimmy asked. He paced a path across the room.

Bubba nodded. "But what's important here is that the iPhone seven is usable as a burner phone because of its GSM compatibility, which means it can be unlocked and used with any carrier that offers a pay as you go or prepaid service. AKA, burner phone."

"We need that passcode," I said.

"Something to note," Bubba said. "Is that the only working two and three G networks left are with Verizon."

"Which means?" Bishop asked.

"That we can track the location of people who call it," I said.

The energy in the room buzzed. We were edging closer to catching Anderson.

"Yes, but if they used WhatsApp like you said," Bubba glanced at me. "We can't get anything from Verizon or WhatsApp."

"Meaning?" I asked.

"A while back WhatsApp deployed end-to-end encryption. Anything shared can only be shared with the intended recipient."

"Which means we'll still see it," I said.

"Only if it's not deleted. Those seven messages, yes. Since they're unopened, we'll see them, but anything else, I can't say."

"Then we go to WhatsApp for them," Bishop said. "Whatever the hell that is."

"It's a private messaging and file sharing app," Bubba said.

"But when I said end-to-end encryption? I meant even they can't see it, so asking the creator is out."

Bishop's shoulders sank. "That's crap."

"To cops, sure. To drug traffickers and stuff?" Bubba shrugged. "Not really."

"Won't matter if we can't figure out Baker's passcode," Jimmy said. "Unless you can get Apple to jailbreak it."

Bubba shook his head. "Jail breaking deletes the data, including all apps on the phone."

"I talked to the hospital earlier," I said. "Baker's daughter Claire arrived a few hours ago." I eyed Bishop. "Let's see if she can help."

Bubba stopped us from leaving. "Hold up. Let's try a few things first. What's Claire's birthday?"

I reached behind me, stretching my arm to the table of stacked files. When I couldn't reach, I sighed, then got up and checked. I read him her birthday.

He shook his head. "What about his?"

We tried that, and it didn't work either.

"R-e-v—" I tapped a finger to count the letters. "E-n-g-e is seven letters. What's a six-letter word for revenge?"

The room went silent.

"Hold on," Nikki said. "I'll Google." Her fingers tapped the screen quickly. "Retort."

"If we don't get it right, it'll lock and we'll have to wait thirty minutes," Bubba said.

"We don't have that kind of time," Bishop said.

"Avenge," Nikki said. "Punish?"

In unison, Bishop and I both yelled, "Punish!"

I took a deep breath. Nikki sat on the edge of her seat. Jimmy stopped pacing and watched Bubba.

"You want me to try that?" Bubba asked. "If it's not right, we're locked out."

Bishop and I made eye contact. He nodded once. "Yes," I said through a tensed jaw.

Time stopped. We needed what was on that phone. It was our connection to Anderson, and it could be the nail in his coffin, but, most importantly, the end of a mad killing spree and finding Ashley.

"Yes," I said.

Bubba glanced at the chief.

"Yes," Jimmy said.

He tapped the screen, his eyes dark and squinted from a furrowed brow. I counted off the letters as his fingers tapped with care. *PUNISH.* His eyes widened. "I'm in!"

38

Bubba handed me the phone. "Just tap the notification and it'll pull up the app."

I rolled my eyes and snatched the phone from his hands. "I'm not Bishop."

"Hey, I resent that!" Bishop whined. "Deserve it, too," he mumbled under his breath.

"The messages are from the mastermind," I said. "Egotistical bastard." I handed the phone to Bishop and let him read them while I filled everyone in. I hadn't read through any more than the seven with notifications. "He doesn't know Baker's in the hospital. His messages are all directives for the next murder. They call her number six."

"No name?" Jimmy asked.

I shook my head. "But it's all set for her abduction late tomorrow night."

"All the women are under protection," Jimmy said.

"Ashley's still alive then," Nikki said. "If she wasn't, wouldn't the next number be seven?"

"Only if he included her in the numbers," I said. "And I'm not sure he did."

"She wasn't an initial part of the plan," Bishop said.

"We need someone posing as Baker on that phone," I said. "That way, if Anderson contacts him, he'll think he's still engaged."

"I'll do it," Jimmy said. He mumbled under his breath, "We need another damn detective."

"We have twenty-four hours tops to find him," Bishop said. He still had the phone and handed it back to me.

"The location. He mentioned the location three times in previous messages. *The location is prepared. All items are ready at the location. I'll provide location an hour before I'm ready for you.*"

I read the messages. "It's not happening in Alabama. If he's telling Baker about the location, it's going to happen here."

"Unless Baker is supposed to drive to Birmingham," Bishop said.

I shook my head. "The first two women were here. He kept the others in the same state." I drummed my fingers onto the table. "Maybe he's got Ashley at the location, too?"

Jimmy had sent Michels home a few hours before, knowing we'd need to say things he couldn't handle. "He's not going to keep her alive. She's too much of a risk."

"I'm there, too," Bishop said. "She's an outlier from his plan, but she's also dangerous. He can't afford to keep her alive."

"Unfortunately, that's where I am. I've wracked my brain for a reason to keep her alive, but I can't find any."

Nikki sniffled. "By now, he's probably gotten everything out of her he needed." Her eyes filled with tears.

"Probably," I said.

Jimmy pinched the bridge of his nose. "The good news is we don't know for a fact, so we can still hit this and hope she's alive."

"Yes," I said.

"Agree," Bishop said.

"It's late." Jimmy pointed to me and then Bishop. "I want you two to go home and get some rest. You need to be at that memorial service tomorrow. And you two," he said to Bubba and Nikki. "You need rest, too. Go home."

"Sir," Bishop said. "Anderson won't show. Especially if he's got an abduction planned."

"The only way he'll be there is watching from somewhere he can't be seen."

"Unless his next murder is in Alabama," Nikki said.

All eyes focused on her.

She blushed. "I mean, the memorial service is tomorrow. He was Johnson's partner. He's expected to be there, right? And we don't know for sure if he knows we're onto him, so..." She let us figure it out.

No one spoke, letting that sink in, until Bishop finally said, "Damn. What if she's right?"

Nikki's face beamed. "It's just a theory."

And a damn good one. I crossed my legs under the table and then uncrossed them. My mind raced. I couldn't sit still. I adjusted my position in my seat, undid and redid my bun, tapped my finger on the table, and then finally stood. I needed to move. Thinking came easier with movement. I stared at the ground as I walked loops around the table a few feet ahead of Jimmy.

"The potential victims are already under protective custody," Jimmy said. "Even if that's the case, he can't get to them."

"Maybe he hasn't played all his cards," I said. I kicked my pacing up a notch. Once I made another full loop around the table, I stopped next to the whiteboards. "What if we've missed a possible victim?"

Bishop shook his head. "We went through every potential victim. There's no way we missed one. Unless it's Ashley."

Bubba slid his chair back a foot, swiveled it around, and searched the files on each murder. He removed the photos from Ashley's files, flipped around and scooted back to the conference table where he laid them out. He pointed to two photos. "There are two girls in these we couldn't identify." He tapped his finger on each woman. "There's not enough of their faces to work with. I searched every social media platform I could. I even contacted the fraternities to see if these were scheduled parties, but they didn't own up to having any parties let alone the ones where the photos were taken."

"So, basically we don't have a clue what this guy is going to do," Jimmy said. He walked over to the whiteboards and studied them.

"If he's there, and he's waiting for Baker to show, he's SOL," I said.

"If he's got a plan to murder, he'll go through with it, Baker or no Baker," Jimmy said. He turned around and pointed to Bishop. "You," he said and then pointed to me. "And you. Go home, pack a bag, get some rest, then head to Birmingham."

"Sir," Bishop said. He checked his watch. "It's past midnight. If the next victim is in Birmingham, odds are he's already gotten to her."

"That could be the case here, too," I said. "I don't understand how the guy stays a ghost."

With straight elbows, Jimmy placed both palms on the table. "I'm aware of each of your theories, but we have people here. If a body appears, we can handle it."

He made a valid point. I eyed Bishop to see if he agreed. When he nodded once, I said, "Screw sleep. I'll meet you at my place in an hour."

39

Kyle's car was in my driveway. It was well past midnight, and I expected him to be asleep. I crept into the house and spotted him snoring on the couch. I tiptoed over to him to give him a kiss.

His eyes popped open. "Hey."

I jumped back and almost fell over my trunk. "Don't do that!"

"Do what? Say, hey?"

"You scared the hell out of me."

He smirked. "Sorry about that. How're you feeling?"

"Sore. Angry. Frustrated. Pick one."

"You should have rested."

"I'll rest when this case is over."

He checked his watch. "Good news?"

I shook my head as I removed my gear. "Not even close. Bishop and I are heading to Birmingham." I caught him up on the case as I tossed a bag of things together for the next twenty-four hours.

"You're not going to catch him alive. You know that, right?"

"I'm going to do my best to try."

"Guys like Anderson, they know what'll happen to them in prison. He's going down in a blaze."

Of glory. "Not if I can help it." I stuffed a black blazer into the bag knowing it would be wrinkled, but hoping I'd be able to iron it before the service, though I wasn't sure how that would happen. "These families need justice." I zipped up the bag and headed back toward my gear. "Bishop's going to be here soon. Can you feed Louie in the morning?"

"Of course." He stepped toward me and, with his hands on my waist, leaned down and kissed me. "Be careful."

"Always am," I said.

He laughed a genuine, full-hearted laugh. "Right."

Bishop knocked on the door. "I'll call or text when I can."

He opened the door for me and shook Bishop's hand. As I walked out, he held the door open, then stood with his hip on the frame and said, "Is this how a wife feels when her husband leaves for work?"

Bishop and I turned around and Bishop said, "Not mine. She rushed me out so she could cheat on me in our bed."

"Ouch," I said.

Bishop waved it off. "Life happens."

I smiled back at Kyle. As I rounded the corner toward the driveway, it occurred to me that I liked having him there to say goodbye to.

Thank God for RaceTrac. It was the only place open with half decent coffee. We each got two for the ride. Just in case. Plus, we'd been going nonstop, and both of us bordered on exhausted. If not for the constant rush of adrenaline and loads of caffeine, we'd be useless.

Neither of us spoke much until we hit I-20 in Atlanta. I'd

already sucked down my first coffee and started on my second, but the drive dropped my energy anyway. If something didn't happen, I'd have fallen asleep in minutes, and the wake up would be difficult. "So," I said making conversation. "How's things with Cathy?"

He shrugged. "We've barely talked since the fifth."

I felt bad for the guy. He'd been through a lot with his ex, all of which happened prior to my job with Hamby, and, as far as I knew, Cathy was the first woman he'd dated since his wife cheated on him. "That must be hard for her to adjust to."

"According to her, it's fine."

I pressed my lips together and released them with a pop. "Did she say that?"

"Yeah. She said it's not a problem."

"Did she say it's not a problem, or it's fine?"

He glanced at me and then back at the road. "Is there a difference?"

"Uh, yeah. A big one."

He looked at me again. His eyebrows crinkled. "I don't understand."

Poor Bishop. No wonder his marriage hadn't worked out. "When a woman says fine, it means it's not fine."

He blinked and his hands gripped the steering wheel tighter. "What the hell is that supposed to mean?"

"It means she's saying it's fine, but it's not, and you're supposed to know that, and fix whatever she says is fine but isn't."

He shifted toward me again. "You're giving me a headache."

"Which did she say?"

"I don't remember."

"Have you heard from her at all since she said those words?"

He nodded. "We talk. I'm a detective. She knows that when something happens, I'll be MIA. She said that was fine with her."

I crossed my arms over my chest. "Fine."

He glanced at me again. "Oh, hell."

I laughed. "No offense, but I can't believe you don't know about the fine thing. It's a universal woman's thing. Everyone knows it."

"Not everyone. I'm honest and literal. If I ask a question, I expect honesty in return. If she's not fine, she should have said that."

I shook my head. "That's not how it works." My cell phone rang. "It's Jimmy." I clicked answer and speaker, and said, "What's up?"

"Ashley's alive."

40

Marshall Medical Center was about an hour from Birmingham. We were already halfway there when we got the call about Ashley. Jimmy organized an Alabama Highway Patrol escort, meaning we followed them at a speed above the limit. Throughout the entire ride, all I could do was internally berate myself for not setting up a decoy abduction for Anderson or whatever minion he sent to do his dirty work. We had no idea how or when he'd move, which made the idea practically impossible, but if we'd lucked out and picked the right next victim, and I posed as her? The satisfaction I'd have would have been priceless.

I wanted to take Anderson down. With my own hands. And I wanted him alive. We needed him alive. His crimes were too big to let him die without giving the families justice.

Ashley's parents and Michels were enroute, but Ashley had specifically asked to see me. I hoped she had something that would get us in front of Anderson. We'd been behind him since the start, and it was time to take lead.

The doctor met us at the nurse's station on Ashley's floor. "Detectives."

I read his ID. "Dr. Parks. Are you Ashley's physician? Is she okay?"

"I am, and she's stable. She was barely conscious when she arrived. The head nurse called me a few hours ago to tell me she's conscious, and the first thing she did was ask to see you." He walked away from the station into the small sitting area along the back wall. "Ms. Middleton has suffered multiple serious injuries. She's lucky to be alive. Had the driver not brought her in when he did, she'd be dead."

"Driver?" Bishop asked.

"A man driving down a back road saw Ms. Middleton lying off to the side. He believed she was near death and rather than waiting for an ambulance, drove her here. Normally, I'd say that was idiotic, but in your friend's case, it likely saved her life."

How did she get on the side of the road? "What are her injuries?"

"Multiple, as I said. She arrived with swelling on the brain, however, we've drained the fluids, and the swelling is decreasing. We performed surgery to repair a compound fracture in her left elbow as well as surgery to repair her knee. That injury will take some time to recover, and it's too soon yet to say if she'll require additional surgery to walk properly."

"It's that bad?" I asked.

"The bottom of her patella—the kneecap—was broken into small pieces. Typically, this happens when a person's kneecap is pulled apart from an injury such as a fall, and then is crushed when the patient lands on it."

"Is that what happened to Ashley?"

"We believe so. She also has several broken ribs and lacerations over multiple sections of her body, many of which required stitches." He glanced up at the ceiling. "Seventy-five total, I believe."

I swallowed back the anger boiling to the surface. Anderson would pay.

"Her right eye was damaged, but we were able to repair it, and our ophthalmologist believes her sight will be fine. Her nose is broken and—"

I cut him off but with respect. "Doctor, do you believe any of her injuries are from an attack?"

He exhaled. "There are multiple fingerprint marks and bruises around Ms. Middleton's neck. She arrived with duct tape around her hands and feet. Whoever did this to her wanted her to suffer."

"We put a BOLO out on Ms. Middleton," Bishop said. "And hospitals within a hundred-mile radius were contacted."

"Ms. Middleton had no identification on her. At the time of her arrival, our primary focus was on keeping her alive. We contacted the authorities approximately six hours ago when she was able to tell us who she was."

"How long has she been here?" Bishop asked.

"Just over twenty-four hours. She was immediately assessed and brought into surgery upon arrival." He exhaled. "She's got a long road ahead, but I think she'll recover physically. Mentally, I can't say."

"Can we see her now?" I asked.

He nodded. "I'll allow it, but please, make it quick. She's been given painkillers, so she's groggy, but she's coherent enough to want to speak with you." He took another deep breath and released it. "Ms. Middleton is a tough young woman, but I should prepare you. She's in bad shape."

He led us into the room. The few steps down the hall dragged by in slow motion. Anxiety pumped through my veins. The urge to run to Ashley upped with every heartbeat. She'd almost died.

Anderson wouldn't get away with what he'd done.

Dr. Parks opened the door to Ashley's room. "I'll give you some privacy, but please don't aggravate her in any way."

"Understood," I said. I took a deep breath and walked in slowly, keeping my shoulders back and head up. I tried to appear positive, but seeing Ashley lying there, damaged nearly beyond recognition, ripped my heart to pieces. All the pain from the wreck no longer mattered. I washed it away without a second thought. Ashley's pain mattered.

They'd put her neck in a brace, so she couldn't turn her head. Her eyes were closed. I leaned over her as I grazed my fingers over her hand. "Ashley? It's Rachel."

One eye was patched, but the other eye fluttered. She groaned. I took a deep breath, willing my tears to stay put. God, if I would have talked to her that night, I could have prevented the trauma she'd gone through.

Her eye finally opened. Recognition flashed across her face. She licked her dry lips. "Anderson. Serial killer."

"We know," I said.

Bishop bent toward her. I heard him swallow. "Did he do this to you?"

Her head moved ever so slightly. She groaned again. Her voice was groggy and barely above a whisper. "Yeah."

Bishop covered his mouth and dragged his hand down his chin. I exhaled and then took a deep breath and exhaled again, focused on staying calm. "Ashley, I don't want you to talk. You've got a lot of recovering to do, but the doctor says you'll be okay. We found the files in your closet. The stickers. You figured it out by the stickers, and that's what you wanted to tell me, isn't it?"

Her head shook from side to side, just a tiny movement. She struggled to keep her eye open. "That was after."

She coughed and the surrounding machines beeped faster.

"No, please, don't talk. Just know we figured it out. We're close, Ash. Anderson is going to pay for what he's done."

Bishop coughed. "I'll get in touch with the local department. We need guards on her ASAP." He excused himself from the room.

I took that opportunity to apologize. "I'm so sorry. I should have talked to you at the party. I could have stopped this."

She shook her head slightly again. "No." She coughed and winced, then groaned softly.

I squeezed my eyes shut, but that didn't stop the tears. Ashley turned her hand up into mine. Her squeeze was barely noticeable.

I smiled at her. Even with all her injuries, Ashley was beautiful. What happened to her didn't take that beauty away. Her face was a mass bruise of purple and red from her left eye down. Blotches of color marked the right side. The side of her head had been shaved, and a large cut had been stitched back together. Though her neck was covered by the brace, I knew the bruises underneath would be just as purple as the ones on her face. What happened? Why did he do this and not kill her? Was that his plan?

She licked her lips. "Water," she whispered.

I grabbed the water off the side table next to her bed. I held the straw to her mouth as she slipped slowly. When I took it away, she cleared her throat again and then whispered, "He tried to kill me." Tears fell from her good eye.

"I know, but he didn't. Someone found you on the side of the road. Do you know how you got there?"

"He threw me down a ravine." She coughed and the buttons on the machines beat rapidly.

"I'm sorry. Don't talk. You need to stay calm, okay?"

"Em," she groaned.

"Michels and your parents are on their way." That lump in

my throat appeared again. Hard as I tried, I couldn't swallow it away. "We're going to find him, Ash, and he's going to pay." I squeezed her hand lightly and told her I'd be back.

I walked out of the room. I needed a minute to think. Bishop stood near the nurse's station with his head dipped down into his phone. I shifted my head back and forth across the hallway, then darted to the right.

The nurse at the station hollered, "Down the hall and on your left."

"Thanks." I jogged there, saw the bathroom sign, yanked the door open, then whipped around and locked it. I bent waist down with my hands on my knees and took in several deep breaths.

41

Bishop and I processed what little we knew about Ashley on the drive back to Birmingham. I contacted Jimmy and filled him in, then asked him to contact Chief Thompson. An hour later we met him at a small café on the outskirts of Birmingham.

"She confirmed it was my detective?" he asked.

"Yes sir," Bishop said. "We think he believed she died in that ravine."

The chief placed his hands on the table and dropped his head. "I thought he was a good guy. He passed the psychological evaluation he went through after his daughter committed suicide." He paused. "How did I miss it?"

"Serial killers know how to play the game," I said. "Anderson didn't break because his daughter committed suicide. He was already broken inside. Her death just catapulted him into action. If it wasn't her, it would've been something else."

He sipped his coffee. "I don't think he'll show his face at the memorial. He's got to know you're onto him or he wouldn't have given that letter to the reporter."

"We've had this discussion," Bishop said. "But we all agreed we needed to go through this, anyway."

I stared down at my untouched plate of scrambled eggs and hash browns. My mind told me to eat but my body had no interest. "He'll be there, watching us." I pointed to the chief. "We need people along the outskirts of the funeral watching for him. Plain clothes. From another department."

I pushed my plate aside and leaned forward. "He thinks Ashley's dead. He doesn't know what we know, but he wants to find out. We get bodies on him at the memorial and follow him. If he's killed someone, he'll have to present his victim, and that's when we'll bust him."

"Our girls are under protective custody. He has no idea where they are. He won't kill here."

"We've got the same," Bishop said.

"Maybe he just needs to think the girl is dead?" I suggested. "Chief Abernathy's got the ability to communicate with Anderson via an app he used with Scott Baker. The chief lets him think he's Baker, and they move forward."

"I'll get in touch with our sister department," Thompson said. "They'll lend us officers."

We showered and changed for the memorial at the Birmingham Police department. A few officers stared me down as if I had holes littering my body like some carnival act. I glanced down at my bruised and swollen hand, but it wasn't just that that caught their eyes. My battered and bruised face drew unwanted attention. I should have let Savannah hide the bruising and teach me how to do it in the process.

A few officers approached and asked questions about the Stuart murders. No one mentioned Anderson. Was that because they suspected him, or simply because his partner had just died, and he needed time off? Either way, I kept my responses short and left out anything that might give away our plan.

The chief updated us on the plain clothes officers set up for the memorial. "We've got everyone ready to go." He checked his watch. "The memorial starts in an hour. It's five minutes from here. I'm heading there now."

"We'll follow," Bishop said.

I texted Michels to see if he'd arrived at the hospital. He responded quickly.

I'm here. She's asleep.

Did she get to see you yet?

Yes. Get the bastard.

We will.

The department held the memorial at a large evangelical church in Birmingham that reminded me of Willow Creek Church in Illinois. The building resembled an event center, and if not for the large cross monument reaching out from the roof, it was barely recognizable as a church to me. I wasn't a fan of the big box churches, or church in general, but I understood the importance of them for memorials and funerals.

We had priority parking, something that struck me as odd for a memorial, but given the circumstances, I appreciated the set up. The parking lot was already full of personal vehicles and various department vehicles. As Bishop parked the car, I prepared myself. The last time I'd attended a law enforcement memorial was for Tommy.

Bishop opened his door then turned toward me with his eyebrow raised. "You okay?"

I nodded as I grabbed the handle to open mine. "I'm fine."

Groups of people crowded around the entrance and inside. Walking inside, I didn't realize I'd held my breath. I blew it out quickly hoping Bishop wouldn't catch onto my growing anxiety.

The place was packed. That wasn't unusual for a law enforcement memorial service. Tommy's had been standing room only. I assumed there would be a short memorial with speeches by the chief, possibly the mayor, and Johnson's ex-wife, Elizabeth. I sent her a text to let her know I was there, and I would be following up with her soon.

We walked around the entire building, conversing with other officers while looking for Anderson. Since the service was in an enclosed space, we didn't expect to see him, but we needed to make sure. He had a better chance of losing us at the cemetery.

Four people stood at the podium and spoke about Johnson's dedication to his job. I felt bad for not really liking the guy after hearing about his successes and involvement in the community. To me he'd been condescending, though I'd learned that was a commonly misunderstood kindness approach in general for Southern men. Guilty as I felt, I couldn't play the *I wish* game. Wishing never did anyone any good.

Chief Thompson also mentioned Detective Anderson, saying he believed he was so impacted by his partner's demise he was unable to attend the services. Nice move on his part. He let everyone know Anderson wasn't there without throwing him under the bus or causing suspicion.

Once the speeches and music finished, we gathered outside and waited as the hearse drove up to the front entrance. Everybody took a moment to acknowledge Detective Johnson as they walked past and headed to their cars. Bishop and I waited to the side as the building emptied. Near the end, a woman walked over.

"Detective Ryder?"

I stepped to the side and turned toward her.

"I'm Elizabeth Johnson."

"Ms. Johnson." Why wasn't she in a car already? "I'm sorry for your loss."

Bishop introduced himself.

She waved to someone in the car behind the hearse. "I'm riding with William's sister, but I wanted to see if we could speak after the funeral."

Bishop shook his head slightly.

"Unfortunately, we have meetings," I said. "But I would like to catch you up on some things later on the phone."

She smiled. "Then I'll talk to you soon." She nodded to Bishop and walked away.

We headed to our vehicle. Our plan was to be the last in line. That way, if Anderson was discovered in the procession, we'd limit our chance of being stuck.

"Do you trust Johnson's ex?" Bishop asked.

"Yes."

"Doesn't seem odd to you that she wasn't in the car ready to go?"

"I'm not sure I'd be comfortable with my former sister-in-law at my ex-husband's funeral. Would you sit with your ex's family?"

"I'd sit with my daughter."

"That's different."

"Understood," he said.

About a third of the vehicles drove in the procession and parked along the small roads near the plot. Johnson was cremated and his remains were being buried next to another plot with a matching stone. The name on the stone surprised me.

I elbowed him. "Read that stone."

His eyes widened. "Damn."

"I had no idea."

"Neither did I. And she was young."

"Three years old. I can't imagine losing a child, but losing one so young," I said. I didn't need to finish that sentence. Bishop had a daughter. He understood.

He dropped his chin and nodded. "It's every parent's worst nightmare."

Everyone confirmed their radio equipment was in check before the service began. There were ten undercover officers inside the perimeter of the cemetery and five in unmarked vehicles on the cross streets outside the gates. The cemetery was small but had sections with mausoleums and trees that provided the perfect hiding places for Anderson. I watched a woman in a tank top and shorts leave flowers at a site about three rows ahead of us. If she was one of the undercover officers, she'd done a great job disguising herself. And I envied her outfit. It was over one hundred degrees, and so humid my hair curled inside its bun.

The service lasted less than fifteen minutes. The cemetery cleared out quickly, with many officers in attendance going back to work at their various departments. Bishop and I hung back in a small, shaded area waiting to make sure Anderson didn't suddenly appear. The odds were he wouldn't, but better safe than sorry.

Elizabeth Johnson stood in front of the two markers. I'd plucked two roses from a vase near the chairs and walked over to her. "The headstone is lovely."

"Thank you," she said. She cleared her throat. "They made it quickly since he was in law enforcement."

"They're good about that."

She glanced around the area. "I wasn't surprised Detective Anderson was a no-show. And I'm sure he wasn't distraught like the chief said. He and my husband didn't get along. William didn't trust him, and I don't, either."

She referred to Johnson as her husband.

She moved closer to me. "You believe he's involved, don't you?"

"I believe we are close to catching the person responsible for several murders."

She turned toward me. "William's included?"

"We're doing everything we can," I said. I couldn't confirm or offer anything more than that. Instead, I placed a rose over Johnson's grave and then put the other one on Ela Jean Johnson's. When I turned around, Elizabeth Johnson was crying.

"He never got over her death. I think that's why he was so committed to his job. Working kept his mind focused away from Ela."

"May I ask what happened?"

"A rare form of brain cancer." She wiped her eyes with a tissue from her purse. "One day she was fine, and then the next, she was gone."

"I'm sorry."

She gave me a partial smile. "They're together now, and one day we'll all be a family like we were meant to be."

Bishop walked over. "We have to get going," he said. He smiled at Ms. Johnson. "Again, I'm sorry for your loss."

"Thank you," she said.

I touched her arm. "I'll be in touch as soon as possible."

We walked back to the car, disillusioned and frustrated. No one reported seeing Anderson anywhere near the burial.

An hour later, we met with Chief Thompson again.

"He wasn't there," he said. "We had men all over that

cemetery and on every street surrounding it. If he'd gone, we would have found him."

"Agreed," Bishop said.

I stared blankly at a photo of the chief and two other men on a golf course. Every chief of police had a similar photo. The mayor, some other key politician, and the chief. I chewed on my bottom lip letting the thoughts racing through my head whip into a funnel cloud until they hit pay dirt. "There's another girl."

Bishop swiveled his head my direction. "I think so, too."

"The ones we have in custody weren't his target. Or he switched targets. He's got a girl, and if she's not already dead, she will be soon."

The chief squeezed the bridge of his nose. "We have no information on any other possible victims here."

I shook my head. "You won't. His murders have all been in Georgia. It's happening there."

Bishop crossed a leg over a knee. "He knows we're onto him. He had a backup plan."

42

We met up with Michels and the Middletons at the hospital. Ashley's condition had improved enough to be moved out of the ICU and into a regular room. The woman was a fighter.

Michels stood outside her room. He hadn't shaved in days and the short beard looked good on him. His lack of sleep was obvious, his sunken eyes supported by bags framed with dark circles. His shoulders curved inward. I walked over and hugged him.

He hugged me back. "You didn't catch him."

I shook my head.

"I want his balls on a silver platter," Bishop said. "And we'll get them."

Michels nodded. "I know. I know." He exhaled. "She wants to see you. She's talking more, but damn, it breaks my heart to see her in pain. It's killing me."

"I know," I said. I'd felt the same way when I'd seen her before.

We walked in. Ashley's parents hovered over her bed. When they saw us, they each kissed her cheek and excused themselves. Mr. Middleton whispered as he walked by, "Catch the bastard that did this to my baby."

I swallowed back the lump in my throat. It wasn't easy. Seeing anyone in Ashley's situation was brutal, but it was personal with Ashley.

Bishop took the side closest to the window. I stood next to her rolling tray. She pointed to her water. "Could you get that for me?" She cleared her throat. Her voice was rough and husky as if she'd just woke up.

"Of course." I held the straw to her mouth.

"I need to tell you what happened."

"Okay," I said.

"But if you get tired," Bishop added. "Stop, okay?"

She nodded. "There were two of them."

"Who came to your apartment?"

Bishop removed a notepad from his pocket.

She nodded. "The first one said he was maintenance. I shouldn't have let him in. Anderson came after."

"What about Scott Baker?" I asked. "Was he there?"

"Just the two men."

"Anderson must have planted Baker's hair," Bishop said.

"What about the photo in the frame?"

She narrowed her eyes. "I...picture frame?"

"There was a frame with a photo of you from the toga party. Michels said it was the frame with the photo of the two of you at a restaurant."

"He must have changed it."

"Did they go through your things?" Bishop asked.

"Only the files I had out, and those were the copies I'd made for Johnson. It wasn't everything."

"Why did you have the files?" I asked.

"I recognized one of the victims in Alabama from the

news. I was curious. I went through Michels's files." She turned toward him. "I'm sorry."

"Don't worry about it," he said.

"Then I saw the girls, and I knew some of them, or at least I'd seen them around. I heard the rumors about what happened to them. I just kept looking. That's when I saw there were prints on the papers with the stickers, but there was no notation about what was under the stickers, so I went to the department and signed out the file to check."

"Why didn't you tell us?"

"Because I wasn't sure what I'd find, and I wasn't authorized to take the files. I didn't want to get anyone in trouble."

"How did you get them?" I asked.

"I said you approved it and would be there to let them know. I'm sorry."

"Don't be," I said. "What you did was genius." Against policy, but genius.

"I found the prints and ran them. That's when I called Detective Johnson and asked him to check his evidence."

"Anderson wasn't his partner when the first murders in Birmingham happened. When he realized the prints were on the backs of the stickers, he had to have known Anderson was involved," Bishop said.

"Yes," she said. "He called me. He was supposed to come to my place." Tears filled her eyes. "I thought it was Johnson. I shouldn't have answered the door, but I saw the guy working on the cameras earlier, so I let him in."

"You wanted to talk to me at the party," I said. "Did you know Anderson was involved then?"

She shook her head. "I wanted to tell you about knowing the girls in the photos. Something didn't feel right about the case, but I didn't run the prints until the next morning. That's when I called Johnson."

"So, you were waiting for him. You weren't sick," Michels said.

She nodded. "I'm sorry."

"Why didn't you tell me?" he asked.

"Because I didn't want to get anyone in trouble."

I handed her a tissue. "Do you know who the man is?"

She shook her head. "It was a young guy, but he's dead."

"How do you know?" Bishop asked.

"I watched Anderson murder him. Loose ends, he called him."

"Why did he take you to the storage facility?" Bishop asked.

"I don't know. We just walked that direction."

"Where was Anderson?"

"He'd left already. We met him on the side of the road. That's where he put me in his trunk."

"Did you try to get away?" Michels asked.

A sob escaped her lips. "He said he'd kill my parents if I didn't do what he said."

"Anderson?" Bishop asked.

She nodded.

"Where did he take you?"

"At first somewhere close to Hamby, but I'm not sure where."

"Can you describe the place?"

"I think it was a warehouse or something."

I treaded carefully. "Do you remember anything that happened to you there?"

"He made me watch him kill that man. And that's where he told me about murdering Detective Johnson." She cried. "He said I deserved the same punishment because I tried to ruin his plan. But I didn't tell him what I knew. I don't know if Detective Johnson did, but I don't think so. He kept trying to make me tell him, but I just kept saying I didn't know it was him. I didn't want to die." The machines next to her beeped faster.

"That's enough," Michels said.

"No, I'm almost done. I need to finish."

"Are you sure?" he asked.

She nodded. "He strangled me. The next thing I knew, I was at the bottom of that ravine. I don't remember much of what happened then. I know I tried to get up, and I must have because I'm here."

Michels stepped to my side. "I think she needs to rest now."

He was right. We said our goodbyes and promised nothing more would happen to her.

Out of the room, I said, "If he strangled her when she was drugged, he probably couldn't feel her pulse and thought she was dead."

Bishop nodded. "He threw her over that ravine thinking no one would find her."

———

We arrived back to our department exhausted and angry, having hit wall after wall regarding Anderson.

As we walked through the pit toward our cubbies, Bishop said, "I need a few hours of sleep."

"I'm going to stick around."

"You need to get some rest, too."

"I couldn't sleep if I tried."

Our phones collectively beeped with text message notifications.

"Shit," Bishop said after we read them.

We took off down the hall without saying another word.

43

Jimmy met us outside the crime scene. Neither one of us was expecting him to be there. "Be prepared. It's bad in there."

A house? It wasn't Anderson's MO. Toys in the front yard. A small wire and wood fence connected to each side of the front. A line of crepe myrtles across the front. Well maintained flower beds. "This is out of character. He's desperate." Anderson didn't leave his victims in their homes. He liked the presentation. He wanted, no, he *needed* his work to be seen.

"Didn't stop him from murdering another girl," Bishop said.

"Bubba went over every photo from the parties," I said. "Not one was a match."

Jimmy nodded. "She's not from our list."

"How long have you been here?" I asked.

"We got the call about an hour ago."

"Why weren't we notified?" Bishop asked.

"The 911 call was brief. The caller didn't stay on the line. We sent patrol, and when they got here, they called it in. It didn't appear to be Anderson, so I came. When I got here and saw what I saw, I realized it was him and called you."

"What makes you think it's him?" I asked.

"It's in the kitchen."

Bishop rubbed his eyes. "Who found her?"

Jimmy exhaled. "Her mother."

"Jesus Christ," Bishop said.

"Where's the mother now?" I asked.

"Ambulance took her to the hospital. She was in shock."

"And her father?"

"He went with her." He sighed. "Let's go."

We slipped on booties and gloves. I set up my phone to take photos.

We walked through the front door. On the left was what I'd grown up calling the front room, or the room nobody sat in. On the right, the dining room. Straight ahead was the hallway toward the rest of the house and the stairs to the top floor. Drops of blood marked the stairway and the hall. Someone had already marked each spot with a yellow marker. I swallowed hard. Bishop mumbled something under his breath.

Jimmy dodged the markers as he walked upstairs. "We believe things started upstairs. After that, we think the victim got down the stairs, and tried to get out through the front door, and when she couldn't, she went toward the kitchen to try the back door, and that's when she died."

We'd walked into a real-life horror movie. My mind darkened to a vengeful, evil black I wasn't sure I'd escape.

Bishop gasped when we entered the bedroom. "Holy Mother of God."

I clenched my fists and counted to ten internally to keep me calm, but it didn't work. Anger lit my stomach on fire, the heat traveling through my veins. I opened my mouth to speak, but I couldn't find the words. It was an awful scene. I understood why the mother was in shock.

Blood had splattered everywhere—the dresser, the chest of drawers, the desk, the bed, all over the walls and carpet. There was so much blood Nikki used sticky notes to mark many of them. "These aren't gun splatters," I said. "She was stabbed."

Jimmy nodded. "Multiple times. So far, we've counted twenty-two times, but we'll get the final number from Dr. Barron."

Bishop muttered a trail of swear words in a tone so scathing Jimmy backed away from him. I touched his arm. It trembled. He was on the edge of losing it. We all were. A feeling brewed in my gut. Something wasn't right. I couldn't quite put my finger on it, but it would come eventually. I turned toward the door and headed to the kitchen.

When we got there, Bishop dropped an f-bomb. I steeled myself. The kitchen opened to the great room, but it didn't appear the victim made it there. I glanced at the floor near the back door where she lay with a white sheet covering her. "Are you sure it was Anderson? None of this fits."

Jimmy walked over to the victim and moved the sheet from her left side revealing the baggie in her hand. "He left a note."

I exhaled. "Shit."

"This one is typed." Cops weren't supposed to disrupt a body before the coroner or medical examiner arrived, but detectives and chiefs of police rarely followed that rule. He carefully removed the bag from the victim's hand, opened it, and then handed it to me.

Ten, eleven, twelve, we'll be compelled.

Dr. Barron walked in. He nodded to us. "My apologies for arriving late. I was in the city."

Barron was a Southerner down to the bone. He liked to fish, drink beer, and tell a joke, but when it came to work, he was one thousand percent on point. No jokes. No small talk. Just work. He squatted next to the victim and said a small prayer before removing the sheet from her. I hadn't seen him do that before.

"Dear God," he said. He studied her body and recorded his notes into his phone. When he finished, he stood up with a loud groan and detailed his findings even though we'd heard them in real time. "I counted thirty-seven stab wounds. Twenty-three on her front and fourteen on the back."

Nikki arrived. "Dr. Barron, she's got something under her nails."

He nodded. "Yes, I will make sure to get that to you." He directed his attention back to us. "It appears she fought off her attacker. She has cuts on her right hand." He glanced down at the note. "I'm assuming this is connected to your current investigation?"

Bishop and I spoke in unison. "Yes."

He exhaled. "Very well. I'll take her when you're ready and get started on her immediately. She's been identified?"

"Kaylee Priest. Twenty-three," Nikki said. She looked at me. "She just graduated from Alabama in May."

Ten, eleven, twelve, we'll be compelled.

"I'm calling Claire Baker. Maybe she'll recognize the name." I excused myself and headed outside. On my way, I noted the front door hadn't been forced open. Did she let Anderson in willingly or had he gotten in another way?

Or had Anderson found someone to replace Scott Baker?

Claire didn't answer her cell phone, so I called the hospital and asked for the nursing station on Scott Baker's floor and spoke to the head nurse.

"I'm sorry, Claire Baker left yesterday afternoon. Have you tried her cell?"

"I have. Is the officer still at Baker's door?"

"Yes. Would you like me to get him?"

"No, thank you. I'll contact him." The something that bothered me earlier nudged at me again.

A few seconds later the officer answered my call. "Officer Winske."

"Detective Ryder here. Who was on when Claire Baker left?"

"I think it was Walsh."

"Did he say where she went?"

"I just came on, but Masterson was here before me, and he didn't mention anything."

"Okay. I want to know when she comes back. Make sure to pass that information along, okay?"

"Got it."

I hung up and tried Claire Baker again. The call went straight to voicemail.

Ten, eleven, twelve, we'll be compelled.

Claire Baker.

I ran back inside.

Alpharetta put two patrol units on Scott Baker's place and allowed one of our patrol officers to assist.

We finished processing the scene and went back to the department. Jimmy ordered Chinese takeout for all of us. I forced a few bites down, but my stomach decided food wasn't the right decision. I couldn't eat knowing there were possibly two killers on the loose.

"She was assaulted. Her father supported Chip Stuart. Now he's in a coma. It's the logical next step."

"There's nothing logical about this," Bishop said.

"You know what I mean. Anderson could have easily manipulated her."

"Yes, he could have," he said. "Let's assume Anderson's our guy."

"He is our guy," I said. "The mastermind."

We'd spread out every document and photo we had from every file associated with the murders. Bishop shuffled through them, pulled one out, and read it out loud. "One, two, three, you can't pin on me. Seven, eight, nine, I'll add to my crimes. Four, five, six, add to the mix." He tossed the paper back onto the table and grabbed a copy of the note from Kaylee Priest's murder. "Ten, eleven, twelve, we'll be compelled." He set the paper back on the table. "Beside the fact that he's all over the place, if she's one of his victims, Kaylee Priest is number six in the rhyme. So, we've got another three murders coming?"

I sighed. "If he has his way, yes."

Bishop shook his head. "We can't even pin all the ones we've got now on Anderson."

"We're close. Just one is questionable right now."

"Good, let's figure it out now. Where are we?" He drummed his fingers on the table. "Okay, here's what we've got. Three murders from over three years ago, and all we have to show of Anderson's involvement are the stickers. Could he have physically killed the Alabama victims?" He shrugged. "We don't know, and Stuart never said who committed those crimes, just that he didn't."

"But Anderson's prints prove his involvement, and that's conspiracy under Alabama law, so, whether he physically committed them, he'll go down for murder on those."

"Right. If they decide to reopen the cases."

"They will."

"Okay then, we can assume Stuart's riddle is his confession

of the second three, seven, eight, and nine, but not the Alabama murders, right?"

"Right," I said. "I believe Anderson killed the Alabama victims himself, but for the next round, he decided to have someone else commit the crime."

"But why? He's a cop. He knows the code. Whether he physically committed the offense or not, he's involved, and he can go down as if he was the one that slit their throats."

"It's not about the physical act. It's about serving justice. We know his daughter committed suicide. It's not complicated. She killed herself because she'd been sexually assaulted or raped. Three years later, Anderson figures out who did it, and takes him out. He takes out the other two because he doesn't want the murder pinned on him. Killing them makes it look like a serial killer. He decides he likes that kind of justice and wants to share it with others. Stuart and Baker."

"I'm with you on that but let me continue. The next three —four, five, and six—he'll add to the mix. We got a confession from Baker about Natalie Carlson, victim number four in the rhyme's order, but he swore he didn't kill Elana Mills, victim five, and we don't have anything from the scene to implicate Anderson. Then we've got Kaylee Priest. There's no way Baker's good for her, and again, no stickers. And if we're paying attention to patterns, Priest is completely off target. We can't say for certain she's part of this at all, which means we can't nail Anderson for those two." He clenched his jaw and spoke through his teeth. "Tell me that doesn't mean we've got another two victims for five and six."

"No, we don't. He left our names with Natalie Carlson. We knew there were going to be two more murders. Elana Mills was the second, now Kaylee Priest is the third."

"Again, nothing from those scenes to implicate him," Bishop said.

"Elana Mills was on the list. That's a connection."

"Maybe, but it's a weak one, and not Kaylee," he said. "We don't have anything for her."

"Not yet," I replied. "But we'll find Claire Baker," I said. "And we'll make her talk."

"You really think she killed her, don't you?"

"Yes, I do. She took over for her father."

"You think she killed Elana Mills, too?"

"I'm working through that."

"Elana Mills's murder was different from Kaylee Priest's."

"I know, but that doesn't mean Claire didn't commit it."

Bishop stared at the table full of scattered file folders and shook his head. "What would compel a young woman to commit that violent of a crime?"

"Rape."

An hour later Nikki stormed into the investigation room. She handed me a paper and bounced from one foot to the other. "Claire Baker applied for an Alabama concealed carry license six months ago." She stopped bouncing then placed her hand on her hip. "And her prints were all over Kaylee Priest's house."

I looked straight into Bishop's eyes.

He exhaled. "Son of a bitch."

"Did you run them against prints found at Elana Mills' scene?" I asked.

"To the best of my knowledge, there weren't any prints found at the scene, but I can contact them and confirm."

"Please do," I said.

I immediately put an all-points bulletin out for Claire Baker, using her driver's license photo for identification. We made sure Birmingham knew, though my gut told me Claire wasn't in Alabama. Bishop interviewed Kaylee Priest's father and then headed to the hospital with his approval to interview his wife. He had two, possibly three, questions of importance. One, did Mrs. Priest know if her daughter knew Claire Baker, two, was she aware of Kaylee being sexually assaulted or raped, and if so, did Kaylee implicate Daniel Travis? Mr. Priest swore on his mother's grave that his daughter and wife would have told him if Kaylee was assaulted or raped, but Bishop and I knew that wasn't always the case.

Someone from patrol purchased two large boxes of freshly brewed coffee from Dunkin', and I poured myself a cup. I stood leaning against the kitchen door frame and stared out into the pit. My mind flipped through scenes of my conversations with Claire and Scott Baker. Claire was angry and combative. She'd never reported her assault, and, therefore, there was no way to prove she'd been raped. The code for rape in Alabama was similar to Georgia's. If Daniel Travis had sexual intercourse with Claire Baker against her will, that was rape. Anything else was sexual assault. But if Travis hadn't technically raped her, that didn't mean Claire didn't think he did. The lines between sexual assault and rape were blurred.

I'd contacted Claire several times, and she'd never returned any of my calls. She'd been contacted about her father's medical condition, but that information was left on voicemail. She'd never called about that, either. She'd just shown up at the hospital.

Kaylee Priest was stabbed thirty-seven times. That was personal. If Kaylee had been raped or assaulted by Daniel Travis and not reported it, Claire could have found out and held a grudge. A grudge like her father's, and one Anderson could have capitalized on.

What got me was the difference in the crimes. The first six, the three in Alabama, and Stuart's, were meticulous and clean. The recent three came off opposite. Scott Baker loved his daughter. He loved her enough to give financial support to the man who killed her attacker. Did he love her enough to convince her to commit murder, too?

44

Jimmy sent us all home stating we couldn't actively search for Claire Baker, and if she was located, we'd be called back in. When Bishop and I argued, he told Bishop he looked like a heart attack waiting to happen. I couldn't disagree. His cheeks had been red for days. He continuously sweated, though that could have been because it was humid as hell. Either way, at his advancing age, I'd told him he needed sleep. He paid me back with a comment about my dark circles scaring small children. Again, I couldn't disagree.

I'd called Kyle, who was at my place bonding with Louie. He met me in the driveway. I rolled down my window. "What is this, valet service?"

He smiled. "Just making sure you got home okay."

I pulled into the garage and killed the ignition. He opened the door for me. "Wow. Such politeness. I don't know what to do with it."

He laughed and kissed me. "I made you some dinner."

"Thanks, but I had Chinese earlier."

"No problem," he said inside. "I'll wrap it up."

"Thanks," I said. "I'm going to jump in the shower." I headed to my bedroom.

"Hey," he said.

I turned around. "Yeah?"

"Michels called me. I'm glad Ashley's going to be all right."

"Physically yeah, she will be, but she's got a long road ahead of her. I just hope she's emotionally strong enough to handle what happened."

"I think she is."

Ten minutes later I wrapped a towel around my body and stepped back into my bedroom. I grabbed a pair of underwear and a tank top and got dressed while Kyle dug through his bag for something to sleep in. "You really should stop carrying that bag here all the time." I walked over to my dresser, opened two drawers, and combined their contents. It wasn't much. "How about you use this?"

He smirked. "Wow, that's a big commitment."

"I know. So, you'd better not blow it."

He stuffed his clothing into the drawer. "Never."

We climbed into bed. Kyle wasn't surprised when I gave him the update on Claire Baker. "We see a lot of women committing violent crimes in my field."

I snuggled against him. He was lying on his back and wrapped his arm around my side. "More than two million commit some form of violent crimes a year," I said. "Granted, men commit the bulk of them, but it's not impossible for Claire Baker to have murdered two women."

"You think she killed them both?"

"Like I said, her father admitted to murdering Natalie Carlson. He swears he didn't kill Elana Mills. And she was found thirty-six hours after she was murdered. So, yeah, it's possible. Since Mills was killed in Forsyth County, Nikki didn't process the scene, but she's checking with them to see what they found."

Kyle's eyes closed and a few minutes later he was out. I wasn't. I tried to sleep, but my brain wouldn't shut off. Finally, after an hour of unsuccessful attempts, I got up and went to the kitchen.

I munched on the dinner Kyle had made while sitting on the couch watching reruns of *The Golden Girls*. Grilled chicken seasoned with honey and Worcestershire sauce, sauteed brussels sprouts, and garlic bread. It was my favorite Kyle meal. The food made me sleepy, and I closed my eyes.

The next thing I knew, Dr. Barron was calling. The ring surprised me, and the plate of food tipped from my lap onto my couch. "Damn it." I picked up my cell quickly and spoke with a hoarse voice. "Detective Ryder."

"Detective, I realize it's late, but I figured if your crime scene tech could wake me up, I could do the same with you."

I pursed my lips and checked the clock. It was five a.m. I'd slept sitting up for three hours with a plate of food on my lap. "Nikki called you this early?"

"No. She called me two hours earlier than this."

"I'm not sure I understand."

"She was looking for help in regard to fingerprints at Ms. Elana Mills crime scene. I made a call to the Forsyth County Medical Examiner, and now, I'm calling you with the results. You've got an excellent tech, Detective."

"Go on."

"She learned there were no prints at the scene, but she hadn't received any information about prints on the body. Per someone at the sheriff's office, they hadn't checked. She couldn't believe that and asked me to check with the medical examiner. It turns out they did, but no one from the county followed up."

Maybe they expected us to since we were involved?

"And Nikki matched them?"

"No need. The prints belonged to Claire Baker, who Nikki suspected. Again, your tech is top notch. I haven't called her back, so please tell her I said that when you talk with her."

"I'll call her now, Doc. Thank you."

He disconnected the call.

I darted to my bedroom and got dressed as quietly as possible, then sent off a quick text to Bishop after I brushed my teeth. I kissed Kyle on the forehead on my way out.

"I have to go," I told him when his eyes opened. "Nikki put Claire Baker at Elana Mills murder."

"That's great." He yawned and then said, "I mean, I'm glad she made the connection."

"I'll call you soon." I kissed him again and said, "Love you." I froze. *Love you?*

He smiled. "I know. I love you too."

Well, hell. I rushed out without another word.

45

I said hello to the officer outside Scott Baker's hospital room. "Has Claire Baker returned?"

"No, ma'am."

"Okay. I'll just be a minute." I walked into Baker's room. It was almost completely dark, the lights from his machines putting out the only light. I leaned over him and whispered in his ear. "Did you convince your daughter to commit murder? She's killed two people. We'll find her, and she'll go to prison for life, that is, if she's not put to death. Your anger ruined her life. Are you happy?"

I ran my hand down the side of his left arm and hit something hard. I jerked my hand away thinking it was a piece of medical equipment, but there was nothing connected to that area from a machine. I carefully lifted the sheet and looked.

A cell phone with a pink cover.

I stuffed it into my pocket and then headed to the station.

Bishop moved my pad of paper aside and set a large Dunkin' coffee in front of me. He took a seat next to me at the table. "Jimmy's on his way. Nikki's here already. She'll be down in a minute."

I already knew that. I hadn't told Bishop about the phone yet.

Just as I was about to, Jimmy opened the door and started talking without as much as a hello. "I've got Bubba and a patrol officer on Claire Baker's contacts. If she's talked to any of them, we'll find out."

"Contacts? How?"

"I found her phone on her father's bed," I said.

"She left it there?"

"Maybe she was in a hurry?"

"Doesn't matter," he said. "She's probably told them not to talk to us."

"Not necessarily," I said. "We haven't put anything out about her. She's not going to make anyone suspicious."

"But her dad's been all over the news," he said.

"Maybe she'll use that as a cover," I offered. "Either way, we have to try."

"So, now we've got two murderers on the run, and nothing pointing us to them," Bishop said.

"We need something," Jimmy said. He picked up the landline, dialed, and put the phone on speaker. Bubba picked up on the second ring. "Nothing yet, Chief, but we're not even a quarter of the way done. She's got twelve-hundred contacts and probably half are in Georgia."

"How'd he get into the phone?" Bishop asked.

"He didn't." I smiled. "I did."

He raised an eyebrow. "How?"

"She used the same password as her father."

Nikki entered the room with a smile plastered across her

face. She caught me watching her, and the smile shifted to a frown. "Sorry, I'm just glad we got those prints."

"Don't be sorry," I said. "Had you not thought of it, we wouldn't know, and that evidence connects Claire Baker to Elana Mills. That will be used to nail her in court."

"Good work," Bishop said.

She blushed. "Thanks, but it doesn't matter if we can't find her."

"We'll find her," Jimmy said.

"We need Jessica Walters," I said.

"Why?" Bishop asked. "I mean, I know why, but explain."

All eyes were pinned on me. I leaned back and smiled. "It's time we put their names out to the public. She can make it national. Anderson will see it, and then..." I crossed my arms over my chest. "Let the games begin."

"I agree," Jimmy said. "But we have to wait until we've contacted everyone on her phone in case one of them watches the news."

"Then we'll help," I said.

And we got to work.

It took us until eleven-thirty to find someone Claire Baker had called. I was right. She'd used her father's situation as an excuse. Bubba had made the call, and once the contact said yes, he put her on speaker. We fed him questions to ask.

"Why are you looking for her?" The girl asked.

"Ms. Simpson, thank you for asking. We have some important questions regarding her father," Bubba said.

"Can't you just call her?"

"We've tried," Bubba said.

"This is about her father, isn't it? I mean, it's not like he's told her anything. He's brain dead."

We didn't bother correcting her misinformation.

At our direction, Bubba didn't let up. "Have you spoken to Ms. Baker recently?"

She sighed. "She called me really upset. She said reporters won't leave her alone about her father. I told her she could stay at my parents' VRBO to get away from them. She clearly needs a break."

"May we have the address?" Bubba asked.

"Uh, I...I'm not comfortable giving you that. How do I know you're not some reporter playing a trick on me?"

I whispered, "Do we have Simpson's address?"

Bubba nodded.

Bishop spoke. "Ms. Simpson, this is Detective Robert Bishop with the Hamby Police Department. I'll happily verify my identity for you. I'd like you to hang up, then call the department and ask for me. You can find the number online. Can you do that for me?"

"Is this that serious?"

Jimmy read the address, then stepped outside with his cell phone. I suspected he was contacting the patrol for that area to send them to her house just in case.

"Yes, ma'am," Bishop said.

She gave him the address, and I wrote it on a piece of paper, then immediately left the room to get a warrant.

We called Daryl Simpson, the property owner to let him know the situation, and that we had a warrant. We requested he stay away from the property, but he ignored the request. He met us at the rental. Bishop and I immediately escorted him to a safe area near the club house and explained the situation.

He rubbed his forehead. "Are you sure she's come here? I have the place rented out starting tomorrow. I'll need to have it cleaned again if she's been here."

"Sir," Bishop said. "We're prepared to enter the home our way, but it would be easier if you could provide us with a key."

"Uh, sure." He removed a key from his key chain and handed it to Bishop. "You're not going to throw things around like they do in the movies, right? I just had the place refurnished."

I rolled my eyes.

Bishop was a lot nicer than me. "We'll do our best."

The property was a small, two-story home in Alpharetta. It sat on a low hill at the end of a cul-de-sac bordered by a small creek with homes on the other side, another one on its left, and the community tennis courts behind it. The lots were postage stamp sized, with the only windows easily accessible from the ground on the terrace level and the back deck. We put our officers at each window and waited for the all-clear.

The front entrance was on a porch that rested at the top of the property's hill. We could get three officers on it if we stood still, and two with limited movement, which is what we chose. Three other officers stood on the steps behind us. Two long, narrow windows framed the door. Inside was a small foyer leading to a family room and the stairs. Given the location of the back deck, I assumed the kitchen was to the right of the family room. Our sight was limited, but anyone walking to the door from the inside could see through those narrow windows easily.

We prepared to enter but wanted to give Baker a chance to come peacefully first. Bishop knocked on the door and announced our presence. When she didn't respond, he waited ten seconds, then knocked and announced again.

Nothing, and no one reported any movement from any visible location inside the home. Bishop gave the nod, then unlocked the door. On three, he opened it while the rest of us prepared for the worst.

46

Claire Baker leaned against the kitchen counter next to the stove. She'd kept herself out of view from our sight points, and her casually crossed arms and legs and the smirk on her face said she'd done so on purpose. We'd come in with guns drawn, and while Bishop and I stayed that way, we directed two officers to detain Baker, sending the rest of the team to clear the rest of the home. I mentally ran through everything I knew about her, trying to find a reason she'd take the leap from prey to predator. Vengeance was a powerful drug, but attaching yourself to a serial killer passed vengeance and went straight to crazy, and she was the third person we'd encountered who'd done just that. First Chip Stuart, then Claire's father, and then her.

And she was completely calm about it. Why? I needed to know why.

The officers who detained her stood with their hands gripping her biceps. Bishop and I shared a look, and he moved toward her and read her the Miranda.

"You have the right to—"

She laughed, and her eyes flicked toward the far corner.

She made eye contact with me and then glanced at the same place again. Bishop continued with the Miranda as I took a step back and casually glanced toward the stairs, letting my eyes wander toward where she'd looked. A chair and a small side table sat in the corner of the room. A reading lamp and a photo frame rested on the table. The kitchen and family room were divided by a large bar-height counter, but it appeared the lamp was taller and would have a clear view of where we stood. I recognized the lamp as a specially designed home security camera immediately because I had one, too.

I turned back toward her. "Bring her outside." Bishop and I shared a look. I flicked my eyes for us to leave the home, too.

The officers brought her to one of their squad cars, but I directed them to one farther from the home.

Bishop and I walked behind them. He spoke softly. "What's going on?"

"The house is bugged." The officers stood with her back against the vehicle. "Leave her out, please. I need all of you inside the home. Look for a bug or camera. It's—"

"I only know of the one," Baker said. Her confident posture from early had deflated into sulking shoulders and heavy sighs.

"Check the entire home. Pay attention to the lamp on the side table next to the chair, but do not go there first. It's a camera. Bring it in." I made eye contact with each of them. "Do you understand?

"Yes, ma'am," they said collectively and jogged back to the house.

Bishop and I framed the front sides of Baker. If she tried to leave, we could stop her. "Camera, right?"

She barely moved her head to nod once. Her skin paled, and she began to sweat. Granted, it was hot as hell outside, but

I knew the sweat was from fear. She spoke softly through lips that barely moved. "I was there when he switched it out."

"Who?" Bishop asked.

She spoke softly. "I want protective custody or put me in jail."

I swiveled around and studied the environment. Homes surrounded us, so it was possible Anderson was in one of them watching us, that we'd purposely been led there. "You know something. Tell us what it is."

Her lips and chin trembled as tears filled her eyes. "Please," she whispered. "He's close by, I know it."

"Who's close by?" Bishop asked. "Say his name. We need you to say his name."

She shook her head in tiny little moves barely noticeable, and then her eyes turned to small slits. She spoke louder through thin lips and a tight jaw. "I killed Kaylee Priest." Her eyes darted back and forth, proving to me her confidence was theatrics. "Give me protection," she said softly.

"You just admitted to killing Kaylee Priest," Bishop said. "Why should we protect you?"

I shook my head and held my palm up toward her. "Wait a sec. We need to make sure Anderson isn't holed up in one of the houses nearby watching us." I whistled to an officer. "Hey, she needs a lift to the department."

"No!" Baker screamed. I turned around to see her shaking and crying. "He'll kill my father!" All pretenses of calm or fear, or whatever emotion she'd been alternating, disappeared. "He's got another girl" She finally broke down into sobs. "I saw her."

Bishop and I exchanged looks.

"Another girl?" he asked. "Who?"

She dropped her head. "I'll tell you everything, just get me out of here."

Bishop put her in the back of the squad car, closed the door and then stepped away, motioning me to follow. "Think she's lying?"

I pulled in and then released a breath. "Maybe, but I don't think we can take the risk if she isn't."

"Agree." He called over the officer assigned to the vehicle and handed him his keys. "We're trading cars. I want a check on every home here. Show them a picture of Anderson. Ask if they've seen him. If anyone acts strange, seems nervous, get inside their house and look. Understand?"

"Yes, sir," he said.

"I'm putting an all-points bulletin out on Anderson," Bishop said. "We don't want another victim."

He got on the radio and sent it out, and then spoke to the chief as I pulled my phone from my pocket and sent a text to Jessica Walters.

Birmingham, Alabama, Detective Edward Anderson is wanted for the kidnapping and attempted murder of Ashley Middleton, the murders of Natalie Carlson, Miles Wentworth, and Kaylee Priest, as well as four murders in Alabama.

The three blue dots on the text thread appeared and then her response popped up. *Got it.*

I stuffed my phone into my pocket. "Walters is running with it."

"Let's get her in. The clock is ticking."

We hit Claire hard with questions on the way to the department.

Bishop gripped the steering wheel with both hands. "Say his name."

I watched her on the video camera in the back of the vehicle.

"Edward Anderson."

A shot of adrenaline went through my body. One more nail in Anderson's coffin. "Who's the girl?"

A sob caught in her throat. "I don't know."

"Where is she?"

She stumbled over her words. "I...I—"

I cut her off. "Where is she, dammit!"

"I don't know!" She yelled back. Her body shook. "Don't you think I'd tell you if I knew?"

"You just confessed to killing Kaylee Priest. How do we know you're not playing us for a deal?"

"I'm not." She bent her head and sobbed into her hands. The few seconds before she collected herself enough to speak again dragged on like hours. "He came to my dad's room dressed like a doctor—"

Bishop's eyes shifted toward mine and then back to the road. "We have guards on your dad's room. There's no way he could have gotten in there."

"He was disguised. He shaved his head and has a short, red beard. I didn't even recognize him."

We were finally getting somewhere. "Did you tell the officer?" I asked.

"No. There wasn't any time, and he said he'd come back and kill my dad if I didn't do what he said."

Bishop turned right onto Atlanta highway.

"He took me to a van, threw me in the back, and blindfolded me. I tried to scream, but he'd stuffed something in my mouth. He didn't take my blindfold off until we were in the room with Kaylee Priest and another girl."

"And you don't know the other girl?" Bishop asked.

"No."

"Did you know Kaylee Priest?" I asked.

She placed her hand over her mouth, gasped, and cried harder.

"Claire," I yelled. "Focus. We need answers."

She went full-throttle into a sob.

We arrived back at the station and sent Baker through booking while we worked with the rest of the team to determine who the other girl was.

Bishop, Jimmy, Nikki, and I stood behind Bubba as he went through the photos again.

He pounded his fist on the table of the investigation room. "I don't know, dammit! None of it makes sense. I haven't been able to connect any more of the girls in the pictures let alone figure out who the hell they are. Another girl is going to die, and I can't stop it."

I squeezed his shoulder. "You're doing the best you can. We all are."

He swiped his hand across his face and his shoulders sank. Jimmy cleared his throat, and we all gave Bubba some much needed space.

"Let's get the photos in front of Baker," Jimmy said. "Maybe she'll recognize one of them."

47

We watched Baker through the camera. She'd calmed down some, though I wasn't sure it was enough to focus on the photos, but we had to try. We walked into the room.

She'd been pacing but stopped and looked at us. "My dad. Is he okay?"

"We put extra guard on him and no one's getting near him without showing ID first," Bishop said.

I set the photos on the table. "Sit. We need you to look at each of these closely and see if the girl Anderson has is in any of them."

She sat and picked up the first photo. Her hand shook. She studied it and then set it next to the pile.

"We're going to ask you some questions while you're looking," Bishop said. "We need you to focus on both. Can you do that?"

She sniffled and nodded.

I sat and prepared to take notes even though the whole thing was being recorded. Claire hadn't asked for an attorney, and we needed to get as much from her as we could before she did.

"Did Anderson say anything about the girl while you were with him?" I asked.

She sucked in a breath and didn't take her eyes off the photos. "Just that she was next."

"What did she look like?"

She bit her bottom lip and held back a cry. "Blond hair." She examined a photo and set it down, then picked up another one. She cried harder and dropped the photo. "Oh, God. The look in her eyes. She was so scared."

"Keep looking at the photos, Claire," I said. "We really need you to focus." The clock on the wall ticked. We were losing time, and we didn't know how much we had to begin with. I changed my focus. "How long were you in the van?"

She looked up at me. "I'm not sure. It didn't seem long."

"Tell me about the ride. Did you stop a lot? Were there a lot of turns?"

"We stopped a lot, but I only remember two turns at the end. I was upset. It took me a while to pay attention."

"Okay. You're doing great," Bishop said. "Did the time between the stops feel fast or short?"

"Short, like there was traffic or something, and he had to wait to get to the light." She set a photo down and picked up another one. "Then it got a little faster, and then we made a turn and another turn into the place."

"Good," Bishop said. "Tell us what happened next?"

Her tears fell and made small splashes on the table. I reached over and moved the photos so they wouldn't get wet.

"He took me into the building."

"What did you see?" I asked.

"Nothing. I was still blindfolded." Her tone gave a hint of annoyance, as if she was losing patience.

"Tell us about the walk from when you got inside and he took off the blindfold," Bishop said.

She breathed in deeply and exhaled, and when she spoke, the annoyance was gone. "I don't know for sure."

Bishop's tone was even and calm. "Claire, this is important."

"I think—we didn't walk far, but we went up some stairs. Just one floor, and then he unlocked a door, and that's where Kaylee and the girls were."

"Was Kaylee bound, too?" I asked.

She nodded. Her soft cries accelerated.

I had to know the truth. "Claire, did you kill Kaylee Priest?"

She cried harder. "I had to, or he would have killed me. He said I had to finish what my dad started, and if I didn't do it right, he'd kill us both." She broke down into sobs. "I'm so sorry. God, I'm so sorry."

"What about Elana Mills? Did you kill her?"

It took her a minute, but she looked up at me, tears streamed down her cheeks. Her eyes were wide and afraid. "Anderson did. He told me." Bishop stepped out of the room as she spoke. "He bragged about everything. He's a psycho. He...he forces people to do things."

Bishop returned with a box of tissue and slid it across the table.

Claire took a tissue and wiped her nose.

He whispered, "All clear by the Simpsons."

I nodded. "What did he tell you?" I asked Claire.

"He said my father was weak." She set a picture to the side. "He said my father couldn't do what had to be done, and he had to do it for him." She stared at the door behind us. "He said killing Elana was messy, but it had to be that way. It had to be the same."

I asked for clarification to see if her story remained consistent. "Did he say this in front of the other girls?"

She nodded.

Bishop tapped the side of my leg with his foot, our sign to move things along quickly. "Claire," he said. "We need to talk about where Anderson brought you again, okay?"

"I told you I was blindfolded. I don't know where he took me." The annoyance returned.

"Describe the room you were in. Was it big? What did it look like?"

She inhaled and exhaled. Was she being genuine? I wasn't sure. "It was long, kind of narrow, but not really. There was a big table with like, kid sized chairs, and it was u-shaped."

The hairs on my arms stood. Something about that felt familiar, but I couldn't put my finger on it. "Were the other women in those chairs?" I asked.

She furrowed her brow. "A crazy psycho kidnapped me and threatened to kill my father. I wasn't really paying attention to the surrounding stuff."

"Close your eyes and go back there. Tell us what you see," Bishop said.

"They were at the end of the room in chairs for like an office or something."

I nodded. "Was it an office?"

"I don't think so."

"Did it have four walls? Any windows? Was the door a double or single?" I asked.

"It had one door in the center of the room. No windows, but there were spotlights in the corners of the ceilings and above the table. When he left, I couldn't face the other girl. I just turned around and stared at some neon-colored swirl painted on the wall."

I sucked in a breath. "I know where he took her."

48

I used the internet on the computer in the investigation room and jabbed my finger at the photo. "It's the roller rink. He's got them in the party room of the roller rink. And I'm pretty sure it's the one on Piney Grove Road in Cumming."

"What makes you think he's at a roller rink?" Jimmy asked.

"Someone recently reminded me of the anxiety places like that gave me, and this place is empty." The sinking feeling in my stomach returned. "The problem is, I'm not one hundred percent confident she's telling the truth."

"Are you over fifty percent?" Bishop asked.

"Yes."

"What's holding you back?" Jimmy asked.

"For starters, she willingly admitted to killing Kaylee Priest, and she hasn't asked for an attorney. But mostly, there were a few moments in the interrogation where annoyance bled through her desperation."

"But you're still over fifty percent anyway?" he asked.

"Yes."

"Then we need to move on this. It's all we've got, and if

Baker's telling the truth, and Anderson's got a girl, God only knows when her clock started ticking," Bishop said.

"I agree. The problem is, how do you know it's that rink?" Jimmy asked. "There must be other roller rinks or kid party places around the area."

"Claire's description of the drive." I clicked on the Yelp reviews for the rink. "And Let's Roll is permanently closed."

"Anderson doesn't give get out of jail free cards to his victims. He kills them," Jimmy said.

"Unless they serve a purpose," I said.

"What purpose does Claire Baker serve being kept alive and released?" he asked.

"To set us up."

Bishop cleared his throat. "It's possible."

I nodded. "Tactically speaking, our manpower alone puts us above him. So we come in at full speed prepared for him to try something."

"What about you?" Jimmy asked Bishop. "You think she's telling the truth or setting us up?"

"I'm about sixty-forty in her corner."

"You support going in without knowing the truth then?"

"I think we have to take that chance," Bishop said.

"Then let's do it." Jimmy moved a step closer to the door and flicked his eyes toward Bubba. "Get on the phone with Forsyth County. Get a copy of that building's interior and exterior layout. Make sure it's the most recent. Tell them we have a suspect possibly holding someone hostage inside. If they give you any trouble, give me the phone."

Bubba nodded and moved to the other side of the table and picked up the landline.

"The rink is attached to an air soft place." He directed his attention to Bishop. "Get on with the Forsyth County Sheriff's office, let them know what we've got, and put them on standby.

I'm taking incident command on this. I'll contact SWAT." He dragged his hand down his face. "Forsyth is going to want their SWAT working with ours. Tell them I'll have an answer on that in thirty."

Bishop nodded, removed his cell from his pocket and stepped out of the room.

Jimmy sent Nikki to notify the lieutenant on duty that we'd need bodies but not likely until after shift change in a few hours. "You," he said pointing at me. "Get Claire Baker to tell you the truth about what she knows. I don't care what it takes. We need information. When we've got our team together, we'll go over the building plans and determine action."

I nodded.

"And Ryder, you know how this works. With SWAT involved, policy dictates you and Bishop stay out of this."

"But I can assist. It's policy."

He set his eyes on mine. "Behind the scenes only. I don't want you or Bishop going rogue on this one. You hear me?"

My adrenaline deflated. "I hear you."

Claire paced in the interrogation room. The photos were sprawled across the table, and she'd thrown used tissues on the floor. A lot of them. She must have cried the whole time we were away. She froze in place. "What's going on?"

"Did you ever go to a roller rink when you were a kid?" I kept my eyes soft and my tone friendly. She'd close up if she knew I suspected her of lying.

Her eyes lit up. "Oh, my God. That's where he took me." She dropped into one of the chairs. "I looked through all the photos twice. I don't think she's in any of them."

A sinking feeling stirred in the pit of my stomach. What young woman her age wouldn't recognize a party room at a roller rink or kids' entertainment center? My confidence in her being truthful took another dive. I straightened the photos into a pile and set it next to my pad of paper, then sat down across from her. "Claire, we need to dig deeper into what happened at that rink. I want you to tell me about Kaylee Priest."

She rubbed her lips together. "He made me do it. I didn't want to, but he said if I didn't, he'd kill me and then my dad." She began to cry again. "Oh, God. That poor girl. She begged me to stop, but I just forced that drink down her throat. I didn't have a choice."

Drink? Kaylee Priest had been stabbed thirty-seven times. Did she mess up? "Excuse me for a moment." I tapped out a quick text to Dr. Barron.

When is the tox report expected back on Kaylee Priest?

The blue dots appeared instantaneously. *Not for a few weeks.*

Claire Baker says she forced a liquid down her throat. She thinks she poisoned her.

There was liquid in her stomach. I sent that and blood samples. I can push for a rush, but you know that's unlikely.

I'd appreciate it. Thanks.

Of course.

Why would she make that up? What was the purpose of dropping that uncertainty into my lap? I pushed forward. "Go on."

She yanked a tissue from the box, wiped her nose, and then twisted the tissue in her hands. "He said I had to finish what my father started." She finally looked up at me. "He made me give her that drink. There was something in it. He wouldn't tell me what it was."

"Did you see her after she died?"

She nodded. "She was just in the chair with her head hanging down." She wiped her nose again. "I didn't have a choice."

"What did he do with her body?"

"I don't know. He just took her away."

"What about the other girl?"

She covered her mouth with her hand again, and through sobs, said, "He just left her with me, and I was—oh, God, I was too scared to help her!" She buried her head in her hands.

Her tears were genuine. Either she was a great actor, or she was telling the truth after all. "Claire, I need you to get through this, okay? And we need to do it quickly."

She nodded, her head still buried in her hands. A moment later, she lifted it and took another tissue, wiped her face, and then added it to the collection of them in her hand. "Okay."

"Tell me why Anderson let you go."

"He said the pawn would lead the queen to her death by the king, and I was the pawn. I don't know what that means. What does it mean?"

Chess. It was all a game to Anderson. He was the king. Who was the queen? My heart rate raced into overdrive. Was the queen the unknown girl or was it us? We had nothing on the girl. Baker either couldn't or wouldn't pick her out of the photos. But us? He made sure we got Claire. He wanted us to come for him. I was right. It had all been a set up. Was Claire involved? I was beginning to think so, but I had to be sure. "Why did you go to the rental home?"

"I didn't want to. He told me I had to find someplace to go."

"Because he wanted us to find you?"

"I don't know. I guess. But he made me call one of my friends and ask to stay there. Said I had to pretend the reporters were bothering me. I knew the Simpsons had that rental, and no one would get hurt if it wasn't rented. That's why I chose it."

I leaned back in the chair and crossed my arms over my chest. I sat there for several seconds, studying Claire Baker. Noting her posture—not stiff, but straight. Someone who'd just experienced a traumatic experience like she'd described would be closed off, afraid. Their shoulders would be curled forward. She'd cried enough to make her face red and swollen, but a lot of women could fake that without effort. What I questioned the most was her release. It wasn't Anderson's MO. Could she have been a part of the plan from the start, or did she participate out of genuine fear? I exhaled. "Tell me why I should believe you."

Her eyes widened, and she blinked repeatedly. "Why would I lie about this? Why would I make this up?"

"As a defense for murdering Kaylee Priest, which you willingly admitted to of your own accord." I purposely didn't mention Priest's knife wounds.

She shook her head and the tear faucets in her eyes pumped into action once again. "No. No, I wouldn't do that."

I moved the file of photos on top of my pad of paper and stood.

"Wait. Don't I get to call an attorney?"

And there it was. Had she done her job? Told us what Anderson wanted us to know? The truth was, I couldn't decide. "Right. I'll have an officer help you with that."

49

I dropped Kyle a quick text as I headed to the investigation room. I let him know not to wait up for me, that it would be a long night. I stuffed my phone in my pocket and forgot about it. I flung the door open expecting to see a crowd of people clustered in the small space, but it was empty. Someone had removed the files and whiteboards. "Conference room," I muttered and jogged down the hall.

I was right. The conference room was two times the size of the investigation room and would fit all the key players for the team. I counted six men leaning over the table studying an architect's drawing of what I assumed was the roller rink. Next to it was a blown-up aerial view of the surrounding area. I recognized three of the men. Bishop, Jimmy, and Sheriff Rodney. One of the other men was dressed in a green t-shirt and baggy camouflage pants. He was SWAT. I assumed the other was a negotiator.

Jimmy looked up and waved me over. "This is Detective Rachel Ryder. She's been actively working the investigation with her partner, Bishop. Ryder, this is Captain Dennis Wood.

He's from negotiations in the county, and this is Commander Max Swift with SWAT."

We all gave each other obligatory nods. I squished my way into the mix next to the SWAT commander and studied the layout. "You got this quick. It normally takes hours."

Sheriff Rodney smiled. "We have access to the system. It works to our benefit."

"Understood." I glanced back at the drawing. "What's the plan?"

Jimmy caught me up. "We're working on it. There are two exits." He pointed to the front entrance and one in the back. "The only windows on the building are on the air soft side, but there is no entrance from the rink to that part of the building."

"We'll put our snipers here," he pointed to a marked building top across the street then two other locations. "And here."

"Command station will be here," Jimmy said. He pointed to an area across the street. "We'll park behind the building in this section. There's enough blacktop for Fulton County's mobile crisis unit."

"What about ours?" I asked.

"Too small. We'll have a lot of bodies there." He used a black marker and numbered three areas on the drawing, two near the entrance and back door. "We'll have men on the doors and here." He marked six openings on the roof. "Two at each of these." He circled one on the right side of the building. "This is where we'll send the drones in. It'll give us a view of the party room." He lifted his eyes to Swift and held up Scott Baker's burner phone. "That's when you get him to give us the girl."

"If she's still alive," I said. They all looked at me. "If he's really got another girl, and I'm not entirely sure he does, he's already killed her by now. And if he hasn't, which I doubt would be the case, he wouldn't keep her there. Either way, Anderson's not going to negotiate."

Jimmy said, "Explain."

"What if Baker is involved? What if this is some elaborate set up for us to find that girl dead?"

Jimmy groaned. "You think she's involved now?"

"More so than before, yes."

"What changed?"

"She claims Anderson told her the pawn would lead the queen to her death by the king. We all know he's the king. That could make Baker the pawn, forced to comply or not, and either the unknown girl or us, the queen." I made eye contact with Bishop. "Which could mean we're being set up to walk into something dangerous or for the delivery of his next victim."

Commander Swift said, "My team can handle anything he throws at us."

"Is that figurative or literal?" I asked.

"Yes," he said.

"You think he plans to blow up the building?" Bishop asked.

"Justice is his driving point. If his daughter's attacker had been reported, she'd still be alive."

Bishop raised a brow then dipped back his head and sighed. "He's not going to blow up a roller rink. That's not his MO."

"MO's change," I said.

Bishop shook his head. "No. If that was the plan, he'd focus on the department in the district his daughter was raped. That makes sense. This doesn't. It's the girl. He's using her as another pawn. She's a bargaining tool."

"Bargaining for what? He's done too much to swing a deal," Jimmy said.

"If we think she's alive, we're not going to take him out. He knows that," Bishop replied. "Maybe he'd rather spend life in jail than get the chair?"

Jimmy shook his head. "It doesn't make sense. He's come this far. He knows he won't last long enough to make it to trial. If he's got to choose between going out on his terms or ours, he'll choose his. Maybe he's going to blow himself up in front of all of us?"

"He's too egotistical for that," I said.

"That's not entirely true," Captain Wood said. He made eye contact with me. "I'm also a licensed psychiatrist. It helps during crisis negotiations. Chief Abernathy provided us with details on your suspect, and with what you've said, I believe Anderson may be conflicted. While he believes he's justly avenging his daughter's suicide, there is a part of him that expects justice in return."

I cocked my head to the side. "Are you saying that he thinks catching him would be justice for the crimes he's committed?"

"I'm saying it's something to consider."

"If he talks and admits to having another girl somewhere, we execute Plan B," Jimmy said. "If not, SWAT takes over." He looked at me, and I looked away. I didn't want him to see the anger in my eyes. I needed Anderson alive.

Four hours later the plan was set and moving forward. Bishop sat at his desk tapping a pencil on his laptop while I chewed a nail and stared at the wall, waiting for the nod to go from Jimmy. I checked my watch. Three minutes had passed since the last time I checked my watch. Time moved like a snail, and I was about to lose my shit. "This is bullshit."

All Bishop said was, "Yup."

I flipped around. "We've busted our asses. Anderson almost killed me and Levy. My entire body still hurts. And Levy? Hell, she almost died. We deserve to be part of the action, not sitting on our asses in the command center watching it."

He continued tapping his pencil on his laptop. "Yup." Tap. Tap. Tap.

"Don't you care? Doesn't this bother you?"

He finally made eye contact. "Yes, I want this guy as much as you do, but we don't get a say in it, Ryder. It's procedure. Does it piss me off? Hell, yes, it does." Bishop kept his voice soft but spoke with a clenched jaw. "I want to be the one to take him out." He poked his chest with his thumb several times. "Those girls are my daughter's age." His face reddened. "My daughter's age."

I bit my bottom lip. Bishop had an up close and personal view of the murders from an angle I didn't. He saw his daughter's face in every one of those girls. I dropped into the chair in front of his desk and adjusted my vest. "I understand."

He stared straight into my eyes. "That girl is already dead, and we know it."

Jimmy walked in. "It's go time."

50

I stood in the command center, a large trailer on an eighteen-wheeler bed, and held my breath waiting for one of the drone officers to update us. I clenched my fists. "This is taking too long. What if Baker wasn't manipulating us? What if he's not in there?"

Bishop stood next to me, straight as a rail. His shoulders had stiffened ten minutes before and he'd yet to relax them. He couldn't hide it. He was as anxious as I was. "It's a big building. Give them some time."

I stuffed my hands into my pockets and rocked on my heels. "What if I was wrong?"

He turned to me. "I trust your gut. You need to trust it, too."

"I'm not sure I can right now." I rocked back on my heels again. "What if he sees the drones? He knows what to look for."

"Listen, if Baker's involved, how can he be sure she followed through and gave us the information? And if she's not involved, there's no way he'd think we could figure out where he was. No way."

"You're right."

The drone camera moved through a door. The entire building was dark as midnight. I couldn't tell where it was or what was around it.

"Drone unit one. Located the party room on the second level. Door is open. No bodies inside."

"Party room clear," Jimmy responded.

My eyes shifted from one drone's view to the other. "That!" I turned toward Jimmy and pointed to the screen. "Right there. It's yellow." By the time I looked back, it was gone.

"Drone unit two," he said. "Move—"

"I saw it, Chief." The camera moved to the right. The yellow and red glow appeared again and quickly darted out of the camera's view. "I believe it's a rodent, Chief."

I closed my eyes and exhaled.

Bishop nudged me with his arm. "Keep your cool, partner."

"I'm cool," I lied.

Ten minutes later the drones finished their search without finding Anderson. We waited around for orders from Jimmy as he and Commander Swift huddled at the front of the truck.

"They're going to send in SWAT anyway," Bishop said. "Anderson's law enforcement. They have to."

Military and law enforcement officers knew tricks that would hide them from infrared heat sensors. Patrol officers carried specially sized thermal blankets in their first aid kits, but a standard sized one, if used right, could hide a body from a sensor, and was readily available at any sports and camping store.

Jimmy walked over. "They're going in."

I checked my watch. They would be inside in seconds, and we'd get the official all clear shortly after. "If Anderson's been in there, we'll find proof."

Three minutes later a voice broke the silence. "Commander Swift, the building's clear, but you're going to want to send the Hamby detectives in. They need to see this."

I pushed past Bishop, knocked the truck door open with my shoulder, winced because it hurt like hell, and sprinted to the rink. I stopped at the door, retrieved my weapon, and kept it at my side. All clear or not, I wasn't taking any chances. I announced myself but it didn't matter. A group of SWAT team members stood in front of me, waiting. Nikki rushed in with her bag and a younger man at her side. He wore a Hamby PD shirt, but I didn't recognize him, and I didn't really care. Bishop jogged in breathing heavily. I secured my weapon back in its holster.

"This way," a SWAT member said.

We walked through the main hallway. The set up was typical of a roller rink. The admission area on the right, a large counter with a wall of cubbies for the skates behind it. Benches in front of us, and the rink in front of them. To the right was a café area and the counter for food service. "Where's the stairs to the party room?" I asked.

"Just up on the right, but you need to go into the kitchen first."

I went ahead of everyone and popped my good hand against the swing door and walked in. My breath hitched in my throat. What once was a kitchen had been turned into something I couldn't imagine. The appliances were gone, in their place were tables with knives, duct tape, rope... things a psycho would use to murder someone. And the blood. The blood was everywhere. My stomach flipped. Bile burned up my throat. My mouth watered. I thought I might throw up. I bent over and took deep breaths until the sensation passed. The door pushed against my butt.

"Ryder," Bishop said. "Let us in."

I stood up, sucked in a breath, and wiped the sweat from my lip. I flipped around and opened the door. Bishop moved to enter, but I stood in front of it to stop him. The SWAT guy made eye contact. "We need booties and gloves. Bishop, it's bad."

Nikki dropped her bag on the café counter. "I've got booties and gloves." She passed them out to the rest of us.

The SWAT member walked over and stood in front of me as I wrapped a bootie over my right boot. "You okay?"

I grabbed the other bootie, slipped it on without looking up at him, and kept my voice low. "No, but I've got a job to do."

He whispered, "Jesus, I've never seen that much blood, and I've seen a lot of shit."

"Yeah," I said. I slipped a glove over my sore hand. It hurt. "Right there with you." I stood just outside the door internally begging my heart to stop pounding and my stomach contents to stay in place while the others finished getting ready.

Bishop eyed me. "What the hell's in that kitchen?"

I sighed. "Have a look."

Bishop raised a brow then opened the door. He stopped short, and I bumped into him.

Then the tech kid bumped into me. "Oh, sorry," he said.

"Oh, my God," Bishop said. I put my good hand on his back and pushed him into the room so the others could get in.

I stood beside him, that familiar bile rushing up my throat once again. I swallowed it and squeezed my eyes shut as it burned its way back down.

The tech kid walked in on my right and gasped. "What the —" He threw his hand to his face and coughed. "I think I'm going to throw up."

I turned toward him. His face was green. "Oh, shit!" I pushed him back through the door, barreling him into Nikki as she stood frozen in the doorframe, her eyes fixated on the back wall. "Move! He's going to be sick."

She stepped backwards but didn't get out of the way fast enough. He roared his head back and projectile puked all over Nikki's shirt and pants.

The SWAT guy spoke into his mic. "We need an ambulance, and I don't know, towels. Someone from Hamby just threw up all over the tech person." He mouthed to me, "I've got this," and I went back into the kitchen.

Bishop hadn't moved. I grabbed hold of his arm and walked him forward. "We need to search it."

"I know, but I need a minute."

Nikki came in wearing a clean shirt. "I carry an extra for emergencies." She turned to the right, then the left, and then looked at me and exhaled. "Okay. Time to get to work. I'm starting on the back wall."

Bishop shook his head. "I'll go right."

"I'll go left."

I took photos of everything as if it wasn't permanently embedded in my brain already. The wall was covered in blood, some darker and dry, some bright and wet. "She's dead," I said.

"I know," Bishop said.

"There's a lot of blood," Nikki said. "I can scrape some of the dry stuff from the walls and floor. It might match the other victims but getting samples of all of it is impossible." She rotated her head from side to side as she studied the wall. "Hmm."

I examined the wall closely. So much blood, at least seven feet high. I struggled to make out which splattered marks came from what blood on the wall. I called Bishop over. "Look at this." I had to jump to point to the one I wanted him to see. "I think someone threw blood on the wall. It's not splattered.

It's thrown." I pointed to a few other areas that looked similar. "Same here, and here, and here."

He stepped closer and studied them. "You're right."

"Looks like that over here, too, but there are definitely real splatters," Nikki said. She walked over to the table with supplies and made a full circle around it, examining items visually and picking some up for a closer look. When she finished, she walked over to my wall. "Look closely." She pointed to a section of red. "This spot's a brownish red. It's darker than the other stuff. Yes, the other stuff is dry, but— hold on." She walked out of the kitchen and returned a few seconds later with a chair from the café area. She set it down and stepped on it then put her nose millimeters from the wet stuff. "This is paint. The smell is faint, but it's there." She climbed off the chair. "I'll conduct a few Leuco-Malachite DISCHAPS tests, just to confirm, but I'm right. It's paint."

"I'll fill Jimmy in," Bishop said.

"I'm going to the party room."

"Be right there."

The new guy and two SWAT members followed me toward the stairs. "I've got this, guys, but thanks." They nodded and walked away, so I headed up the stairs and flipped on the light for the party room and stood in the doorway. The small, dim light blinked twice and finally came to life, and I wasn't at all surprised by what I saw.

I called Bishop up. He stood behind me. "What the—she lied." A trail of cuss words flew out of him. "She's in on it."

The party room was entirely empty. No table, no kid chairs, and only one small light dangling from the track over where the table would have gone. "Blue walls," I said. "Just blue." My head pounded. "I need to get back to the department. She's mine."

The kid who'd thrown up all over Nikki walked in. "Uh, I'm better now. Nikki sent me up here to help."

Bishop eyed him up and down. "You sure?"

"I went to college and everything. I can do this."

"Without puking again?" I asked.

His pale cheeks turned pink. "Yes, ma'am."

While Bishop explained what to look for, I got on the radio with Jimmy. He wasn't pleased.

———

Bishop and I headed straight to the jail at the department.

The attendant greeted us with a sour face and practically dead personality. "Her lawyer showed up about three hours ago. Didn't stay long." He pointed to the video of her cell. "She cried after he left, but she's been asleep now for about an hour." He stood and stretched, then wobbled the two feet to the electronic door, swiped a card over the sensor and tapped in a code on the number board. The door opened. He handed me a key card from his desk. "Don't make her upset. I don't want the other inmates waking up."

"Of course," I said, though I didn't mean it.

Baker's cell was three down on the right. There were no occupied cells before hers and six more collectively past it. She lay on the cot, her body in the fetal position as it had been on the security screen. I swiped the lock, and the door clicked open.

Bishop closed it behind him.

"Baker," I said. "Time to have a little chat."

She didn't move.

I kicked the bed frame and said, "Wake up, dammit," but she still didn't move. "Oh, shit! No!" I bent down and checked her pulse on her neck. Nothing. I checked under her nose and over her mouth, but she wasn't breathing. "Get the AED and the paramedics!"

Bishop rushed out of the room while I turned her onto her back and climbed onto the small cot. "Don't you do this, Baker." I began compression. "One. Don't you die on me! Two." I counted each compression. At thirty, I tilted her head back and breathed into her mouth, two times, then two more times. I checked her pulse. Still nothing, so I started again.

Bishop returned with the AED, and after multiple attempts, the paramedics arrived and took over, but it was too late. Claire Baker was dead.

Jimmy stopped me from ripping the jail attendant's head off. He stood in front of me. "Stand down, Ryder."

I breathed through my nose, letting the anger dig deep into my bones. No way was I letting it go. Jimmy ordered Bishop to *keep me calm* while he figured out what happened.

The attendant explained that he'd followed procedure. He allowed Baker and her attorney to meet privately. They spoke for about an hour. She signed paperwork, they shook hands and he left. Baker was returned to her cell where she cried herself to sleep. Or so he thought.

Jimmy held out his hand. "Sign-in sheet."

The attendant handed him the clipboard, then clicked through the items on his computer and pointed to the lawyer's photo. "I did everything right, Chief."

I moved to view the photo and my heart raced. "That's Anderson!"

Bishop and Jimmy looked closely. Bishop dropped an F-bomb.

"Baker said he'd shaved his head and grown a red beard." I bent my head, rubbed my eyes, and pinched the bridge of my nose. "He made her do his dirty work, and then he killed her. I should have believed her."

51

Jimmy stood in the doorway of Bishop's cubby. "Go home and get some sleep. You both look like hell. If there's a dead girl, we'll know soon enough. I'm heading home now, too. Let's resume at eight." He walked out of Bishop's cubby.

Bishop yawned. "He's right. Tonight was all theatrics, and we fell for it. We won't get him if we keep falling into his traps, and we're doing that because we're exhausted and malnourished."

I sat there chewing on my nail, my eyes focused on the floor.

"Ryder."

I looked up at him. "Exhausted and malnourished. I heard you."

"Nikki confirmed the paint. Barron's taken Baker's body to the morgue, and he's promised to test the patch from Baker's stomach, though we all know it's fentanyl. There's nothing for us to do. Let's get out of here."

Kyle's vehicle was in my driveway. I'd told him to go home, but he went to my place anyway, and I was glad. I fed Louie some pellets and quietly got in the shower as Kyle snored on my bed. I finished and slipped into bed beside him and kissed him on the cheek. He still hadn't shaved. I kissed him again, and he lifted his arm and pulled me into his chest. I fell asleep within seconds.

My phone alarm buzzed me awake at seven o'clock. Kyle was already up and dressed, sitting on the bed tying his shoes. "Leaving already?" I asked.

"Meetings." He secured his weapon onto his belt. He turned and smiled, then his smile switched to a frown. "Rough night?"

"Very." I dragged myself out of bed. "I don't know when I'll be home next."

"Understood. I'll check in later." He walked over and kissed me. "I do want to hear what's going on."

"Okay," I said. "Later."

He looked me in the eye and kissed me again. As he walked to my door, he pointed to the dresser and said, "I brought some things." He winked and headed out.

I smiled and little fluttery things happened in my stomach.

Every local radio station reported on Anderson as I drove to work. Jessica Walters broke the story and the rest of them ran with it. When I arrived at the department, the lot was packed with reporters. I groaned while parking my car. Two reporters rushed over. "Here we go again." I opened the door and was bombarded with questions and microphones in my face. "No comment," I said over and over. I grabbed my things and jogged to the door.

Bubba met me on the way to the interrogation room. "The tip line is nuts. They've had over a thousand calls since the news broke last night. Don't these people have anything better to do than call us with stupid stories? Anderson's an alien. He landed in this dude's backyard." He laughed. "Bet the guy wears tinfoil on his head."

I chuckled. "There's a lot of them out there. Any credible sightings?"

He shook his head. "But the chief spoke to that Walters reporter. He gave her the photo of Anderson impersonating Baker's lawyer. She said she's going live in fifteen minutes with it."

"Perfect." I set my things on the table as my cell phone rang. "Ryder."

"It's Dr. Barron. I was able to call in a favor on those test results for Kaylee Priest. There was fentanyl in her stomach, but as you know, once the heart stops beating, blood flow stops. I can say with certainty that Ms. Priest died from a stab wound, not fentanyl poisoning."

"I understand. I just wanted to know if she had anything in her system."

"Then your answer is yes."

"What about the transdermal patch on Baker?"

"I have confirmed that to be fentanyl also, however I've got to complete the autopsy for a final cause of death."

I thanked him and disconnected the call, all the while drumming my fingers on the table. There was a way to find Anderson. He wasn't invincible, contrary to what he thought. He'd stepped up his game and wanted us to believe he was smarter than us. He'd proven that with the little horror movie mockup at the roller rink. He'd slip up soon.

Bubba sat across from me, his fingers pounding on his laptop keyboard. "Hey, Bubba?"

He looked over his screen. "Yeah?"

"We need to get that photo of Anderson, and his real

license photo to all the hotels in a, uh, let's say thirty-mile radius from here. Is there a quick way to do that?"

"Sort of. I can send it out to the corporate locations of the major chains and ask them to distribute it locally. But the smaller, mom and pop ones? I'd have to search for those and send them individually."

I gave him a cheesy, toothy, fake smile and raised my eyebrows.

He shrugged. "I'll get it done."

"You're the best."

"Tell that to my parents."

I laughed. "Oh, one more thing." I had a hunch, and I wanted to test it. "Can you run Claire Baker and get her tag number?"

"Now, that I can do quickly."

"Thank you."

Two hours later we still had no solid leads from the tip line or the news reports and no dead female bodies. But we did have a list of hotels to call, including the mom and pop motels, and Baker's vehicle make, model, and tag. A white two-thousand-nineteen Subaru Outback.

Jimmy put three officers on the hotel calls, but Bishop and I wanted to hit the smaller ones personally. First, we drove to the hospital where we expected to find her vehicle, but it wasn't there. We stood in the parking lot surveying the cluster of cars and limited free spaces.

"He can't have unlimited financial resources, and stealing vehicles is a lot of work," I said. "He's using Baker's Subaru. Otherwise, why isn't it here?"

"Maybe it was towed?"

"Easy to find out." I tapped a message out to Bubba asking him to check with the hospital.

Bishop pulled a pack of cigarettes from his pocket.

"Hey, you quit."

He snapped open a lighter and lit one up then took a long, slow puff, let it work its magic, and released the smoke through his nose. Just the act of smoking triggered a pleasure point in my brain. God, how I'd missed that. Thankfully, not enough to start up again. He dropped the cigarette and smashed it with his boot. Bishop was the one puff and smash king of smokers.

"That's not quitting."

"If Cathy can have cheat days on her diet, I can have smoking cheat days."

Couldn't really argue with that. "Let's hit the motels. There's only five of them." I pulled up the motel list.

He rocked his neck back and forth. It popped twice, and my stomach did a flip. "Gross."

"It feels great, though."

I rolled my eyes and gave Bishop directions to the first motel. "Anderson has fake IDs. We know that from the license he used to get into the jail."

Bishop's nostrils flared. "We should have caught that."

"I know, but my point is, he could have a hundred fake IDs, and just as many disguises. We need to take that into consideration." I'd told him to turn right, but he went straight instead. "You missed the turn."

"Anderson's not at a hotel. It's too obvious. We're thinking like detectives dealing with a murderer. We need to think like detectives hunting a dirty cop."

I'd thought we were. "Meaning?"

"If I were Anderson, I'd hide out in the place you were

least likely to look." He made a right turn, and I knew exactly where we were headed.

52

Bishop drove up and down every street in a two square block radius of Scott Baker's place in downtown Alpharetta. The area had become a hot spot for millennials and others who wanted a taste of the city life, just not in Atlanta. Alpharetta fit that perfectly with its clusters of eclectic shops, unique restaurants, microbreweries, and self-pampering, wellness boutiques.

Townhomes and apartments framed the retail and business district with buildings up to ten floors high, but there was limited private parking, and much like Chicago, people had to park a good distance from their home.

"There," I said, pointing a few cars up from us on the right. "A white Subaru."

The vehicle was jammed into a space, and there was no way to see the tag. Bishop and I couldn't determine the year either, so he drove past it, swung a hard right at the entrance to an apartment building, and parked to the side. I pulled my hair out of its bun and fluffed it a bit to hide my face, then casually walked up and down the sidewalk to get a glimpse of the tag.

The car was Bakers. I pumped my fist and whispered, "Bingo!" Once around the corner, I jogged back to Bishop's vehicle. "It's hers."

He immediately got on his cell and called Jimmy on speaker.

"We'll get bodies out casing the area, and I'll contact Alpharetta PD to increase patrol while we're formulating our plan," he said.

My eyes met Bishop's. We both knew it would take several hours to set up the team again, but we didn't think we had that kind of time.

"Chief," I said. "We might not have that kind of time."

"I don't care. I'm not letting you two approach the residence, not without substantial back up. We have no idea what the hell you could be walking into."

"We're staying close. If he leaves, we'll follow," Bishop said.

Jimmy huffed. "Do not approach that apartment. Do you understand?"

"Yes," Bishop said.

He didn't give me a chance to respond. "Ryder? Verbal confirmation."

"Yes, Chief."

He disconnected without even saying goodbye.

Bishop grabbed a gym bag from the floor of the back seat, set it between us, and opened it. He removed a red and blue Atlanta Braves baseball cap, a red and black Atlanta Falcons baseball cap, a baggy black t-shirt for a local pizza place, and a smaller, but still baggy women's red t-shirt with a peace symbol printed on it. He tossed the t-shirt to me.

I bit back a smile. "You carry undercover clothing for me in your bag?"

"You stand out like a sore thumb." He put the car in drive

and parked behind the building in a private area. "I'm not sitting in this car."

"We're under strict orders to not approach the apartment."

"I know, but he didn't say anything about casing the area. If we're lucky, Anderson will show up."

I scooted my seat back and changed my appearance while Bishop did the same. Since my utility belt would be obvious, I stuffed my weapon into the back of my pants and let the baggy shirt hang over it.

"Jesus, it's hot out here," Bishop said. "My head's already soaked under this cap."

I pointed to my long hair hanging out from under the cap and down my back. "Stop whining."

"No one's forcing you to have long hair."

I rolled my eyes. "Whatever."

We did a fantastic job of meandering around the area, moseying in and out of stores and cafes like visitors.

Bishop pointed to a tea place. "Oh, thank God, I'm already dehydrated." The place was empty, so we stepped right up to the counter. Bishop studied the menu on the wall. "What's bubble tea?"

I shrugged. "Something I've never had."

The young girl behind the counter explained. I didn't hear a word. I was too busy cringing at the piercings on her left cheek. Those had to have hurt.

"Tapioca?" Bishop asked. "Just give me an iced coffee, two sugars, and lots of cream."

"And you?" When I didn't say anything, she said, "Ma'am?"

"Oh, sorry. Just water."

Bishop paid the bill. I walked over to the shelves next to the windows to keep watch.

"Do people really drink tea with tapioca in it?" Bishop asked me.

"Apparently."

"That's disgusting."

An attractive woman wearing a floral sundress walked by. She caught Bishop's eye. I glanced at the retro vinyl music store across the street. The door opened, and out walked Anderson. "There," I said. "Across the street. Blue doo-rag on his head."

"Shit! You take this side," Bishop said. "I'll cross over to his. Get back up from Alpharetta now." He darted across the street before I could argue.

Anderson walked into a store two doors down. Bishop grabbed a seat on the bench just to the right of it. I leaned against a store window across the street and called for backup, making sure dispatch had all three descriptions. An Alpharetta patrol unit passed by shortly after. I eyed the driver. He gave me a small nod.

Anderson walked out of that store and down the street toward Baker's apartment. He walked into the Subway restaurant. Bishop hung back then walked toward it and looked inside before turning around and going back again. I crossed the street, passed the Subway, and took a seat on a bench. Another patrol drove by.

Bishop and I could only communicate through our phones. I sent him a text.

Backup in the area. Contact for permission to approach?

He called me. "He's got six people in front of him. Get APD inside with us."

I made the call, and, within a minute, five plain clothes and four patrol officers from Alpharetta were standing at the corner. We made a plan, and I sent a text to Bishop with the details.

Two plain clothes officers walked into the Subway and two stood outside the entrance. The patrol officers positioned themselves directly across the street, while the others stood two stores down balancing out the sidewalk on the Subway side of the street.

I watched Anderson closely. He glanced at the men in line several times. Plain clothes officers have a presence that's easily read by other cops, but our plan was to stay back until the last person in the restaurant before him left. We made sure no one else entered the building.

As he went to pay, he reached behind him and instead of removing his wallet, pulled a gun from his pants. It happened quickly. Bishop and I stormed in, guns drawn. The plain-clothes officer next to him smacked the gun from his hands as Anderson turned to shoot, and then grabbed his wrist and twisted, pulling Anderson off balance. It didn't drop him, but the head butt stunned him enough for the officer to drop him to his knees and then stomach and cuff him.

53

Alpharetta didn't read Anderson his rights, graciously handing him over to our custody. Our patrol had arrived in the thick of the takedown, and a caravan of patrol officers made sure Anderson didn't pull any tricks on the way to Hamby.

Bishop and I drove behind the patrol escorting Anderson. Neither of us spoke for the first few minutes until Bishop finally said, "It should have been us that took him down."

"I know." I was upset about that, too, but I knew we had to handle it that way to cover our asses.

"A plain clothes there said they offered, and you said no. Why the hell would you say no?"

"We both know Jimmy wanted us to stand down on all aspects, not just approaching Baker's residence."

"I don't care. It should have been us."

The procedure for arresting an officer is different from a citizen, and we were required to follow that procedure regardless of the alleged crimes. That meant we couldn't even book

Anderson until he had a chance to meet with his union rep let alone question the monster. While we waited, we put our case against him together.

I sat on the edge of my seat typing out my report, just waiting for Jimmy to give us the go-ahead. I called Kyle to catch him up, but my call went to voicemail. The union rep took her time, but finally, seven hours later, we got in front of him, his union rep, and an attorney.

Bishop and I sat across the table from them. Anderson's wrists and ankles were cuffed. He wasn't a threat anymore. In fact, the queen was about to kill the king.

I looked him in the eyes. He showed no emotion. "Check."

He blinked.

I had to stop the urge to celebrate.

The attorney slid over one-page documents to both Bishop and me. "This should be all that you need."

I glanced down at the paper. It was a signed statement claiming he was not responsible for all three Alabama murders three and a half years before, Daniel Travis and the two other men here in Georgia six months before, Johnson and Wentworth's murders, Natalie Carlson, Elana Mills, Kaylee Priest and Claire Baker's murders, Ashley's abduction and murder, and the attempts to murder both myself and Lieutenant Lauren Levy.

I tossed the paper back across the table. "BS."

The attorney opened the folder, retrieved another two documents, and handed them to us. "You'll find a handwritten, detailed alibi for my client during the times those crimes were committed. Now, I'd like to have my client processed and put into a protected cell."

Bishop laughed. "Protected cell my ass. Your boy's going to Fulton County. He's going to hang with the big guys."

I watched Anderson, but he still showed no emotion. I

leaned forward and looked him in the eyes, staying as calm as possible even though my insides were on the brink of exploding. "Why?"

"Don't answer that," the attorney said.

"With all due respect, regardless of your client's refusal to admit his responsibility in the long list of felonies he's committed—"

"Allegedly committed," she said.

I rolled my eyes. "We all know he's guilty. How about we just cut the bullshit and have an honest discussion?" I smiled at Anderson. "Maybe you'll get a better last meal."

His face remained stoic.

"Okay," Bishop said. "How about this?" He focused on Anderson. I knew where he was going. Give him the opportunity to brag without it being a confession, OJ Simpson style. "If one were to commit multiple murders, what would be the reason? Justice?" He smiled. "To avenge one's daughter's suicide?"

Anderson swallowed hard. He turned to his attorney and whispered in her ear. She whispered something back. He nodded then turned to us. "Because they could."

I jumped out of my seat, but Bishop pulled me back down. "Easy, partner."

"How did you manipulate Chip Stuart, Scott Baker, and Claire Baker to help you?" I asked.

"My client has not confessed to any such actions, Detective Ryder. Now, I believe we are done here." As she gathered her things, Anderson placed his hand on her arm. She jerked it away.

He smirked at me. "Based on our mutual investigation, it is my assumption that Chip Stuart was an idiot on many levels, but I suspect he was the perfect minion. He likely begged to kill and was given the education and resources to execute a plan effectively." He smiled up at the video camera in the corner of the room. "Someone like Stuart would work efficiently and would be clean, meticulous, and eager to please. Now, Baker? Well, as detectives, we all know anger is a powerful tool easily triggered into action. Unfortunately, anger causes mistakes, which is why Mr. Baker was arrested for the murder of Natalie Carlson. A murder which I am being charged with, by the way."

I ignored that. "And his daughter?" I asked. "Theoretically speaking, of course."

"With a young woman like Miss Baker, I believe fear would be a motivating emotion. I suspect whoever committed the heinous crimes instilled a great fear in her."

"You threatened her father's life and made her think she murdered Kaylee Priest," Bishop said.

Anderson sneered at Bishop. "I am simply speaking hypothetically. I have not confessed to anything."

I cleared my throat and smiled. Even though he thought he was in charge, and he believed he'd won the game, he hadn't. I handed the statement back to his attorney, all the while keeping my eyes glued on Anderson's. "You're going to need to edit this." I paused for effect. "Ashley Middleton is alive." I smiled. "Checkmate."

54

Bubba, Nikki, the kid that barfed, who I still hadn't officially met, Jimmy, Bishop, and I stood outside the Fulton County jail and answered questions from all the major news outlets in the state. We were exhausted, but we wanted the word out.

After we finished, Jessica Walters walked over and shook my hand. "You kept your promise."

"Not really," I said. "Look around."

"No, not here. Your chief made sure what I got earlier was exclusive. He said that was your promise, and he intended to keep it." She shook my hand. "It was a pleasure working with you. I hope we don't have to do it again." She smiled and walked away.

The projectile throw-up kid stood next to me and giggled. "This was amazing."

We had different opinions on the situation. "What's your name?"

"Oh, I'm Ethan Bauer." He pointed to Jessica Walters. "That news reporter? She's hot."

I turned and stared at him. "How old are you?"

"Twenty-two." He shuffled his feet. "I know I look younger, but it's the truth."

"Well, Ethan, let me give you a piece of friendly advice. Never make that kind of comment in front of a woman again. And never, ever make it about a woman old enough to be your mother." I cringed. "That's just gross."

His jaw dropped. I winked at him and walked away.

I finally had a chance to call Kyle again, and he answered. "I know it's late," I said. "Have you watched the news?"

"Briefly. It's been a busy night."

"Oh, are you at work?"

"Actually, I just swung by my place to pick up some stuff, and I'm pulling into your driveway now."

"Great. I'll be there in fifteen. I'm beat, but I want to spend some time catching up."

Fifteen minutes later I drove up to my driveway, but Kyle's truck wasn't there. I figured he ran out for a minute and headed inside.

I almost had a heart attack when I saw him feeding Louie. A bag sat on the floor next to him. He wore a baseball cap, but I could still tell that he'd cut his hair short, and he still hadn't shaved. I eyed the bag as he turned around. "That isn't stuff for your drawer here, is it?"

He took off the cap and revealed his bald head. "No. I've got an assignment."

No truck in my driveway, a new look, a big bag. I didn't like where things were going. "Can you tell me about it?"

"No."

I exhaled. "When do you have to go?"

"My ride will be back in a half hour."

My arms stilled at my sides. "Oh. How long will you be gone?"

"I don't know."

"Will I hear from you?"

"I can't say for sure." He walked over and wrapped his arms around me.

He was going dark. Undercover. Walking into a danger I couldn't comprehend. I understood what that meant—I might never see him again. I pressed my face into his chest, an explosion of emotions overwhelming me. I didn't want him to go. I wasn't ready. I was afraid of losing him. Tears slid down my cheeks. I pulled away from our embrace.

He smiled down at me and wiped a tear with his thumb. "I'll come back."

I couldn't fight the emotion rising up my throat. I let out a soft sob and laughed a little. "You'd better. You know what? It's really shitty that the first time I tell you I love you is when you're leaving me for God knows how long."

He smiled.

"Don't smile. I wanted it to be different."

"I think it's perfect." My electronic doorbell rang. He eyed the door behind me then smiled at me again. "I love you, too."

I called Savannah a few hours later. I hadn't slept at all.

"Hey you, my butt-kicking-girl-cop-best-friend. I didn't expect to hear from you today," she said. "What's up?"

I hated being emotional, but there I was sobbing into my best friend's ear. "He's gone."

"Who's gone?" Scarlet wailed in the background. "You've got a lot of men in your life. I can't pick one."

I appreciated her ability to make me laugh when I was miserable. "Kyle went dark. Undercover."

"Oh, he finally left? I'm sorry."

"What do you mean he finally left?"

"Oh, whoops." She giggled. "He told Jimmy, and Jimmy told me. He wasn't sure when he was going, but he knew he was. Honestly, I thought you'd figure it out when he started growing that God-awful beard."

"You should have told me."

"It wasn't my secret to tell."

"Sometimes your Southern values are annoying."

She laughed. "Honey, that's not my Southern values. Southern women gossip. I keep secrets. Now do you understand why I put pressure on you about being honest with him?"

I sucked in a breath. "I was."

"Oh, yay! It's about damn time. Me and the little monster are coming over. I'll pick up breakfast. Sound good?"

"Sounds perfect."

55

Bishop had a get together three nights after we escorted Anderson to Fulton County jail. There was so much to celebrate. Lauren Levy and Ashley were both out of the hospital, and though they couldn't come, we still honored them with a video call. Michels held the phone for him and Ashley, and his bright eyes and toothy smile were a joy to see.

I was not allowed to bring anything, and I was completely fine with that. Bishop handled the barbeque, wearing a cooling cloth around his neck, and Cathy made sure everyone had a drink and a small plate of appetizers.

I leaned against the kitchen counter with Jimmy after she walked out. "Hmm. You see what I see?"

He chuckled. "Looks like they're an old married couple."

I peeked out the window. Cathy stood next to Bishop with her hand on his lower back. "Sure does."

"You did good work with Anderson. I know you and Bishop wanted to be the ones to take him down, but you did the right thing."

"Doesn't mean I liked doing it."

He laughed. "I can respect that."

We walked onto the deck where everyone had gathered. Jimmy scooped Scarlet from Savannah as I stood away from the crowd. Bubba and Nikki chatted with Ethan, who seemed to fit in well with them. Bishop and Cathy shared a kiss. All was good. I missed Kyle, and I worried about him, but I had my people, and I didn't have to cook.

Jimmy's cell phone rang. He handed Scarlet back to Savannah and dug it out of his pocket. "Abernathy." He listened for a moment and then walked into the yard away from us. We all stopped what we were doing and watched him. He nodded a few times, turned around and faced the fence, then ran his free hand over his head. He dropped the phone to his side and turned around. "Edward Anderson was killed in the shower thirty minutes ago."

EPILOGUE

Four months later, Scott Baker woke from his coma. The doctors wouldn't let us in with him for another month, but they assured us they would not discuss his daughter. When we finally got to him, she was his first concern.

"Claire is dead." The cockiness he'd once exuded had disappeared. In turn was a man weakened by physical damage and internal conflict. His gaunt cheeks and sullen eyes told me more than he'd ever said verbally.

"Yes," I said.

"I know everything."

"We're not making a deal."

"My actions killed my daughter. I don't deserve to live." He looked at Bishop. "I owe this to her."

Baker had documented every conversation he had with Anderson. Initially for posterity, but ultimately, he'd revealed, because he believed he'd need it for his defense. A defense he'd decided he didn't deserve.

Anderson, or the Mastermind as he liked to call himself, had killed the three men in Alabama. He learned of their crimes through a private chatroom online where he'd posed as a victim himself. Originally, his goal was to find the person who raped his daughter. When he couldn't, he sought justice another way.

Baker believed Anderson manipulated Stuart. Baker had not been manipulated. He had willingly approached Anderson after learning of his existence from Stuart. He'd wanted justice for his daughter, just as Anderson had wanted it for his.

Even though Baker worked with him by choice, Anderson threatened to murder his daughter if he was ever implicated in the murders.

Louie and I hadn't received any communication from Kyle. All Ashley could say was that he was still alive. I took solace in that because it was all I had.

DEADLY MEANS
Rachel Ryder Book 7

One after another the extravagant homes of Hamby are being robbed...until the unthinkable happens.

Three home invasions in a wealthy golf community have Hamby on edge. At first, only cash is taken. But with each break-in the crimes escalate. Jewelry is stolen. Victims are beaten. Then events take a deadly turn when the fourth attack leaves a young woman dead.

Shocked by the murder and desperate to stop an increasingly brazen criminal, Detective Rachel Ryder and her partner Rob Bishop are quick to take on the case.

But they soon discover that all is not glitz and glamor in this high society neighborhood. Behind mansion doors are scandals that the ritzy community is determined to hide. After all, the rich and powerful don't want the skeletons in their closets exposed to the world, let alone to Detective Rachel Ryder. And they will stop at nothing to make sure their secrets stay locked behind their lavish gates.

Strap in for the next exhilarating crime thriller in USA Today bestselling author Carolyn Ridder Aspenson's Rachel Ryder series.

Get your copy today at
severnriverbooks.com/series/the-rachel-ryder-thrillers

ACKNOWLEDGMENTS

So many people helped get this book to publication, and I am so grateful. Severn River Publishing deserves a gold medal for managing the production of this book. A huge thank you to Julia, Amber, Mo, and Keris. You all rock! Thanks to my developmental editor, Randall Klein for guiding me through the thirty-nine page outline process and for creating the best story possible. To my other editor, Kate Schomaker, for polishing the manuscript until it shined, and to Anne Damman for nailing the characters for the audio files.

As always, a big thanks to Ara Baronian, BTD Director; GPSTC, for his continued support in keeping the law enforcement details real.

And to my husband Jack for being the best thing to ever happen to me. LUMI

ABOUT CAROLYN RIDDER ASPENSON

USA Today Bestselling author Carolyn Ridder Aspenson writes cozy mysteries, thrillers, and paranormal women's fiction featuring strong female leads. Her stories shine through her dialogue, which readers have praised for being realistic and compelling.

Her first novel, *Unfinished Business,* was a Reader's Favorite and reached the top 100 books sold on Amazon. In 2021 she introduced readers to detective Rachel Ryder in *Damaging Secrets. Overkill,* the third book in the Rachel Ryder series was one of Thrillerfix's best thrillers of 2021.

Prior to publishing, she worked as a journalist in the suburbs of Atlanta where her work appeared in multiple newspapers and magazines. Writing is only one of Carolyn's passions. She is an avid dog lover and currently babies two pit bull boxer mixes. She lives in the mountains of North Georgia as an empty nester with her husband, a cantankerous cat, and those two spoiled dogs.

You can chat with Carolyn on Facebook at Carolyn Ridder Aspenson Books.

Sign up for Carolyn's reader list at
severnriverbooks.com/authors/carolyn-ridder-aspenson